MURDER
In The Library

BOOKS BY KATIE GAYLE

MURDER
In The Library

KATIE GAYLE

bookouture

Published by Bookouture in 2022

An imprint of Storyfire Ltd.
Carmelite House
50 Victoria Embankment
London EC4Y 0DZ

www.bookouture.com

ISBN: 978-1-80314-172-5
eBook ISBN: 978-1-80314-171-8

To librarians, who keep the magic of libraries and books alive and hopefully seldom find dead bodies amongst their shelves.

From her perch on the low stone wall outside her back door, Julia surveyed her domain with a quiet satisfaction. The garden was just beginning to turn. The last of the summer flowers were in bloom, but the oak was touched with yellow and a light smattering of fallen leaves lay on the ground under the silver birch. Soon everything would be aflame with autumn colours.

Her six hens scratched and pecked the ground, their heads rising and falling jerkily as if controlled by some invisible puppet master. She loved the low contented clucking and chirping sounds they made, and their industrious manner.

Jake watched the chickens through the wire of the coop with the resigned air of a Labrador who would dearly like to mess with the fowl, but knew it was more than his life was worth. His velvety brown muzzle rested on his neatly crossed paws, and his tail slapped lazily on the grass. He was growing up and calming down, and even his bird-chasing obsession seemed to be coming under control.

Julia took a sip of her tea and rested her mug on her knee. She reached down with her other hand to give Jake a pat. 'Good boy,' she said. 'What a good chap you are. You'll get your walk this afternoon, when I get home.'

Jake, unfortunately, recognised the word 'walk', but did not take on board 'when I get home'. He leapt to his feet with a delighted bark, sending the hens dashing for the shelter of the henhouse as if the farmer was after them with a cleaver.

'Off, Jake,' she said, pushing the bouncing, bounding dog away, but not before he'd knocked the mug with his head, spilled her tea and landed his big muddy paws on her trousers.

'Down!' she said firmly. He complied, as he usually did, once the damage was done.

Julia brushed at the dirty streaks on her thighs, knowing it was futile. 'Now I'm going to have to change before I go to work,' she said, getting up.

'Work' was rather overstating things. Julia volunteered once a week at Second Chances, the charity shop in Berrywick village. It was really a way of getting out and about and meeting a few locals in her new home, while making some small contribution to the world now that she was no longer working as a social worker. The prospect of retirement had terrified her rather – she'd wondered how she would fill her days without her demanding job and her husband. She had a horror of waking up in the morning without a thing to do, but it turned out that village life, the garden, the shop, Jake and her new friends and chickens sucked up a surprising amount of time.

In a clean pair of trousers, Julia left the house and headed into the village. She was due at the shop at nine, but gave herself a few extra minutes, knowing that there was a good chance she'd be stopped by a chatty local between home and the village main street.

As she walked out of her gate, a neighbour passed by, making the same joke he'd made for the past three months: 'Found any bodies this week, have you?' She gave him a stiff smile, and shook her head. It was hardly her fault that a body had been buried under her garden shed nearly twenty years ago! Or that two more bodies had appeared in quick succession after she'd found the first one.

Her route was particularly popular with dog walkers. She passed a few of the regulars – the woman with the brace of yapping Yorkies, the bouncy jogger with the loping Great Dane – heading for the path along the river. They greeted each other with a smile and a hello.

'Nice day for it,' said Yorkie lady. 'I hear there's rain coming later, though.'

'Ah,' said Julia, gazing obediently at the sky. She never knew how to take the weather conversations which seemed to make up about half of all casual interactions. She had a brainwave, and answered: 'Thank you. I'll remember to take the washing in.'

The Yorkie lady looked satisfied with that, and they parted company.

A man with a metal detector who plied the river banks and fields around the village was hard at work along the side of the towpath. She saw him often, but they'd never spoken. He was always in deep concentration, headphones over his ears, eyes fixed on the ground, looking for treasure. Perhaps today would be his lucky day.

'Well, hello!' Wilma, the store manager, said cheerily when Julia reached the shop and opened the door. It was unlike Wilma to be at the shop so very promptly. 'Busy day ahead. We're going to freshen up the window display. Jolly things up.' She clasped her hands together in excitement.

'Wilma's had a super idea.' Diane caught Julia's eye and gave her a tiny smile and a hint of an eye-roll, recognising Wilma's obsession with creating the window displays. 'The natural history of the Cotswolds.'

'In honour of Vincent Andrews,' Wilma said breathlessly, looking at Julia in eager anticipation of a reaction.

'Vincent...?' The name rang a bell, but Julia couldn't place him.

'Andrews! Don't tell me you don't know him? He is a legend. An icon. A local treasure. A son of the Cotswolds.' Wilma looked astonished, even outraged, at Julia's ignorance.

'The tennis player?' she hazarded.

'Of course not! Tennis player, my word. That's Andrew Vincent. Vincent Andrews is the famous author. Very famous.'

'Oh yes, of course,' Julia could see she'd offended Wilma. 'Yes, V.F. Andrews, the historical novelist. I didn't know his first name. But I know he's coming to the village, there's a do at the library on Friday. Tabitha got me a ticket.'

'He'll be here tomorrow, I hear. I thought Second Chances should give him a good welcome, seeing as he's a local fellow made good. We'll be doing a pastoral Cotswolds theme,' said Wilma, sweeping her hand over the shop, as if over a meadow. 'Sheep, flowers, you know, um...'

'Wellies, straw hats...' said Diane, helpfully.

'Wonderful idea,' said Julia. 'Shall I get started, see what sort of props I can find in the storeroom?'

'Yes please,' said Wilma. 'Diane can help.'

The tinkle of the doorbell cut their conversation short. A young woman came in, towing a little boy.

'Just for a minute, Sebastian,' she was saying. 'Just a quick look...'

'Oh hello, Sebastian,' Julia addressed the boy with a smile. 'Nice to see you.'

'Hello. Where's the naughty dog?' asked the boy.

'Jake's at home, he doesn't come to work,' she said. Sebastian looked disappointed – she was clearly a less interesting prospect without her dog – and turned away to investigate a shelf of toys and puzzles. Julia turned to his mum. 'Hi, Nicky.'

'Oh hi, Julia! I'd forgotten you work here sometimes. I was on my way past, going to the post office, I was, and I thought, well, why not pop in and take a look at the second-hand books, see if I can find anything by V.F. Andrews? There's a few I haven't read, and seeing as he's coming here to Berrywick... and he's so dishy, did I say? I'm sure you've seen him. Quite the dish. Dark, kind of Pierce Brosnan vibes, but more, you know, intellectual. Nerdy, but smouldering, and with a sort of twinkle, if you know what I mean. Like he'd be fun, once things got going. Not that anything's going to be got going, of course not. I'm a happily married woman, I am. Aren't we all? Or, maybe, oops...'

Nicky stumbled over her words and coloured slightly, presumably remembering that Julia was in fact newly divorced and her husband was engaged to be married to another man, and that Wilma had lost her husband to lung cancer the previous year.

'Ah, yes, well... Anyway, what I mean is, do you have any of his books?'

There was a brief lull after Nicky's stream of joined-together-words. It was rather like being enveloped in a very large wave and tossed about so you didn't know which way was up, and when you finally came up for air, you were sort of dazed.

The three women blinked, as if to clear the sand and seawater from their eyes. 'We've kept a few of the newer ones for the display, but the rest have been snapped up,' said Diane, who recovered first from the onslaught. 'If I'm not mistaken, Olga Gilbert bought the last couple last week, isn't that so, Wilma?'

'Sorry, Nicky, that's right. Nothing left here. Did you try the library?'

'Oh yes, I did, but there's a list. Have you ever? A list? For a library book? Like it's a designer handbag or something? Ah well, nothing to be done. I'll have to wait, or buy one when he comes to do his talk. Get him to sign it,' she said, with a wiggle and a giggle as if she'd said something risqué.

While Julia searched for 'pastoral' items for the window display, and Wilma fiddled about in the window, Diane took care of the shop. From the stockroom, Julia could hear her disappointing V.F. Andrews' eager fans – 'All sold out, I'm afraid.'

Oh yes, Berrywick was all a-twitter over V.F. Andrews.

2

'The Fringe must have made a killing this week,' Diane said, surveying the chattering crowd of locals, milling about and finding their seats. 'Half of Berrywick has a new hairdo.'

This was rather rich coming from her, Julia thought, as Diane's own long red hair was newly washed and blow-dried, and emitted a sweet lemony fragrance when she moved. But Julia didn't mention that.

'Oh yes, everyone does look spiffy,' she said, wondering if she might have made more of an effort herself. She was in a good pair of camel-coloured trousers which accentuated her trim figure, but on top she was wearing the ubiquitous puffa jacket that seemed to have taken over the world. Julia had held out for a year or two, and then succumbed, and once you had one it was hard to take it off. You found yourself wearing it for weeks, then months, then whole seasons. But she had at least accessorised with a pretty scarf, jauntily tied, and diamond studs in her ears.

Nicky squeezed down the row of seats towards the two women, uttering apologies to the seated, and waving and calling to the standing. Julia had only ever seen her dressed in jeans, usually adorned with a smear of Sebastian's ice cream. This evening, she was wearing a lovely, drapey dress of deep purple paisley. And make-up.

'That's a very pretty dress, Nicky, you look great,' she said as Nicky sidled past to take an empty seat between Diane and a slim, dark-haired woman a bit older than herself. Nicky thanked Julia and greeted the dark-haired woman enthusiastically.

'Olga! Well goodness me, aren't you looking fine? And your hair! I hardly recognised you.' Nicky blushed and added, 'In a good way.'

Julia couldn't help but sneak a proper look at Nicky's neighbour after that, under the guise of looking for someone at the back of the crowd. She was indeed very smartly dressed in a silky grey top, tight-fitting black trousers and high-heeled black boots. The aforementioned hair looked fresh from the salon, but the woman's face was pinched and worried.

Nicky had recovered her composure, and waded back in. 'I was just talking about you the other day. In the charity shop. Isn't that so, Julia? You bought the last V.F. Andrews, you wicked woman!' Olga gave a tight smile, while Nicky laughed loudly at her own joke.

Julia had put her handbag on the chair next to her, which she was keeping for Sean O'Connor, her friend and the local doctor. The resident library cat, who confusingly shared its name, Tabitha, with the librarian – the cat was known as Tabitha Too for clarity, or just Too for short – had squeezed in next to the handbag. The library was packed and seating was at a premium, so people kept coming over to try and sit on what looked from a distance like an empty chair, and then turning a bit grumpy when they discovered it wasn't. Julia found this mildly stressful. She craned her head to find Sean and was pleased to catch sight of him in the doorway, craning his head to find her.

She waved and caught his attention. He smiled his Sean Connery smile, his blue eyes crinkling attractively at the corners, his even teeth showing. It was rather uncanny, being – what? Friends with? Sort of perhaps dating? – anyone at her age, let alone with arguably the sexiest of the 007s. She tried not to overthink it, just to enjoy the friendship.

He sat down next to her, lifting the cat and putting it on his knee, and leaned in for a kiss on the cheek. His skin was warm and smelled clean and soapy, which she preferred to the cloying smell of aftershave.

'Hello, Julia, thanks for saving me a seat. He's right popular, our Mr Andrews, isn't he?'

'He certainly is. Half the village is here. Do you see your cousin anywhere? Is she coming to see her son-in-law wow the locals?'

'I haven't seen her; it's a bit of a bunfight.' Sean scanned the room and then pointed. 'Oh, there she is, second row from the front. That's Eleanor, wearing the red jacket and the peacock feathers.' Sean paused for a moment, as if taking in how startlingly odd Eleanor actually looked. 'And that's her daughter, Sarah, Vincent's wife, sitting next to her.'

Julia spotted the deep red velvet jacket, which was randomly decorated with peacock feathers arranged on the body of the jacket with no rhyme or reason, and the back of two heads, the one above the red jacket silver-grey with a well-cut sharp bob, the other younger and streaked with expensive-looking gold and blonde highlights. The daughter, Sarah, turned to speak to her mother, sending the glossy hair swinging, revealing a glimpse of a chiselled profile and strong, high cheekbones.

'We'll go and say hello afterwards,' said Sean. 'And of course you'll meet all three of them on Sunday, for lunch.'

'I'm looking forward to that,' said Julia. And she really was, even though it seemed rather daunting, meeting Sean's

extended family, as well as the famous Vincent Andrews, of
course. The two of them had thus far only had walks and drinks
at the pub and, once or twice, a casual supper in her kitchen.
'I'm making an apple pie.'

She was interrupted by the *tap tap tap* of a finger on a
microphone, which set off a resounding electric shriek. All
conversation ceased, as sixty pairs of hands covered one
hundred and twenty ears. Too woke from her feline dreams
with a start and jumped off Sean's lap, looking furious.

'That's one way to get people's attention,' said Julia.

The initiator of the awful shriek was the human Tabitha,
Berrywick librarian and one of Julia's oldest friends. She was
seated upfront at a small table next to a good-looking man. Julia
recognised V.F. Andrews from the dust jackets of his books,
although the real-life Vincent Andrews was a good few years
older than his photo – mid-forties, Julia thought – with a gentle
streaking of grey at the temples. He had what Julia's mum
would have called 'film-star looks' – his almost-black hair parted
on the left and flopped over his forehead in a charming, boyish
way. His features were even, his smile warm and wide. The soft
blue cotton shirt beneath his jacket was the exact faded denim
colour of his eyes.

A slight and serious young woman in top-to-toe black,
whom Julia had seen hovering around Vincent, bustled up offi-
ciously with a glass of water, which she placed at his elbow. Her
shoulder-length hair was mostly as black as her clothes; the only
colour on her person came from a flash of blue at the tips of her
hair and the silver glint of a nose stud. Vincent put his hand on
her shoulder and gave her a broad smile. Julia noticed a warm
flush come to the girl's pale cheeks, softening her demeanour.
Vincent was a charmer, all right.

'Good evening, everybody,' Tabitha said, this time without
splitting their eardrums. 'A very warm welcome to Berrywick

Library, and a special welcome to our guest this evening, the bestselling, award-winning author, V.F. Andrews. Vincent needs little introduction. I think most of you are familiar with his very popular historical novels set in these parts. He's been described in *The Times* as, "Marrying a rollicking good tale with emotional resonance and a surprising historical veracity and depth."'

There was a smattering of applause at that. Julia noted Nicky as one of the more enthusiastic clappers, as was Olga, next to her, who gazed at Vincent as if transfixed and sat up so straight and tall that she seemed about to levitate from her chair. Tabitha smiled into the crowd as she waited for the clapping to die down. Julia admired how calm and friendly her friend was, how much herself, even in front of an audience. She didn't seem nervous, or feel the need to project anything other than her own warmth and quiet intelligence.

Tabitha turned to Vincent and continued, 'Thank you, Vincent, for being with us this evening, for making time for our little village on the book tour introducing your seventh novel, *The Raven's Call.*'

'Nothing but a pleasure,' Vincent said, turning the full beam of his charm towards her. 'As you know, I'm from around these parts...' That last, said in a strong and – to Julia's ears, perfect – regional accent, drew laughter from the crowd. 'Grew up not twenty miles from here, in Hayfield. And my wife, Sarah' – he gestured towards the front of the audience and smiled lovingly at the chiselled blonde – 'has family right here in Berrywick, so really, we feel as if we've come home.'

There was an appreciative, 'Aww,' and a bit more clapping from the audience. He'd been up there three minutes and already he had them eating out of his hand.

.   .   .

For the next twenty minutes, Tabitha and Vincent chatted about his books, his background, his inspiration. Tabitha asked about his method and practice – 'Just sit down and keep at it...' – and about his research – 'I have a great love of history, and fortunately I have a patient wife who doesn't mind that I've got my nose in a book half the time,' with another smile at Sarah in the front row.

The conversation turned to his new novel, which Julia had not yet read. Set in the 1930s, it was the most modern of Andrews' books, the rest of which ranged from the time of the Battle of Hastings to just before the First World War. According to the critics, this latest was an engaging tale of intrigue and betrayal, with a bit of romance thrown in. Like all his books, it was set in a charming little village in a beautiful rural landscape, and featured a strong, clever female protagonist.

Julia had read two of his older books, and found them well-written. The stakes were just high enough to make you care and keep turning the pages, but never so high that you were put in a state of anxiety and had your afternoon on the sofa ruined. She could see why he had such a devoted following.

Come question time, a rash of hands went up. Vincent looked as if there was nowhere he'd rather be and nothing he'd rather do than answer their questions. He fielded a number of rather predictable fan enquiries: 'Where do your ideas come from?' and 'Can you tell us what era the next one will be set in?'

Next to Nicky, Olga held her hand high, but Vincent picked a tall, handsome woman on the other side of the room. She stood to ask: 'It's quite unusual for a male writer to write strong female main characters. Why and how do you do it?'

'In my experience, it's women who get things done, who make the world go round – isn't that so, Sarah? Where would I be without you?' He looked down at his wife again, to the delight of the audience. 'I don't think women are portrayed strongly enough in modern fiction, or film for that matter. That's particularly true of historical fiction – there's a sense that men make history, which is far from the case.' There was a light smattering of applause at this.

He pointed to a raised hand towards the back of the room, giving the woman his encouraging smile.

'I read your new book and it seems to me that the village is our village. Not the Tesco and such, or the new shops, obviously, but the basic arrangement of the place – the road, the post office, the lake, the river. It's Berrywick, isn't it?'

He chuckled. 'A generic Cotswolds village, I'm afraid, based on some I've visited, and my own imagination. I don't like to disappoint you, but Berrywick hasn't been immortalised in this V.F. Andrews novel.'

There was a smattering of good-natured laughter, but the woman persisted, 'It's very similar though, isn't it? Even the pub on the river.'

'And the people,' someone interjected from the back. 'I reckon I know some of them.'

Vincent Andrews leaned in and scanned the back. 'Fiction, ma'am. And of course, on one level, we are all the same, aren't we? No matter where you go, or in what century, there's a butcher and a baker, a flirtatious wife and a cuckold husband, a harsh father and a saintly grandmother. I'm sure if you went to a village in Africa or India you'd find a sad and lonely man holding a grudge about unrequited love years ago.'

More chuckles. There was a bit of a disruption as a man sitting a few seats away from Olga got to his feet and edged his way past Julia and Sean and the rest of the row to get to the exit. Julia noticed that he had a slight limp. There was some tutting from their neighbours who presumably felt – not unreasonably – that he should have waited for the end of the talk.

'What're you in such a rush for then, Mike?' someone piped

up at the back, drawing laughter from the audience. Julia saw the poor chap redden.

Olga had her hand up again, but Vincent pointed to an older fellow who asked a very long, boring question about the historical accuracy of certain minutiae related to local history. It was one of those questions which was not in fact a question, but actually a statement, or, rather, in this case, a mini lecture. Having been in many a seminar and lecture in her time, Julia remained astounded at people's inability to determine the appropriate length and structure of a question. She wondered if Vincent wished he'd taken Olga's question instead. But Vincent Andrews, it seemed, was not new to this game. He managed to sidestep the question with alacrity, saying cheerfully, 'Well, Harry, I think you've answered your own question!' And then, turning to Tabitha, 'That's a fine note to end on, don't you think?'

Only Julia, who had known Tabitha for many decades, would have noticed the momentary flash of irritation which crossed her face at having her guest take charge of wrapping up the session. She was her unflustered and equanimous self when she smiled and said, 'One last question from me. I was intrigued by the story of the rise of young female journalists in the thirties. How did you come upon this fascinating period, and how did you find so much rich and intimate detail about such women's lives?'

'Oh, you know. We historical fiction types are like magpies, always on the lookout for a glittering gem that can form the cornerstone of a new novel. I read a little something years ago and filed it away to use one day.' He tapped his head, drolly. 'And I'm pleased to say that day finally came.'

His answer was rather unsatisfying, but there was a bit of applause from the crowd. Tabitha decided to wrap it up. 'And we're all very pleased that it did! Thank you, Vincent, and thank you all for coming. Please join us for cheese and wine in the foyer, where we also have books for sale. If you don't have cash, there is a credit card machine. Is that right, Phoebe?' The all-in-black woman who had brought Vincent the water smiled and nodded in the front row. 'And Vincent has promised to sign each and every one, so get your personalised copy.'

With a scraping of chairs, and a rising chatter, the well-groomed citizens of Berrywick headed to the door.

3

'Core the apples and slice fairly thinly,' Julia read out loud. Jake listened intently from under the kitchen table, alert for any indication that her words might herald a walk or a snack. Labradors were simple beasts, with simple pleasures, and the baking of pies wasn't one of them. Eating pies, yes, undoubtedly. But baking them, no.

Julia wondered exactly how thin 'fairly thin' was, in pie terms. The recipe writer had that jaunty, chummy style that urged you to add a 'sprinkle' or 'good lug' or 'generous dollop' of various ingredients. The tone was intended to be empowering – 'go on, you can do it!' – but Julia found it a little imprecise for her liking.

Julia had been up early, and decided to research apple pie recipes for tomorrow's lunch with Sean's cousin and family, before heading back to the library at ten to help Tabitha clean up after last night's event. She wasn't much of a baker – her ex-husband, Peter, had been the chief cook, and if there was baking to be done either he'd done it, or they'd ordered from one of the many overpriced bakeries in their old neighbourhood. Cooking was one of the skills and interests she had planned to develop in her new life as a country lady – both for her own survival, and for her enjoyment. Her neighbour had come by yesterday with a basket of apples from her tree, which was laden with fruit, so an apple pie it would be.

Her Google search for 'easy apple pie' had turned up 1,700,000,000 results. How could that be? Had every adult on earth contributed an apple pie recipe? Or were there a few thousand people generating apple pie recipes endlessly, day and night? This sort of thinking made her head spin. Her own mother had had *The Good Cook's Encyclopedia*, a compact book with an orange cover that had taken care of all her recipe needs for a lifetime, whether she'd intended to cook a Madeira cake, beef Wellington, or haggis.

Julia had ended up picking an apple pie recipe rather randomly from the first three, on the basis that there couldn't be much difference between it and the 1,699,999,999 others. Apples, pastry, butter, sugar, cinnamon – that would surely do the trick. Having made her decision and read through the recipe, she felt a sense of achievement. Almost as if she'd actually baked the pie. She put down the iPad and drained the last of her tea.

Jake took this as a sign that the morning might be about to improve, and got to his feet. 'Okay, Jakey boy, let's go and feed the chickens,' Julia said. Jake dashed for the door, his tail wagging. It wasn't a walk, but it was something. Better than all this sitting about, that was for sure.

Julia picked up the small bowl of kitchen scraps from next to the sink, and the two of them went outside into the crisp morning. The days were getting shorter, and the sun was only just appearing above the far hedge, below a layer of grey clouds, bathing the garden in a wan light.

The chickens noted their arrival and rushed to the gate. Julia went in and tossed the peels and bits and pieces onto the ground. While the hens fell upon them, she moved to the nesting boxes. One hen was sitting. She slid her hand under its soft tummy and retrieved a warm egg, and then another. 'Clever girl,' she said, placing the egg carefully into the empty bowl which had held the scraps. One more egg lay nestled in another box. She picked it up. Locking the chicken coop, she took the eggs inside, and picked up her umbrella. The weather report had predicted rain later, and she didn't want to be caught in a downpour.

'Be a good chap, Jakey,' she said, as she headed out of the gate and turned towards the village. 'I won't be too long.'

The clean-up wouldn't be a big job, she thought as she walked along the path that took her to the main road into the village. The glasses and side plates needed to be washed up and packed into their boxes for delivery back to the church, from which Tabitha had borrowed them. The stacking chairs would be piled up and put in the storeroom. The rest of the furniture, which had been pushed out of the way at the edges of the room and in between the shelves of books, would be pulled back into place.

When Julia arrived at the library, Tabitha was unlocking the big glass door. 'Right on time,' she said, turning to Julia with a smile. 'Thank you for offering to help. It's much easier with two. And more fun.'

'My pleasure,' said Julia, following her in. 'There's not too much to do. I should think we'll be done by noon.

'I tell you what, why don't we have lunch at the Buttered Scone afterwards? My treat. As a thank you for your help.'

'Thank you. Offer accepted!' said Julia. Their local tearoom did a smoked trout salad with seed bread that she was particularly partial to. 'Let's get started. Shall we do the glasses first?'

'Right. Let's get on with it.'

They worked contentedly side by side, chatting. The time passed quickly. A few loads of washing up later, the glasses were sparkling along the counter of the library's little kitchen.

The side plates needed only a quick going-over, and they were stacked in the drying rack.

'They'll be dry by the time we've sorted out the furniture, and I'll pack them up and take them back to the church on Monday,' said Tabitha.

The two women headed into the library's reading and study area, where they had watched Vincent charm the crowd the night before. The light plastic chairs stacked easily on top of each other. They stacked them five high, for ease of moveability, and pushed them to one side, next to a display cabinet of local historical artefacts, which had been set up specially for the event. Then they turned to the comfy reading chairs which had been pushed against the far end of the room, making a last row. With the chairs out of the way, Tabitha and Julia took one end each of a small square table. There were four of these tables, but they weren't too heavy. They positioned the first one where it belonged and went back for the next.

'We should have rustled up a few strong young people for this job,' said Tabitha, standing up to stretch her back. 'Instead of two sixty-year-old women, one of whom leads a rather too sedentary life and seldom lifts anything heavier than a le Carré novel.'

'Nonsense, we're doing brilliantly,' Julia said, with a little more breeziness than she felt. 'And besides, you read that Robert Galbraith book last month and that's nearly as heavy as one of these tables.'

Julia was in fact rather pleased with her new-found fitness. Walking a crazy chocolate Lab every day (sometimes twice a day) and working in the house and garden had been good for her. She reached for the fourth and final table, at the front of the next aisle. As she pulled it towards her, she noticed a black leather shoe behind it, in the shadows next to the stacks. *Odd*, she thought to herself. How would you lose a shoe in a library? Probably fell out of a child's school bag. Julia remembered the frustration of the missing bits and pieces that had 'disappeared' from her Jess's school bag in the ditzy teenage years.

She gave the table another hard pull towards her, backing out of the stacks. Straightening up, she saw that there was not only a shoe in the shadows, but also a sock and the bottom of a trouser leg.

And inside the trouser, and the sock, and the shoe – was a leg.

4

'Tabitha!' she shouted, although the librarian was right behind her. 'There's someone here. Come and look.'

Tabitha came forward. 'Good Lord, good God, oh good heavens,' said Tabitha when she saw the leg. 'It's a man. Is it...? Is he...?'

'I don't know,' Julia answered the unasked question. The leg was certainly immobile, and lying at an odd angle. The man lay in such a way that the leg was sticking out, but his body was behind the end of the row of shelves. Julia hesitated to go further. The man might be dead, and she knew enough to know that her footsteps might disturb important evidence.

'I think we should phone the police,' she said. 'And maybe an ambulance.'

'He might just be asleep. A glass of wine too many, perhaps? He might have been locked in by mistake,' Tabitha said.

Tabitha was by nature an optimist. Julia was more pragmatic, and strongly suspected this was not the case. But she didn't want to call the police and an ambulance for a sleeping drunk.

'Let's go around and get a closer look,' she said, and stepped further into the stacks, Tabitha close behind. They shuffled past the protruding leg trying not to disturb anything, until they could see the rest of the man, lying on his back at the end of the Natural History row. The two women gazed down at the body, which was instantly recognisable. The floppy hair, the straight nose, the soft blue shirt.

'V.F. Andrews,' murmured Tabitha in a shocked whisper.

It was undeniably Vincent Andrews, and he was undeniably dead. A hole pierced his throat, and blood had seeped from it into the soft blue shirt. The carpet underneath him was soaked red-brown.

'Call the police,' Julia said curtly, as she dropped to her knees and leaned over the body. Vincent was still and grey, and lying in a pool of his own blood, but she nonetheless pressed a finger to his jugular, searching for a pulse. Unsurprisingly, there was none.

Tabitha's voice came to her as if from far, far away. 'I am reporting a death... Berrywick Library... Yes, it's on the main road. Berrywick. No, *inside* the library... I think he was shot.'

She ended the call and the two women looked at each other. They spoke at the same time.

'I don't understand how...' Tabitha started.

'When on earth...?' said Julia.

They both stopped. After a moment's silence, Julia was the first to speak. Her instinct, after years as a social worker working with at-risk youth and their families, was to ask questions and try to build a picture of what had gone on. The first question in her mind was how on earth nobody had realised that Vincent Andrews – the man who had drawn crowds of Berrywick residents – had never left the library last night?

'Surely Vincent left the library before you locked up last night?' she asked Tabitha.

Tabitha frowned. 'I didn't see him go. I saw him signing the books, of course. And I saw him gathering up his things while Phoebe packed up the credit card machine and the cash box. Sarah and Eleanor were waiting at the front, I think, while she did that. I remember that Eleanor was humming, in that odd way she has. I was doing a bit of a clean-up of the glasses, so I was in and out. But when I locked up, the library was empty. Or I thought it was.'

'Who was the last to leave? Do you remember?' asked Julia.

Before Tabitha could answer, the sound of brisk footsteps came from the foyer. DI Hayley Gibson came hurrying in, with DC Walter Farmer following behind.

'Julia!' Hayley said in surprise. 'What are you doing here?'

'I came to help Tabitha clean up the library after last night's event. That's when we found the body.'

Hayley raised an eyebrow, as well she might. This was not the first, nor even the second, but in fact the fourth body that Julia had come across in Berrywick. 'You do have the most peculiar luck, Julia,' said Hayley. Then she became brisk, switching into her no-nonsense work mode.

'Where is it?' she asked. 'And do we know who it is?'

Tabitha moved aside to allow her access. 'Over here. It's Vincent Andrews. V.F. Andrews, the writer.'

Hayley Gibson looked down at the body. 'You sent me the invitation to the talk, I remember,' she said to Julia. 'I couldn't make it last night. Meeting with the local firefighters. Seems I should rather have been here.'

She knelt down so that she could have a better look at the body, and carefully put on a pair of disposable gloves that she took from her pocket.

'He wasn't shot,' she said, as she slightly moved Vincent's head, better exposing the source of the blood. 'That's not a bullet wound. It looks as if he was stabbed, or impaled.' She stood up, and glanced around the area. 'No sign of a weapon? A knife, anything sharp? I take it you didn't move anything?'

'Of course not,' said Tabitha, sounding mildly affronted. Julia knew that Tabitha had read more than a few police procedurals in her time, so would know this sort of thing. In addition to not being a complete idiot. 'As soon as we found him, we phoned you.'

'Secure the crime scene,' Hayley instructed the young DC, removing her gloves and shoving them in her pocket. 'And close the main door. The library's closed. We can't have anyone in here. Crime scene are on their way.'

She turned to Tabitha. 'Talk me through what happened last night.'

'He was here yesterday evening for the talk, of course. It went really well, even if he did cut me off before we were quite done. Still, nobody seemed to mind. After that, he was at a little table in the foyer, where people were buying books, and he was signing them. He was quite chatty, giving everyone the time of day, and it was getting late, so I started clearing up. I didn't see him leave. Sarah, his wife, and Sarah's mom were hanging about, looking anxious to go, so I thought they might leave soon. He was just there one minute, and gone the next. I didn't think too much of it, although I was sorry not to have thanked him and said goodbye and all that. Still, I thought I could always write a card. Not now, obviously...'

'So you have no idea when he actually left? Or if he left at all?'

'Well, there was no one here when I locked up. But as to his movements, you'll have to ask his wife, Sarah. Or Phoebe, the publicist from Prime Publishing. She was selling the books. She was still there the last time I saw him.'

'What's the wife's full name? And where is she?'

Tabitha looked at Julia, who answered. 'Sarah Andrews. She and Vincent were staying at a B&B in the village. I don't know which one, but I can ask Sean – Dr O'Connor – she's his cousin's daughter.'

'Please do.'

Julia stepped away from Hayley and Tabitha, and took her phone from her handbag. She dialled Sean.

'Hello, Julia,' he answered, sounding a bit surprised at the morning call.

'Sean, there's been an incident. I'm sorry to tell you, but Vincent Andrews is dead.'

'Dead? Just last night, he was... How? Heart attack?'

'Sean, he was killed. Murdered.'

'Murdered? My God. Where are you? Where's Sarah? She must be distraught.'

'That's just the thing. Vincent was killed in the library. I'm there now. It seems he died last night. The police are here and they need to reach Sarah. Do you know where she is? Where they were staying?'

'Yes, they are at the Carriage House in Fairmile Lane. I recommended it because it's close to the library.'

'Oh yes, I know the place. I've passed it on the way to the Buttered Scone. I'll tell DI Gibson. She'll have to go and speak to her, give her the bad news.'

Hayley was gesturing to Julia that she had something to say to Sean.

'Hang on,' Julia said to Sean, 'Hayley wants to say something.'

The policewoman held out her hand for the phone. 'May I?' Julia handed it over.

'Hello, Sean, my condolences... Yes, yes indeed. A thought. Would you be able to come with me to the B&B? She might need a family member... Yes. As soon as Crime Scene get here, I will go. I'll let you know when we're leaving. Thank you.'

She handed the phone back to Julia. 'Thanks.'

Julia nodded, and spoke into the phone. 'I'm so sorry, Sean, it's awful.'

'I can't believe it,' he said, sounding old and shaky. 'Murdered in the library. In Berrywick.'

'I know. Terrible. Just unbelievable.'

Awful, terrible, unbelievable. There were so few words, and they were so inadequate for the task of describing the brutal, incomprehensible reality of death.

'Julia, will you come?' Sean asked. 'Will you come with me to tell Sarah? I would appreciate you being there. She's not, well, she's a little fragile, and this... You being a social worker, it might be helpful.'

'Ex social worker,' she said. 'But yes, if you want me there, I'll come. As long as it's okay with Hayley. I'd better ask.'

Hayley waved her assent, impatient to get on with the investigation.

'Okay, Sean, I'll get a lift with Hayley. I'll meet you there,' Julia said, relishing the idea not one bit.

5

A shower of emotions passed over Sarah Andrews' face – a welcoming smile for Sean hid a hint of surprise at his unexpected appearance on her doorstep, and a frown crept in when she saw and tried to place Julia. When her eyes fell on Hayley, a stranger with an official air, in a navy trouser suit and practical shoes, she looked confused and then concerned.

'Sean,' she said. It was something between a statement and a question.

'May we come in, Sarah? There's something we need to talk about,' Sean said in his calm, low voice. There was no hint of the distress that he had shown on the phone when he'd first heard about Vincent's death. Julia had to admire his professional demeanour.

Sarah clutched her green velvet dressing gown together, cinched the tie tighter, and stood back without a word, letting them file past into the little sitting room of her suite in the B&B.

'I think you met Julia at the event last night, and this is Hayley Gibson.' Sean paused.

'Detective Inspector Hayley Gibson.' Hayley offered her hand.

The mention of her rank brought a look of panic to Sarah's face.

'Detective? Sean, what's going on? What's happened? Tell me.'

Sean took a moment, the four of them standing in the middle of the room, suspended in that long silence before the words were out and real. It struck Julia that between the three of them, they had a great deal of experience in delivering bad news. It was her opinion that it never got easier.

'Sarah, it's about Vincent. I'm sorry, but...' He faltered, cleared his throat and tried again. 'It appears that, um...'

Hayley stepped in, saying plainly, 'I'm sorry to inform you, ma'am, that a man we believe to be your husband, Vincent Andrews, was found dead this morning in Berrywick Library. We're going to need you to come and identify the body, but it does seem clear that it was Vincent, I'm afraid.'

Sarah turned pale and seemed to reach for something to support her.

Sean took Sarah's arm and walked her a few steps over the plush carpet to a small, dusky pink sofa. He lowered her onto the sofa and sat down next to her. Julia and Hayley stood awkwardly in the little space in front of them. The B&B wasn't set up for company, its inhabitants no doubt supposed to be out and about seeing the sights and sampling the eateries. Hayley gestured to Julia to take the single armchair. She sat down.

'I'm very sorry for your loss, ma'am,' Hayley said.

'Vincent. Oh my God. I can't... But yesterday...' Sarah said, in dull disbelief, and then asked, 'What happened?'

Sean opened his mouth to speak, but before he could, Hayley answered quickly, 'The post-mortem report will only be available in a day or two, so we don't have the full picture right now, but I would like to ask you a few questions, if I may.'

'Of course,' Sarah said.

'When did you last see your husband?'

'At the book event at the library last night. People were queuing up and he had all those books to sign and he was always happy to chat, so I knew it would take a while. I was tired, so I left before him and came home. My mum was leaving and she gave me a lift. I went straight to bed. When I woke up this morning, he wasn't here.'

'He hadn't come back at all?'

'No, not that I was aware of.' Sarah looked at Hayley, her blue eyes wide. She reminded Julia of a child who wanted to show the teacher that they were trying their best, even as they got the answers wrong.

'Weren't you concerned?' Hayley's tone had changed from gentle to slightly accusatory. Julia wondered if she thought that Vincent's death could have been avoided if only Sarah had been a more concerned wife.

'Of course I was. I mean, of course I wondered where he was.'

'Did you phone him?'

'No.'

There was a pause, Sarah's answer hanging like a bubble in the air before them. It did seem odd, Julia thought, not to phone when one's husband failed to return home at night in a strange village. She could not imagine not phoning her own ex-husband, back when they were married, if he had disappeared in the middle of the night. Not that that was Peter's style at all. Before Hayley could ask a follow-up question, Sarah said quietly, 'I didn't phone because we'd had a bit of a spat before I left the library.'

Sarah dropped her head, and Sean reached out and took her hand. 'It happens to us all,' he said gently. 'Nothing to be embarrassed about.'

'What was the fight – sorry, the spat – about?' Hayley had, Julia noticed, taken out her notebook and a brand new fresh-looking pencil.

Sarah hesitated, reluctant to divulge the details. 'It's personal. Nothing serious. Just the stuff of a long marriage. I would rather not say.'

Julia noted a barely perceptible change in Hayley's expression with this talk of spats and secrecy. Like Julia, Hayley would know that no one was more likely to get into a murderous rage than a spouse or lover. The perp was seldom a stranger. But Hayley had clearly decided to keep up the momentum of the conversation, rather than push the issue of the cause of the fight. She made a small note in the notebook, and then continued. 'Was it usual for him not to come home? Where did you think he was?'

'It has happened before. Once or twice.' Sarah looked around at the three faces watching her. 'I thought maybe he must have taken a room somewhere else. To punish me, you know. He was so cross. And there are plenty of B&Bs around here. I didn't think that something could have happened to him. I didn't.' At this, tears began to run down Sarah's cheeks. She was gulping for air. 'I was so cross with him for not coming home, and now it turns out he was dead. Oh, I feel so terrible now. The last thing I said to him...' She started to weep properly, her face in her hands, the curtain of expensive blonde hair falling forwards from its straight parting.

'I just... Can I? A moment, please,' she gasped in ragged breaths.

Sean stroked the hand that he was holding, saying, 'Try to breathe slowly, you're hyperventilating. It's the shock.'

'Should I make some tea?' Julia asked. All those years of training and work experience, and this was the best she could come up with in a crisis. Tea. But Sean looked relieved and grateful.

'Yes, thank you. If you would. Put some sugar in it for her.'

Julia walked through to the little kitchen area and switched on the kettle, which was already full. While the water heated, she wondered about the Andrews. Vincent had made quite a show – and a convincing one – of complimenting and smiling lovingly at his wife from up on stage, and yet the two of them were having a 'spat' not an hour later. It was odd, to say the least. And then he turned up dead the very next morning. Was the content of the spat somehow related?

There was a little tea station with teabags and sugar. She opened the fridge and found a small jug of milk covered in cling film.

She looked around while she waited for the kettle to boil. Clearly no one was expected to actually cook anything in the kitchen – and why would they, with all the gastropubs and cream tea servers in the village and its surrounds? The place had been equipped with the barest minimum of equipment – four white cups sat on four white saucers on a little shelf, a pile of four pale green bowls sitting on four darker green plates beside them. Three glass caddies held teabags, coffee and sugar. She took a bag and popped it into a cup.

The kettle boiled and clicked off. Julia poured the water over the teabag and looked around for a teaspoon. From a cutlery tree hung four spoons, four knives, four forks and four teaspoons. She gave the tea a stir, removed the teabag and dumped it in the little bin. She added milk from the jug in the fridge and then remembered the sugar. She added a teaspoon and stirred, thinking, as she did so, how unknowable and mysterious other people's marriages were. And one's own, in fact, as she herself had discovered.

As she stirred and pondered, her eyes fell on a small knife block, a piece of blonde wood with three slits for three knives, the largest of which was missing. In a kitchen where everything was so minimally equipped, and so perfectly aligned and matched, the missing knife looked out of place.

The skin on Julia's face and arms prickled.

She searched the tiny kitchen – the sink, the single drawer – to see if she could find the third knife. No sign of it.

Could it be the murder weapon? Had Sarah killed her husband with the kitchen knife? It sounded crazy, and far too much of a coincidence that Julia would be in the kitchen and notice its absence. But surely stranger things had happened? She needed to tell Hayley.

Julia picked up the cup and returned to the sitting room, where Sarah sat with her head resting on her knees, Sean patting her back. He looked up at Julia gratefully. 'There you are, thank you. Come now, Sarah, take a sip.'

Sarah raised her head and reached for the cup. She blew on the liquid and took a tiny sip. 'Thanks,' she said. 'Sorry, just the shock...'

'No need to apologise,' said Sean kindly.

Julia tried to catch the detective's eye, to give her a sign that she needed a word, but Hayley was clearly eager to get back to the inquiry.

'If I may continue?' she said. Sarah nodded.

'You mentioned that you had a row that evening, nothing serious, you said, the stuff of a long marriage. I'm sorry to have to pry at a time like this, but we do need to get a full picture. How would you describe your marriage, overall? Was there a lot of conflict between you?'

Sarah's face changed, as if a realisation had come to her. The teacup rattled gently in its saucer. She put it on the table and asked, 'I should have asked this before. But how exactly did my husband die?'

6

'Killed?' Sarah asked. And then, rather redundantly, 'You mean on purpose? Are you saying Vincent was murdered?'

'I'm sorry, Mrs Andrews,' said the detective. 'As I said, the forensic investigation is in process, but it appears that he was stabbed in the neck with a sharp object.'

'In the library? By whom? And all the people there... I don't understand...'

Julia had seen this before – the confusion that terrible news brought, the brain's inability to process what had been said, and what had happened. Either Sarah Andrews was in shock, and struggling to grasp the reality of her husband's murder – or she was a very good actor.

'Neither do we, as yet. We are investigating. That's why we are here, to get as much information as possible about the time leading up to his death.'

'Of course,' she said. 'Vincent, oh my God. He was just...' She gestured to a black jacket hung over a chair next to a small table. 'He was just here. Alive.'

It was one of the great unfathomables of life, Julia thought, that anyone who died was, just milliseconds before, as alive as any of us.

Hayley spoke. 'Mrs Andrews, the rows between you... Was there ever violence?'

'Physical violence? Oh goodness, no. Vincent would never hurt me. We argue. Argued. But no violence, no, never. I can't believe you would ask me such a thing, at this time.'

'Now, Sarah, DI Gibson has to look at all the possibilities, make the proper inquiries,' said Sean, in a conciliatory tone. 'To find out what happened and to rule things out.'

'I understand,' Sarah said. Turning to Hayley, she said, 'Our marriage was good, but not perfect. Like any couple, we were not without our problems. Yes, we argued a bit. No, it never got physical.'

'What was last night's argument about?' asked Hayley.

Sarah shifted in her seat on the sofa. She seemed reluctant to answer. After a pause, she sighed, and spoke. 'Vincent was an attractive man, charismatic and charming. And, in recent years, a little famous. An *artiste*.' She said the word ironically, with an exaggerated French pronunciation and an edge of bitterness. 'It's hardly surprising that women liked him. And to be honest, he liked the attention. That's what the spat was about.'

'Was there a specific incident? At the book event, perhaps? Something that triggered the row?'

'Yes. Phoebe Ailes, the woman from the publisher, the one selling the books. She arranges the events, the publicity and so on. She's very starry-eyed about him, the successful author, you know. She's not the first... Anyway, she was flapping about gazing at him adoringly and laughing at his jokes. I felt he could do more to keep her at bay, and I said as much.'

'Is it her job to come along to these things?' asked Hayley.

'Sometimes, although she wouldn't usually be at such a small gathering, selling in person. She lives not far from here, apparently. Said it was no trouble to come. I felt... Well, I didn't think she needed to be here, and to stay over, for a little thing at an unknown library in a little village in the Cotswolds.' She paused, and then added, 'No offence.'

'What did Vincent think?'

'Oh, the usual. He swept it all away. Said we should let the publisher do their job and it wasn't up to me to micromanage things, their staff, you know. Phoebe was merely being helpful and professional. I was misinterpreting and overreacting as usual. Like with his so-called research weekends. He could put things in a way that made me feel ridiculous, like I was imagining things that didn't exist.'

It's called gaslighting, thought Julia. Convincing someone that what they experienced was not real. It was often a factor in toxic and abusive relationships. She'd seen it many times in the course of her social work.

'Maybe he was right, maybe I was imagining things. I made a big deal out of nothing. I never thought that our last conversation... and now he's...' She dissolved into tears.

'Now, now. This isn't your fault,' said Sean. 'Perhaps you need a rest.'

'Yes, I think so,' Sarah said. 'I would like a break.'

Hayley shot Sean an irritated look, and turned to Sarah. 'Of course, Mrs Andrews.'

Sarah looked stricken. 'Vincent's mother... Oh God. I'll have to phone everyone.' She wilted visibly at the thought of it all, her head dropping.

'I'll stay with you,' said Sean, patting her shoulder. 'I'll give you a hand with it all.'

'I'm sorry for your loss, Mrs Andrews,' Hayley said. 'I'll phone you later to make an appointment for a formal interview, to help with the investigation. There will be more questions, as I'm sure you'll understand.'

Sarah nodded dully and her hand floated in a weak wave of assent.

'One last thing, if I may.'

Sarah raised her eyes to Hayley.

'Where can I find Phoebe Ailes?'

7

The women walked in step, their feet on the gravel path unnaturally loud in the quiet of the Saturday morning. Hayley Gibson was silent as they made their way from the front door of the B&B to the road. Her face was pale and her thin lips pressed together. You could almost hear her brain whirring. Julia followed her cue, not saying a word. She knew that the detective had been irritated by the abrupt end to the discussion with the victim's wife.

Hayley opened the little gate, standing back to let Julia go ahead of her, and then closed it behind her with a firm click. She fished in her jacket pocket as she walked towards her red Polo, pulling out a key and pointing the remote control towards the car to unlock it.

'There's something I need to tell you before you go,' Julia said.

Hayley stopped short, her arm held horizontal, the remote in her hand. She looked at Julia expectantly.

'There was a knife missing from the B&B. In the kitchen.'

'How do you know?' Hayley lowered her arm.

'There should have been three in the knife block and I noticed there was one missing.'

'It could have been anywhere. In the dishwasher.'

'There was no dishwasher. But I looked around. No sign of it. Everything was very neat and ordered. I would have seen it, if it was there, I think.'

'It could have been broken. Stolen by a previous guest. Thrown away by mistake.'

'Yes, that's possible.' Julia was less certain of herself now. There were of course a hundred possible explanations for a missing knife, now she thought about it. 'Anyway, I thought you should know.'

'Thanks. I'll keep it in mind. Let's see what forensics says about the weapon.'

'Sure, it was just a thought.' Julia hesitated. 'Do you think Sarah might have killed her husband?'

'A spouse would always be of interest at this early stage,' said Hayley, noncommittally. 'But it's too early to make any sort of assumption.'

'Of course, yes. But it's odd, don't you think? She didn't notice he wasn't home, and when she did, she didn't phone him?'

'Yes. And their last interaction was a fight. Or a spat, as she put it. It's a pity we couldn't continue talking. I'm going to have to conduct a formal interview to get more information.' Hayley raised her arm again, and this time hit the remote. The car gave two beeps, and the rear lights flashed briefly. 'But in the meantime, I'm going back to the office. Try to locate Phoebe Ailes. See if I can get forensics to buck up, at least on the weapon. Get some people looking into Vincent Andrews.'

'I suspect you'll find a woman or two lurking in the background, or turning up amongst the suspects,' Julia said, then blushed, feeling she'd overstepped. The two women had an odd sort of connection, having been thrown together in a murder investigation just weeks after Julia moved to Berrywick. It was a friendship of sorts, and there was mutual respect, but it was hardly Julia's place to proffer motives for crimes that Hayley was investigating. 'Sorry, of course it's none of my business.'

Hayley leaned one arm on the roof of the car and looked at Julia. 'Well, you did find the body. Again. And besides, what you say does seem likely from the little I got from Sarah. Did you meet Vincent Andrews last night?'

'I saw him in the conversation with Tabitha. He was good. Came across as very warm and personable. People liked him – women especially, I would think. It was clear that he enjoyed the attention of the crowd. Tabitha introduced us briefly afterwards when he was getting ready for the signing. I saw enough to know that he could turn on the charm. Had that slightly long handshake, good eye contact, and that boyish grin.'

'Right. Know the type.' The way Hayley said it, she had no love for 'the type'. Julia wondered briefly about Hayley's personal life, about which she knew next to nothing. Was there a bad relationship there? A charming someone who had broken her heart?

Hayley opened her car door. 'Lift home?'

'Not to worry, it's an easy walk and I've got to stop in at the library to see how Tabitha's doing. We were going to have lunch, but I doubt we'll do that now, under the circumstances. And you've got plenty to do, I'm sure.'

'Oh yes. That I have, starting with finding Ms Ailes, who may or may not still be in Berrywick, staying at who-knows-what address,' said Hayley. She got into the driver's seat and said rather irritably, 'It would have been helpful if Sarah had at least a phone number, but there you go. That's detecting for you. Bye then, Julia.'

She slammed the door, turned on the car and drove off with a wave of the hand.

. . .

The body had been removed from the library. Julia was grateful not to have to confront the bleak topography of the dead man under a sheet, the jutting toes and knees and nose. The front door of the library had been closed and locked when she arrived, but she had seen shadowy figures moving behind the frosted glass panels. A bit of knocking and banging had drawn the attention of a young uniformed policeman who, after some explanation and the intervention of Tabitha, had allowed Julia in with stern warnings about not disturbing the crime scene.

Tabitha looked about a hundred years old. Of all Julia's contemporaries, Tabitha was the one who had retained the most youthful energy into her sixties. Her golden-brown eyes were bright. Her curls, though greying, were soft and lively, and bounced when she walked or moved her head. Tabitha's collection of earrings, baubles and bangles was legendary, and she met the world cheerfully accessorised every day, accompanied by the gentle tinkling of silver and beads. If her look was lively, her spirit matched it. She was whip-smart and well-read and interested in everything and everyone. But no amount of bounce and bangles could disguise the sadness and exhaustion on Tabitha's face now.

'How are you?' Julia asked, the words weighted beyond the commonplace greeting.

'In shock, I think. I can't believe that V.F. Andrews is dead. Killed in the library. *My* library. And just last night.' Tabitha's voice shook.

'Shall we go outside for a bit? We can get some fresh air.'

'I don't know if I can.'

Tabitha glanced over at the crime scene, the area where Vincent had died. Also the area where their book club took place on the third Wednesday of the month, and where school children did their homework, or slouched on the sofas and read comics while waiting for mum to choose her next novel. The young policeman who had let Julia in had gone back to join his colleague, a serious-faced young woman, who was busy with yellow crime-scene tape. They both wore plastic booties over their shoes, as did a third person, who was writing notes on a clipboard and speaking into the phone tucked under her chin. Julia had the odd impression of being inside a television show.

'The police. They might need me.'

'They'll be busy for a bit by the looks of things,' Julia said, taking her friend's hand. 'Tell them you'll be outside if they want you. I'll make you some tea and we'll sit in the sun.'

The two women sat on a bench in the little garden in front of the library. The day was chilly, and they wrapped their hands around their cups for heat. Tabitha sipped her tea, and then gave a soft sigh as she lifted her face from the warming steam rising off the cup. 'Thank you,' she said, giving her friend a smile. 'I needed that. How was Sarah Andrews?'

'Shocked. Sad. Angry.' Julia filled her in on the conversation. The argument. The women.

Tabitha shook her head sadly. 'Imagine, the last words she said to her husband were angry ones.'

'I know, it's awful.'

They sat in silence for a moment, watching a robin redbreast which had landed on the bird table Tabitha had put in at a height designed to keep Too, the library cat, from making a meal of the birds. The robin pecked enthusiastically at a pile of seeds.

'What did the police say?' Julia asked Tabitha.

'They weren't very forthcoming. Ongoing investigation and all that. But I overheard a few things.' Tabitha said this mildly, but Julia knew that she was smart and curious, and had probably made it her business to 'overhear', whilst giving the impression of an older lady pottering about the library.

'It seems he was killed where he lay. The pool of blood apparently indicated that the body hadn't been moved. It happened sometime late last night, which of course we knew.

No obvious injuries, it seems, other than, you know, the wound that killed him. It didn't look as if there had been a fight. No bruises or scratches on his face or hands.'

The robin was joined by two little brown birds. What they were, Julia had no idea. She had thought vaguely that she might take an interest in birds once she moved to the countryside. Learn their names and habits. Maybe buy some binoculars. Make a list of birds she saw. But she'd realised that she only liked birds in the most general manner. She was happy to see them out and about and enjoyed their songs and antics and activities, but had no need to know any more about them.

'I'd better go and see if they need anything inside,' Tabitha said, interrupting Julia's ornithological musings.

'Finish your tea. They'll call you if they need you. Did they say anything about the murder weapon?'

'There was quite a lot of humming and haw-ing about that. Not clear apparently. It seems it was a rather unusual, um, wound. Not a bullet though, they knew that much. More of a stabbing; there's a hole.'

Julia's thoughts turned to the knife block, and the missing kitchen knife. What sort of hole would that make, she wondered with a shiver.

'What does Hayley think happened?' Tabitha asked.

'She didn't give an opinion. Just listened to what Sarah said.'

'Do you think she did it? Sarah? Does the detective think so?'

'I don't know. She didn't say. Hayley needs a lot more information before she can start making that sort of judgement. First, she's going to track down the publicist, Phoebe, I think her name is.'

'Phoebe Ailes, from Prime Publishing.'

'Yes, her. See what she can find out from her. Put the time-line together. Who left when, I suppose. Find out if there was a relationship between Andrews and her. Or Andrews and anyone else. That sort of thing. Sarah didn't know where she was staying, and it's Saturday so there'll be no one at the publisher's offices.'

'Well, I've got her email address, if that helps,' said Tabitha, reaching for her phone. 'She was the one I dealt with about the details of the event. I'll send it to Hayley, shall I?'

'Yes, definitely. That might save her a bit of trouble.'

Julia heard footsteps on the path. She looked up and to her surprise, there was Phoebe Ailes herself. The girl hadn't spotted the two women, who were screened by a lush stand of hydrangeas.

Phoebe peered through the frosted glass of the closed library door, her hand on the door handle. She hesitated, and then pushed. The cops hadn't locked it again after Tabitha and Julia went out.

Julia watched as the younger policeman stepped up to her, blocking her path.

'Oh,' Phoebe said in surprise. 'I think I left my jacket here.' The girl's voice stopped abruptly and her face froze when she took in the scene. The police, the plastic booties. The tape.

'What's going on?' she asked. 'What happened here?'

8

'I'm sorry, ma'am. I'm not at liberty to say. Police matter. You can't come any further, this area is closed for a police investigation,' said the young policeman, holding up his hand.

'What? Oh, oh, my goodness. Sorry. I had no idea. I just came to look for my jacket, but I'll go.'

'Thank you, ma'am,' he said, and turned back to join his colleagues, closing the door behind him.

Phoebe turned quickly, and walked back down the path.

'Ms Ailes?' Julia called after her, standing up. It wasn't Julia's position to confront the woman, but neither could she simply let her leave. At least she must keep her in the village, and put Hayley in touch with her.

Phoebe looked in surprise at the hydrangeas, the bench and the two women.

'Hold on a moment, please,' said Julia.

'Yes... But who...? Can I help you?'

'I'm Julia Bird. I saw you last night. Could I have a moment? There's something I need to tell you.'

Julia gestured to the bench, upon which Tabitha still sat. Tabitha patted it encouragingly. Phoebe hesitated – she seemed flustered by the whole strange business – then nodded, sitting down.

'You remember Tabitha Fullergood, the librarian?'

'Yes of course. Hi, Tabitha,' Phoebe said. 'What's going on? Did something happen after last night's event? A robbery or something?'

'Not exactly,' Tabitha said, struggling to find the words.

Julia stepped in. 'It's rather more serious, I'm afraid. A death. The police want to speak to people who were there last night, and I mentioned you...'

Phoebe interrupted. 'Someone died? Oh my word. Who?'

Julia took a deep breath and answered, 'Vincent Andrews.'

It seemed impossible that Phoebe's pale face could become any paler, but what little colour she had drained away, leaving her grey with shock. 'Vincent? No. Oh my God. I don't understand.'

Julia put a hand on the young woman's shaking shoulders. 'The investigating officer was looking for your number. She wants to speak to people who knew him, and who saw him last night. I'm going to call her and tell her you're here.'

Phoebe nodded dumbly, as Julia reached for her phone and called.

'Hayley, Julia. Phoebe Ailes is here at the library. I thought you'd want to know.'

'I'm coming right over,' said Hayley. 'Good thinking, Julia. Thanks.'

Julia was pleased that Hayley was praising her rather than telling her to keep her nose out of things for once.

The call ended; she turned to Phoebe. 'Detective Gibson is only a few minutes away. She's going to turn around and come here, if you don't mind waiting.'

'I don't know how I can help, but of course I'll wait. I don't understand... What happened?'

Julia didn't want to offer any information that might jeopardise Hayley's interview. 'I'm not sure. We should probably wait for the detective, she can fill you in.'

Tabitha patted Phoebe's back. 'It must be a terrible shock for you. Were you close?'

'Oh yes. I mean, no. Well, not *close*, exactly, but we worked together a lot. He was our top author, and it was my job to look after him and his publicity. I organised all the tours and events and things. His books are brilliant, people love them. He was a popular speaker.' Phoebe sounded as if she was personally responsible for Vincent's speaking prowess.

'I can see why. I enjoyed the chat yesterday. He was clever and charming. I could see how the audience responded to him,' said Julia.

'Oh, they did,' Phoebe sounded quite proud of her dead author. 'Everyone liked him. Too much sometimes; it was hard to get rid of some of them. I'd often have to rescue him from an over-enthusiastic book club lady.' Her face grimaced in irritation at the thought, and then softened into tears.

'Oh, Vincent, poor Vincent. And he was about to get a television deal. Frederick Eliot, my boss, told me he was on the verge of making a deal that would take Vincent to the next level. I really thought it would happen this time.' The tears were flowing down her cheeks. Julia watched one leave her jawline and plop onto her sharp collarbones before continuing its journey into the scoop neck of her dress – a rather too flimsy one for the weather, in the same blue as her hair.

'How long have you worked together?' Julia asked, wondering when Hayley would arrive.

'About three years. It was my first proper job out of university, I was just an assistant, but Vincent always noticed me and made an effort to get to know me. He was so kind. And then I got promoted, and started working on the events and publicity for his books. It can be lonely for the writer, all the travelling, and stressful. But I took care of everything. He was so appreciative of everything I did. Said he didn't know what he'd do without me. I just can't believe he's gone.'

While Tabitha comforted Phoebe through a fresh round of tears, Julia scanned the road, wishing that Hayley would get a move on. She was finding the situation rather tricky. She wanted to quiz Phoebe about her relationship with Vincent, but she knew it wasn't her job. And she didn't want to give out any information that DI Gibson might not want Phoebe to know.

Traffic was light on a Saturday morning. She watched the passers-by. A couple of middle-aged cyclists out for a ride, decked out in top-to-toe Lycra. A picture perfect family, mum, dad, son, daughter. There was Moira, with her clever border collie, Sammy, walking at heel without a lead. Maybe when Jake grew up a bit, and with lots of practice... No, she had to admit it was unlikely.

At last! Hayley Gibson came into sight, her little car moving down the narrow road at pace, and pulled up in front of the library.

'Here she is,' Julia said with relief. Phoebe sat up straighter, and wiped her sleeve over her face in a childlike gesture that made Julia sad for the poor girl.

Hayley Gibson got out of the car, slammed the door and walked over to them.

'Hayley, this is Phoebe Ailes. Phoebe, DI Gibson.'

'Thanks, Julia, much appreciated.' Hayley spoke brusquely as usual, but her eyes spoke of genuine gratitude.

'Don't mention it. I'll be going, leave you to it. Just need to pop in to get my handbag.' As Julia walked back to the library, she remembered Phoebe's jacket. 'Oh, Phoebe, shall I ask the uniforms to have a look for the jacket while I'm there?'

'What do you mean?'

'The jacket. The one you left.'

'Oh, that jacket. Of course. No, don't worry. I remember now, it's not there. I left it somewhere else.'

Tabitha and Julia walked back into the library, so that Hayley could speak to Phoebe in private.

'Nearly done here,' said the female police officer to Tabitha. 'You can open again Monday.'

'Thank you,' said Tabitha. 'I'll wait for you, lock up afterwards. No lunch at the Buttered Scone, I'm afraid, Julia.'

'No. I'd better be getting home to Jake at any rate. Lord knows what carnage he's caused. Last week I was out a bit too long for his liking and he dug up a potato plant from the vegetable garden and put it on the doorstep as a welcome gift, along with a mysterious yellow sock.'

Tabitha smiled. 'Tell you what, why don't we have breakfast tomorrow? Meet at the Scone at nine.'

9

Julia hadn't been seated three minutes when Tabitha appeared. One of the contributing factors to their long friendship was that they were both reliably punctual. It really made a relationship much more relaxed. No anxious waiting, wondering if you'd got the time wrong, or if the other person had forgotten. No grumpy foot tapping and pretending to be busy on your phone.

Julia was at her usual table on the pavement, just to the left of the entrance to the Buttered Scone. She sat outside, because of Jake, but close enough to chat to regulars seated inside by the window, which opened wide. Fortunately it was a reasonably warm day – she had no idea what she'd do when the weather turned. Tabitha took the seat opposite her.

'Well hello, Tabitha!' Flo looked positively delighted to see the librarian, which Julia took to mean that news of Vincent's demise at the library had made its way to the Buttered Scone. Sure enough, knives and forks were put down on plates and heads turned at the three or four tables that were already occupied. The faces looked over eagerly – with a bit of luck there would be some inside info, food for gossip and discussion for the rest of the day.

'Nasty business,' tutted Flo as she gave Tabitha a menu. 'You all right, love?'

'Yes, thanks, Flo.'

The waitress was not to be deterred. 'Who'd have thought, a body in the library? And a famous one at that,' Flo said, and waited expectantly, an encouraging half-smile on her face.

Tabitha wasn't biting. She nodded and opened the menu, scanning the options, even though she, like all the regulars, would know every one of them by heart. 'I'll have a coffee please, black. And the scrambled eggs and bacon. Thanks, Flo.' She closed the menu firmly and handed it over.

Julia and Tabitha had barely had time to greet each other when they were again interrupted, this time by Pippa. 'Well hello, darling Jake,' she said, greeting the half-grown dog before the humans. 'Aren't you a love?'

Jake enthusiastically agreed that he was, indeed, a love. His tail thumped the table leg, sloshing Julia's tea into the saucer and setting the cutlery rattling.

Julia found Pippa's adoration of Jake amusing, given that Jake had driven her completely mad when he – together with his better-behaved siblings – had lived with her in anticipation of their being trained as guide dogs. Jake alone had failed to make the grade, due to his extreme naughtiness, his unwilling-ness to take instruction, and his uncontrollable urge to chase birds. Pippa had been delighted to palm Berrywick's Naugh-tiest Chocolate Labrador off on Julia.

'Awful news about Vincent Andrews,' Pippa said. 'Awful for you, Tabitha. I knew him a bit, you know. He was at school with my brother. We lived over that side back then.' She did the sort of hand wave that people in the village did when indicating all and any places beyond the confines of Berrywick, whether that be the next village over, or Australia. She sat down on the spare seat, without so much as a 'May I?' and continued.

'He and our Duncan were best mates. Naughty, they were.

You wouldn't believe the pranks they pulled on the citizens of Hayfield. Never thought Vince would end up a famous author. Certainly showed no talent at school. Then again, I never thought he'd end up murdered, for that matter. Gave no sign of it.'

'Well, I suppose no one ever thinks they're going to be murdered,' Tabitha said, rather weakly.

'Lovely chap, though,' continued Pippa. 'Had a nice way with him. Friendly, sweet. And when he grew up a bit, ooh, the girls liked him.'

'I can imagine,' said Julia truthfully – she had no trouble believing that.

Flo was back with Tabitha's coffee, and took the opportunity to join in the conversation. 'Good looking fellow, he was. Like a more macho Hugh Grant. Or a more literary Matt Damon.'

'Quite right. Indeed,' Pippa said, pleased to have a rather more expert and engaged discussant in Flo.

'And even a hint of our Mr Cumberbatch I thought. Around the eyes,' Flo said seriously, as if she had given the matter a good deal of thought and attention.

'He was quite the charmer, even back then,' said Pippa. Leaning in to Flo she said, in a confiding tone, 'He and Olga were an item, would you believe it?'

Flo clearly would not, judging by the exaggerated look of shock on her face and the barely contained squeal of delight.

'Yes, indeed. For a good year or so. Until he went off to uni. She was still at school, a year or two behind him. Teenage heartbreaks are the worst, poor girl. And his parents moved around then, so he wasn't even back for the holidays.'

'Olga? The Olga who works at the vet's?' Flo said, still in disbelief. 'I'd never have thought.'

'Yes, Olga Gilbert, from the vet's. I know it sounds crazy...'

There was an impatient ringing of the little bell on the

kitchen counter, signalling the presence of Tabitha's scrambled eggs and bacon and Julia's Gruyère omelette.

'Hang on a mo,' said Flo, and dashed over to grab them off the counter. She was back in a minute, sweeping past a big bearded man who was trying to get her attention as if he were invisible, and plonking the plates down rather abruptly in front of Julia and Tabitha.

'Go on then.' She stood over Pippa expectantly, her hands on her hips.

'Well, she was a fine looking girl. Very fine. And clever, too. Oh, they were quite the couple.'

Flo looked doubtful. Julia herself had no view on Olga. She had never seen her at the vet. She had of course noticed her in passing at V.F. Andrew's book event. His last ever book event, as it turned out. Olga had had a tense and weary air. She was tall and thin and very well dressed. Rather *over*dressed. Julia remembered that much, and waving her hand about. Poor thing, it must have been hard to see her first love swanning about looking handsome with his bestselling books and his beautiful wife. And he hadn't even picked her at question time! It said something about Vincent's charm – or Olga's own mental state – that she might still be carrying a flame for him after twenty-odd years.

'Next thing we heard about young Vince was when he popped up with a bestselling historical novel ten years later,' Pippa continued. 'You could have knocked anyone who knew him over with a feather, I tell you. An author! Who would have thought?'

By this stage, there was quite a bit of arm waving and throat clearing in the restaurant, as the other customers appealed for coffee refills, breakfast orders, and bills. 'Customers will be needing me, mustn't tarry,' said Flo, as if they'd been detaining her against her will. She went off muttering, 'Olga Gilbert, well I never.'

Pippa, after trying unsuccessfully to engage Julia and Tabitha further on the subject of Vincent's literary merits, good looks, and recent death, left with a mumbled excuse about dogs and walks.

Tabitha and Julia finished the rest of their breakfast in peace and quiet, undisturbed by nosy villagers. It was as if they made an unspoken agreement not to discuss Vincent Andrews. They hardly spoke at all, other than to remark on the tasty marmalade and the pleasant weather. Tabitha mentioned a programme she was enjoying on the television, about a shepherdess in Scotland. Julia updated her on the chickens' performance in the laying department – very satisfactory. They were good enough friends that they were comfortable with the silences between them.

They finished, split the bill in two without fuss, and went their separate ways – Tabitha to the library, and Julia for home. She intended to take a scenic route down the main road for a while, and then into Fairmile Lane and onto the path by the river, stopping at a field where Jake could run off the lead without causing any bother to anyone, human or avian.

She was passing Sarah Andrews' B&B when, rather to the sinking of Julia's heart, Sarah's car drew up alongside her and parked on the kerb. There was an awkward moment of greeting. 'How are you?' Julia asked, and then could have kicked herself. It seemed like an inappropriate question, given the circumstances. The woman's husband had been dead not even two days and was presumably chilling in the morgue at this very minute.

'Oh, fine,' said Sarah, although clearly she couldn't be. There was an awkward pause.

'You?' said Sarah, eventually.

'Fine, fine,' said Julia. She found herself casting around for something more to say. Even the traditional English space-fillers like 'lovely weather' didn't seem appropriate. After another awkward silence, Sarah said goodbye, opened the back door of her car and reached in for a handbag, a jacket and a long, furled red umbrella.

'Bye, then. Take good care of yourself,' Julia said, and turned to go.

She hadn't gone more than a few yards when Phoebe Ailes emerged from the cottage next door to Sarah's B&B. She closed the door hard. Sarah turned at the noise and stared at the younger woman in shock.

'You!' she said. 'You're next door?!'

'Hello, Mrs Andrews,' Phoebe said, almost in a whisper. 'I'm so sorry for your loss.'

'He put you next door?' Sarah demanded, storming over to her. 'Or did you do the bookings? I suppose you did.'

'I did. The publisher always arranges... I was just...' Phoebe stammered, and then regained her composure. 'It was convenient for everyone to be close to the library.'

'Oh yes, how convenient. He could just pop over for a visit. That's what you were hoping for, I suppose? A little one-on-one time with the star author. The two of you and your stories.'

Sarah was white and cold with rage. She seemed to have forgotten Julia's presence, and Phoebe hadn't noticed Julia at all. Julia stood rooted to the spot, her back pressed against a perfectly clipped box hedge. Jake took his cue from Julia and sat down, his body flush against her leg, sensing some sort of danger.

Phoebe shook her head. 'No, Mrs Andrews. It wasn't like that at all. I was doing my job.'

'You were always googly-eyed at him. Don't think I didn't notice the way you followed him about, the way you touched his arm. It was pathetic. He wouldn't look at a scruffy thing like you. Blue hair. We laughed at your blue hair.'

'That's not true!' said Phoebe, in a strangled shout that was both angry and hurt. 'He did look at me. I don't mean... It wasn't like that. We were friends. *Good* friends. We talked about things.'

'About what? Like how clever he was? How much you *admired* him, your special friend Mr Bestselling Author, the literary sensation? Oh, you don't know the half of it. Anyway, when was all this talking, before or after the two of you...'

'No! Shut up! That's not how it was. And anyway, maybe if you hadn't been so...'

Sarah seemed to grow a few inches, filled as she was with pure rage. 'I *beg* your pardon? If I hadn't been so what, exactly?'

'If you hadn't been so cold, and angry. And suspicious. Anyway, now he's dead. And I think I know who's to blame...'

Julia watched in horror as Sarah raised the furled umbrella and swung it at Phoebe. Fortunately her aim was poor, and it caught the girl a glancing blow on the upper arm. Phoebe yelped and grabbed her arm in pain, then launched herself at Sarah, who got in a few more umbrella strikes while Phoebe gave a couple of ineffectual blows with her fists.

It had been a long time since Julia had stepped in to break up a fight, and she didn't relish the idea of getting close to that swinging umbrella. But it looked like she would have to. She moved towards them, her arm up, ready to intervene, saying, 'Come on now, let's all calm down... Break it up.'

The umbrella, aimed at Phoebe, glanced off Julia's left shoulder. 'Ow,' she said, more in shock than pain. She rubbed the site where a bruise would surely appear, letting Jake's lead slip from her grasp. He ran into the fray, barking madly, growling and nipping, more in panic than in anger.

It was Jake's hysteria that finally stopped the fisticuffs.

10

Julia reached over and turned on the lamp on the table next to the sofa. She'd lain down in the clear afternoon light, and now found herself in the gloom, squinting over the pages of V.F. Andrews' new book. It was testament to his skill that two hours and fifty pages had somehow gone by almost unnoticed.

The bucolic descriptions of the Cotswolds village and its surrounds – the babbling brooks and stone cottages and pretty gardens – were delightful, and familiar to Julia in their similarity to Berrywick. She remembered that a couple of the locals at the book event had remarked on the same thing – familiar places and even faces. Vincent had brushed it off. But it really did seem as if he'd used the geography of this village for his fictional one. Clever idea, really – easier than inventing a whole new Cotswold village out of your head and remembering where to turn left, and what side of the road the pub was on. Julia was too much of a newcomer to recognise any of the characters. The main narrative centred around a beautiful and spirited young woman, Camille, who was a reporter on the *Wiltshire Observer*. Her neighbour and long-time suitor, Mick Garland, a decent fellow with freckles and a limp from an accident with a horse, was tossed aside for a higher status and better looking chap – a fellow journalist named Felix Port – leaving Mick bitter and angry and pathetic. Poor sap. There was a supporting cast of well-drawn parents, newspaper editors, friends and villagers.

What set the book apart was the historical detail. V.F. Andrews created a world which was as real as our own, layered and detailed and – to Julia's eye – authentic. He had a light touch. The attention to time and place didn't overwhelm the story, but rather buoyed and held it, making it sparkle in the light. Julia had been fascinated by a short detour into the rise of female reporters in the 1930s.

Rather reluctantly, she marked her page with a bookmark, and put the book down on the side table next to a buttery orchid in a willow-pattern pot. The situation with the umbrella-wielding widow and the possible 'other woman' had unsettled and exhausted her, but the lie down had restored her somewhat. Jake seemed to have had a similar reaction to the conflict. He'd been contentedly asleep next to the sofa, but was now on his feet, his eyes boring into her like two manic, glowing chestnuts. Time to get up. She would take Jake for a short walk in the gloaming before feeding him his supper and settling down for the night.

Despite his inability to concentrate in puppy class, Jake had remarkable observational powers. He could recognise individual pairs of shoes, for example. If Julia reached for her walking shoes or wellies, he would run to the door and leap about like an excitable bear cub. Her smart pumps elicited a despairing sigh. If the slippers came out, he flopped down ready for bed. He was particularly alert at key dog-central times of the day – morning and evening walk times, and supper time in the late afternoon. He responded to the rattle of his lead, the opening of the fridge door and the particular squeak the dog biscuit tin made when Julia opened it to give him a treat.

Jake was currently leaping and whining and chucking his not

insubstantial brown body at the kitchen door. 'Go outside and wait, I'll be there in a mo,' Julia said, opening the door to let him out. As she did so, she found herself face to face with Sean, the knuckles of his right hand raised, ready to knock. They both started in surprise, then both laughed gingerly, then spoke at the same time.

'Oh, I...'

'Sorry, I...'

The interaction had a strange mirroring quality which they both recognised, and laughed again.

'Walk with me?' she asked. 'We're only going down to the river. A quick one to get Jake out of the house.'

'I'd like that,' he said, stepping aside to let her out. 'Sorry I didn't phone first. I was nearby and I thought... Yesterday was so awful, I don't think we even said goodbye when you left Sarah's. I was going to phone you but there was so much to do as a family. The press, telling friends, the autopsy, funeral. Poor Sarah.'

'I hadn't thought about the press,' said Julia. 'Of course, it would be a story, the murder of a famous author.'

'We haven't mentioned the cause of death in the press release, so that part isn't public knowledge. Yet. It will get out, for sure.'

They turned into the road, walking in step, heading in the direction of the river path.

'How is Sarah? I saw her this morning, outside the B&B,' said Julia, hesitating over what to say next. 'She...'

'She told me about the, um, the contretemps with the publishing lass.'

'Phoebe Ailes. Sarah hit her with an umbrella.' Julia felt sorry for Sarah, of course, but was disinclined to give her a free pass on the physical violence.

'Phoebe, yes. Phoebe reported it to the police. Common assault, I think it's called. Detective Gibson came round. Sarah phoned me; she has no one else, really. Didn't want to get her mum involved. Eleanor can be quite... reactive. Protective of her daughter. It was God's own job sorting that out, I can tell you. But it looks like Phoebe isn't going to press charges.' He looked exhausted at the thought of it.

'That's a relief, I suppose,' said Julia. 'No fun for you, being in the middle of all of that. But at least you managed to calm things down.'

'Sarah's still furious. Shouted at DI Gibson. And she was raging about Phoebe. She was even cross with Vincent, which seemed a bit unfair under the circumstances, him being dead.'

'It's not uncommon for trauma or shock to be expressed as rage. I've seen it often. Anger seems easier, somehow. Easier than grief.'

Sean nodded. 'You're probably right. I've seen it in my patients too.'

They walked on, each in their own thoughts. Julia's turned to Sarah and Vincent. She just couldn't square this angry, hurt woman and the dead philandering husband with the loving couple she'd seen on Friday night. His warm looks, and his flattering references to his beautiful, understanding wife. Had it all been for show?

They reached the river path and turned into it without consultation. When Julia stopped to let Jake off the lead, Sean stopped too. She liked how comfortable their friendship was. Jake bounded about, stopping to sniff and follow a scent, then getting distracted by a bird or a breeze or a better odour.

The clouds held the last of the daylight and were reflected in the river, tinging the slow ripples pink. It was a windless evening, with a pleasant chill. Little birds swooped to catch insects on the top of the water. A light bobbed ahead of them, upriver. As it moved closer, Julia saw it was attached to the head of the metal-detector guy, who was coming up the path, sweeping his instrument over the ground, his headlamp showing the way.

'Hello, Harry,' Sean said, as he came up to them. 'Nice evening for it.'

'Ah yes, good to get out, clear the head,' the man replied, without slowing or taking his eyes from the ground.

'Bye then, best to Felicity,' Sean said, and they passed.

'It's an odd hobby,' Julia said, when they were out of hearing range. 'Finding old bits of metal.'

'It's quite popular in these parts. There are some interesting finds around here. Very old agricultural implements, household items and so on. Harry's a proper history enthusiast, he knows his stuff.'

Darkness was coming in fast and they picked up the pace a bit without having to say a word to each other.

'Makes sense. I suppose it's no weirder than playing the bagpipes or breeding Siamese fighting fish.'

'Growing enormous pumpkins.'

'Extreme ironing.'

'What?'

'Oh, it's a thing, I saw it on YouTube. Ironing in remote and dangerous locations. Mountain tops and so on.'

Sean opened his mouth to comment on that, or to lob the next in the volley of ridiculous hobbies, when his phone rang in his pocket.

'Sorry about that,' he said, reaching for it. 'I'd better check, might be a patient. Oh, it's Sarah.'

Julia walked on a few yards to give him some privacy for his phone call. She whistled for Jake. It was getting too dark for him to be off the lead. He got into enough trouble in the sunlight; she didn't want him bounding off the edge of the path into the water or something.

'Come on, Jake, come in,' she called, rousting the dog from a bush. He was damp and covered in sticks and leaves. In his mouth was a piece of pie crust.

'Where did you find that? My word, you can find food anywhere, can't you? You should've been trained as a truffle hound, not a guide dog. Although you'd swallow anything edible you found.'

Jake tossed the pastry up in the air and swallowed it neatly as it came down. He looked mighty pleased with himself.

'Good boy,' she said, clipping on his leash, and patting one of the drier patches on his back. 'You fine truffle hound, you.'

'JULIA!'

Sean's voice came crashing into the evening's peace. She looked up to see him walking fast towards her. 'We need to go now. Sarah's been arrested.'

'Oh no! Honestly, I think that's a bit much after what she's been through. I mean, it was only an umbrella.'

'She's been arrested for Vincent's murder.'

11

DI Hayley Gibson didn't look pleased at the arrival of Sean and Julia. No doubt, relatives – and their friends – added an additional layer of complexity to an already difficult situation. She was clearly busy and in the middle of something, or several things, moving briskly across the office, a couple of files in one hand, her phone in the other. She did not give the impression of someone willing to stop and discuss matters.

Julia hung back, letting Sean take the lead. She had no official role here, being neither a friend nor a relative, nor professionally involved in any way.

'Good evening, Detective,' said Sean. He spoke formally and calmly, but Julia knew him well enough to see that he was agitated: a slight flush to his neck, and a tremor in his hands. 'I am here about the arrest of Sarah Andrews. Can you tell me why she is being held? What are the charges?'

Hayley stopped her walk and addressed them. 'Sarah Andrews has been arrested in relation to the murder of her husband, Vincent Andrews. Certain evidence has come to light regarding his death. More than this, I'm not at liberty to say.'

'I believe she doesn't have a lawyer. Isn't it her right to have legal representation?'

'It is indeed. She may consult her lawyer, as I've told her.'

'I'll arrange it.' Sean paused, and then said, in a slightly less formal tone, 'Can I speak to her please, just for a minute or two? So I can sort things out with the lawyer, and inform her family?'

Hayley hesitated, and then said, 'All right. I am a bit worried about her, and you are a doctor, so I can make an exception. Two minutes, max. DC Farmer will be in the room.' She turned to Julia. 'Not you, I'm afraid.'

'Of course,' said Julia, who had no expectation of being included in such a meeting. Hayley led Sean through a door to the left of the counter. Beyond it, Julia caught a glimpse of a corridor with more doors leading off. The door closed behind them, leaving Julia in the waiting area.

She took a seat on an uncomfortable plastic chair, one of a row of five, two seats away from a woman who appeared to be drunk and trying her best not to show it. The woman swayed almost imperceptibly, and a sweet scent came off her. Sherry, Julia thought. Or port. She wondered what the evidence might be. Had they found the murder weapon? Was it the knife? Or was it something the forensic team had turned up? Or something else altogether – video footage, or mobile phone messages, or what have you?

The woman sitting near Julia answered a phone that had begun ringing in her pocket, proclaiming '*I like to move it move it!*' at a thousand tiny decibels. She launched into an outraged tale about someone called Greg who was, like Sarah, being held in custody: 'Disorderly, my foot. Good heavens, our Greg was only having a bit of a sing. I mean, if you can't walk about your own village of an evening and sing a song... Yes, I know, I know, lovely voice. And then he tripped. Those cobblestones are a menace, don't I always say? Tripped, he did, and the bottle fell... Well, yes, he was carrying a bottle. Beer. There's no law against *that*, far as I know. Anyway, it fell against this car. Some fancy bloody car some poncy bugger had parked right in the way. Rude fella, he was, there'd been a few words between them a bit earlier... Oh, nothing, just blokes sounding off, you know. Anyway, when he tripped, Greg's bottle fell against the car's headlights and broke them... What? Yes, both of them, as it happens. That, and a bit of a scratch to the paintwork. And a dent... Mmm, no, not too big. Well, big*gish* I suppose, depending. So yes, damage to property. Whoever heard of such a thing? Ridiculous charge.'

This intriguing story was just wrapping up when Hayley appeared. Julia got up and walked over to her.

'Is Sarah a suspect? I don't mean to interfere, but surely you don't think she killed him? It just seems so...'

Hayley cut her off, speaking quickly and quietly, 'Because it was your tip-off, I'm letting you know, we found the knife. We're waiting for forensics, but in the meantime Sarah has some questions to answer. Julia, this is a serious situation, and with you and Sean being... friends... and them being related, you understand I can't discuss it with you any further.'

Greg's tipsy friend got up and beckoned to Hayley. 'Hey, ma'am, police person. What's happening with Greg, then? The accidental car damage? Can he come out? It's getting past my bedtime, have to say.'

'The desk sergeant will update you when there's more information,' Hayley said. She turned away, her black boots clicking determinedly across the lino, carrying her through the door to the offices and cells before the woman could continue. With some grumbling, the woman sat down again, muttering about the state of the police services. She looked to Julia for support. Julia avoided eye-contact, and was relieved when the door opened a few minutes later and Sean came through it.

'Let's go,' he said brusquely. He looked grim. Julia stood up and followed him into the street, now dark. Sean unlocked his car without a word. They got in. He sat in the driver's seat and slammed the door.

'How was she?' Julia asked.

'She's terrible. Of course. She's just lost her husband, a grieving widow, and now she's been arrested. It's outrageous. Of course she didn't have anything to do with his death. I've left a message for her lawyer.' He looked at his phone again, and tossed it onto the shelf between the seats. 'Nothing from him.'

Julia had never seen Sean angry before. He was clearly the quiet, seething type of angry person. His face was pale, with heightened colour on the cheeks which made his blue eyes glint.

'What did she say?'

'They found a knife in the B&B. A kitchen knife, apparently.'

Julia nodded, as if this talk of kitchen knives were all news to her. He continued, 'But it was found in the bathroom, wrapped in a hand towel. There are traces of blood. It's gone for tests. Sarah says she knows nothing about the knife, she's never seen it. She reckons the killer planted it. Or someone else did, to frame her for the murder.'

'But who? And with what motive?'

'She was so distressed, she wasn't making much sense, and we only had a minute or two to speak. She was still spitting about Phoebe, but then she did say, "Or one of those women."'

'Women? Plural?'

'It seems so.'

'I must say, Vincent did seem like a man who liked the attention of women. And vice versa. And the way Sarah reacted to Phoebe made me think this wasn't the first time she'd had her suspicions. That kind of thing tends to get messy pretty quickly. But still. *Murder?*'

The word, spoken out loud, seemed to fill the car with something dark and heavy. It shocked them into silence for a minute, and then Sean spoke. 'Look, marriages can be tricky, granted, but there's no way that Sarah killed Vincent. It just didn't happen. The police will come to that conclusion too, I know they will, but in the meantime, I need to get her out of there. Surely they can't hold her.' He pulled the car out of the parking space and into the road. Julia hadn't thought that a person could drive angrily, but there was a quietly furious energy to his gear changes, and the way he used the accelerator.

'They can hold her for up to twenty-four hours, after that they have to charge or release her,' said Julia, who had some experience of this in her previous life, running a busy Youth Services centre in London. 'They'll push forensics on something like this. A murder, a high-profile victim. It'll be at the top of the queue. They'll likely have results tomorrow.'

'Well that's good to hear. But it still means she'll be in for the night. Imagine.'

'Awful for her. I'm sorry, Sean. But hopefully they'll be quick and she'll be out in the morning.'

She put her hand on his knee and gave it what she hoped was a comforting pat. He rested his hand on hers, and seemed to relax a bit. 'Thank you for being here, Julia. It means a lot to me. I'm sorry I've been so moody.'

'No need for an apology. It's a horrible situation.'

'I just hate to think of her there, and after what she's been through. But you're right. It'll be sorted out tomorrow and they'll release her. She's told me not to mention it to her mum. Doesn't want to worry her. And one never really knows how Eleanor will react to things. Sarah will be out tomorrow and Eleanor none the wiser.'

'You'll get hold of the lawyer and they will take over any further discussions with the police and deal with the media when this story gets out.'

'Oh God, the media. I'd forgotten.' Sean sighed.

'He's well-known, but not madly famous. It'll blow over.

When forensics are done, the body will be released, there'll be a funeral. Poor Sarah will have some closure, time to heal.'

Feeling a little calmer, they sat in silence for a little while, the headlights sweeping the deserted road. An owl flew low across the road in front of them, its wings huge in the beam of light. It turned its round face towards them, its big yellow eyes momentarily holding their gaze, and then swooped up out over the top of the car and away into the night.

12

Julia nominated Monday as a bonus Sunday. The weekend had been extremely stressful, what with the discovery of the body, and then spending so much of her time between the library, the police station, and Sean. She deserved a quiet day of rest and relaxation and she was going to have it. She was, after all, a retired woman of leisure. She was resolved to put thoughts of the murder out of her mind, at least for the morning, and read and nap.

She woke at her usual hour – she had never developed the ability to sleep in – went to the kitchen to make a tray of tea, and came back to bed with her book. She decided against the V.F. Andrews, on the basis that it wasn't conducive to her peaceful morning, given the author's recent death. She picked up her Kindle and one-clicked an alluringly light and tasty morsel, set in a coastal village on a Greek island, without any murders in it. She turned her phone on silent and put it face down on the nightstand where it wouldn't tempt her.

Propped up against a mountain of cushions, a cup of tea on the side table, the morning light streaming in, she felt a sense of calm come over her. She reached for her toast – well-browned, generously buttered, topped with her home-made strawberry jam and cut on the diagonal (the only proper way to cut toast, in Julia's view). She took a bite, put down the toast and picked up the Kindle with a contented sigh. This was just what she needed: a morning of rest and relaxation in bed with tea, toast and a book.

Jake, of course, didn't believe in rest and relaxation. Jake thought rest and relaxation was rubbish. He whined and pawed at the side of the bed, trying to entice her out on a walk.

'Stop that,' she said firmly, but he didn't.

'Come on then.' She let him up on the bed, even though she'd sworn not to. Just this once. Jake took this as an invitation to climb on top of her and lie across her tummy, smiling eagerly into her face and blocking her view of the Kindle.

Julia shoved him off, swung her legs off the bed and said, 'Come on, out!'

Jake was delighted at this turn of events. He leapt off the bed and dashed ahead of her into the kitchen and to the door. She opened it and let him out. He looked at her expectantly, hoping they would be leaving for the lake shortly.

'Later,' she said, and went determinedly back to bed.

Julia began to read. She got to the end of the first page and realised she had no idea what she'd just read. It had gone through her eyes but had somehow got lost on its way into her brain. She reread the page and moved on to the next one. The second page was a little better, and she started to settle into the gentle world of azure sea and golden, sun-warmed skin. By page three, her mind was calmer, and she was looking forward to a nice morning on the island's beaches, prior to lunch in a taverna with the heroine, the newly single Jemima, and the mysterious stranger with the black eyes and firm pectorals.

Julia lowered the Kindle.

Why was Jemima newly single, come to think of it? What had become of her previous boyfriend? Had Jemima of the

violet eyes and shining auburn locks stabbed him to death with
a kitchen knife before swanning off to Greece? Julia told herself
not to be silly. It was hard to picture and highly unlikely, especially in a holiday rom-com. But still, it happened, didn't it?

Page four.

Julia concentrated as hard as humanly possible on page
four, and it was indeed beautiful on the beach, but her mind
kept returning to the corpse of Vincent Andrews and the stab
wound in his throat. She imagined Sarah stabbing her husband
in the throat with a kitchen knife. She tried and failed to banish
Sarah and her knife and her dead husband from her brain. She
was ruining her indulgent morning.

She gave up on the Kindle, dropping it onto the bed with a
sigh, and picked up her phone to check her messages and scan
the news headlines.

'Oh heavens,' she said out loud. 'Another one.'

AUTHOR MURDERED IN COTSWOLDS LIBRARY

The stories had started almost immediately – but this one
seemed more in depth than the previous paragraphs that Julia
had spotted. A front page story on the *News Today*, accompanied by a smouldering photograph of Vincent in a black polo
neck. The picture looked about ten years old, and she assumed
it came from a book jacket. She scanned the story. Most of it
was familiar to her, of course – author of seven books, new one
recently published, in town for a book event, a signing at the
library, accompanied by his wife. There was nothing useful. 'A
local woman who declined to be named' had apparently said,
'He was in good spirits and it was a very nice evening. I can't
believe that it ended in this brutal way.'

A few more media outlets had picked up the story. One ran
a short feature on other famous deaths in libraries – there were a
surprising number of them in fiction. One mentioned the recent

murders that had occurred in Berrywick – the ones that Julia herself had discovered, and largely solved. A publishing news site referred to Vincent as 'The jewel in the crown and chief rainmaker at Prime Publishing' and gave a breakdown of how many copies of each book he had sold – loads and loads, as it turned out.

The phone rang. It was Sean. Just days ago, Julia had got a little zing of pleasure when she saw his name appear. Now she felt a prickle of dull dread. It seemed unlikely to be good news.

'Hi, Sean. What's up? Has Sarah been released?'

'No. They're still holding her. The police have applied for an extension. I didn't know that was possible.'

'If the crime is serious, like murder, they can apply to hold a suspect for longer.'

'I still can't believe that they even think this is possible. You only need to look at her to know she couldn't have done something like that.'

In Julia's quite extensive experience, you couldn't tell much by looking. Sure, you got your classic hoods and goons with angry faces and scarred knuckles, your skinny falling-apart junkies, and so on. But you also got perfectly innocuous middle-aged blonde ladies who turned out to be murderers. She did not share this opinion with Sean.

Sean cleared his throat and said, 'Julia, I need a favour. I wouldn't ask if it wasn't such a desperate situation.'

She waited.

'Would you phone Hayley Gibson, see what you can find out?'

It was the last thing Julia wanted to do, but she did it anyway. She couldn't refuse to help Sean help his cousin's daughter. She was quite surprised when Hayley answered – she had expected her to kill the call given what she had said at the station about not wanting to discuss the case any further. Julia got straight to the point.

'I'm phoning about Sarah. I hear she's being held for longer. I know you can't tell me much, but is she a suspect?'

Hayley hesitated and said, 'Off the record. The bloodied knife doesn't look good for her, Julia. And the physical attack on Phoebe points to a propensity for violence. It was enough to get an extension to hold her for ninety-six hours.'

'Do you really think she killed him?'

'Honestly, Julia? I think she did. She's trying to point us towards other suspects – that Phoebe woman as a spurned or jealous lover, possible business connections. As if publishing people are in the business of killing each other. I'm going to look into them, but between you and me – and please, don't go into detail with Sean – I think she's the most likely culprit. Forensic results will be here today and we'll know more.'

'Well, thanks for your honesty.'

'I shouldn't be talking to you about this at all. And just to be clear, this is a one-off – don't ask me for more.'

'I won't. I promise.'

'Oh, Julia, last bit of advice – the best thing Sean can do now is to get her lawyer to come and see her.'

'I'll let him know. Thanks, Hayley. Really. Thanks. I owe you dinner.'

Hayley made a sharp noise between a grunt and a laugh. 'At the very least.'

13

Phoebe's cottage was a mirror image of Sarah's. The same wallpaper, the same framed prints of local birds, the same beige carpet subtly patterned to hide wear and tear, the same stiff seating arrangement of the rather uncomfortable sofa and single chair. Julia found it oddly disconcerting.

When Phoebe saw Julia and Sean at the door, she seemed relieved. 'I saw them take Sarah away,' she said. 'What's going on?'

'They've taken her in for questioning,' said Julia, not wanting to go into detail. Phoebe was, after all, a possible suspect in the case.

'Poor Sarah!' Phoebe said, with what seemed like genuine pity. 'I can't imagine how she must be feeling right now, her husband dead, and her locked up. It's appalling.'

'That's very decent of you, considering,' said Sean. 'You don't think she did it?'

'Sarah? No. Of course not. She adored Vincent. Why would she kill him?'

Well, that was a rather awkward question. Julia caught Sean's eye and saw the same reaction in him.

Julia took a deep breath and answered, 'I believe the police might consider a possible motive could be jealousy? Sarah seemed to worry about him with other, um, women. You experienced it yourself, after all.'

'She was jealous, no doubt about it. And I can't say I blame her. Women did like him, he was nice looking and kind. It didn't hurt that he's kind of famous. And he was nice to chat to; honestly, he was just a regular chap, not at all what you'd expect – stand-offish, or too clever to have a normal conversation. We never talked about history and literature, just regular stuff, you know. Music, where we go on holidays.'

Sean cleared his throat and made some humming and hawing noises. Julia guessed what was coming, and she wasn't wrong.

'Phoebe, if I might ask. Your relationship with Vincent...' Sean, it seemed, could not quite bring himself to spell it out. But luckily, Phoebe understood.

'Like I said, we were friends. Hand on heart, there was nothing physical. If I'm dead honest, he is – was – a bit of a flirt. But I soon realised that that is all a show – he's actually a very loyal guy, wouldn't ever cheat on his wife. We were colleagues and friends. Good friends.'

'I'm not sure Sarah sees it that way. How's your arm, by the way?' Julia asked, remembering the scuffle with the umbrella.

'Oh, it's fine,' Phoebe said dismissively, giving it a rub.

Julia thought back to the incident. 'You said something about her... About knowing who's to blame. What did you mean?'

'I shouldn't have said that. I just meant that she would chase him away with her jealousy. The truth is, Vincent had plenty of opportunities, but honestly, he loved Sarah. He'd be devastated to think of her accused, locked up. Devastated.' Her voice broke. She took a couple of slow breaths, and then continued, calmer.

'That day, with the umbrella, she was just worked up. She lashed out. But you can't blame her, she was in shock. Her husband had been killed, after all. And I shouldn't have been next door. I should have given them more space, it's just that...'

'What?'

'Vince asked me not to leave him alone. There is an old girl-friend of his in the village. He said she was a bit too keen to see him on the book tour. She sent him messages, which he politely answered, and then it got a bit much so he stopped responding. She stalked him on social media too. Eventually he blocked her.'

'Olga?' Julia asked.

Phoebe looked surprised. 'Yes, do you know her?'

'No, not really. I just heard they'd been an item way back. Village grapevine.'

Phoebe tucked her smooth hair behind her ear, a gesture Julia had noticed she employed when considering what to do. She must have decided to speak. 'Sarah had a radar sense for troublesome women. And Olga fit the profile. Overeager, a bit unpredictable. He didn't want any contact between them. He asked me to stick close. Be a bit of a buffer, I guess. I don't know if there was an incident, or he just thought she was a risk. But...' Phoebe stopped talking, her eyes widening.

'What?' asked Sean. 'Go on, spit it out.'

'Vincent seemed nervous of Olga. Almost, I don't know... scared?'

The ringing of Sean's phone broke the thoughtful silence that followed Phoebe's revelation.

'Sorry,' he said, answering it. 'Dr Sean O'Connor. Yes, thank you for getting back to me... Yes, in custody. It's absurd, she's a grieving widow and being treated like... Okay, thank you. Shall I meet you there?'

The call brought their discussion to an abrupt end. Julia walked out with Sean, who already had his car keys in his hand.

'I'll ring you later, let you know what the lawyer says,' he said, unlocking the car. He opened the door and turned to her. 'Thanks for your help. You've been a great support,' he said.

'Oh, it's...'

He leaned in for a kiss, which landed awkwardly on her talking mouth. She stopped talking and leaned into it, enjoying the closeness, the feeling of his lips against hers.

'Oh,' she said again, as they drew back. They smiled shyly at each other.

'Later,' he said, and the word and the burr gave her a little jolt.

A minute later he was gone, leaving her standing outside the B&B. Julia remembered that she hadn't asked Phoebe a question that had been bothering her all day. She went back to the B&B, knocked on the door, and leaned in. 'Phoebe, why did you come to the library the day after the murder? I know it wasn't to find a jacket.'

'Oh yes, a silly lie,' said Phoebe, blushing. 'I was looking for Vincent. I hadn't seen him leave that evening. He was there one minute, gone the next. We were supposed to meet for coffee the next day to discuss the rest of the book tour, but we hadn't made a time or place. I messaged him in the morning but he didn't pick up my message. I didn't want to knock on the door. Sarah, you know. So I took a walk up the road. I thought he might have gone for a walk, he often did, or that I'd see him in one of the cafés. When I passed the library, I went in on a whim. But then when I saw the police, I got a bit of a fright. Said I was there for a jacket.'

Julia wasn't entirely sure if she bought this. Why would an innocent person be frightened into inventing an imaginary jacket just because the police were at the library? Surely you'd just ask if the person you were looking for was there, if you had no suspicion that they might be dead? On the other hand, there was something innocent about Phoebe. Something wholesome, despite her blue hair. Perhaps the sight of the police had really thrown her.

Julia said her goodbyes and wondered what to do next. What she really wanted to do was meet Olga. If Olga was as obsessed and unhinged as Phoebe said, could *she* be a suspect for Vincent's murder? This was, of course, none of Julia's business. Her role in this matter was 'friend of victim's widow's mother's cousin'. By no stretch of the imagination did this give her the right to start interviewing suspects. But still.

She started walking in the direction of home.

But, thought Julia, Olga did work at the vet. Pippa had done the first round of inoculations, but it was about the right time for Jake's booster. What if she fetched Jake and took him for his shot this afternoon? If Olga was there, and they got to chatting, well, what of it? She had no intention of questioning her. No, not that. Just getting a feel for her. Julia had very good instincts, after all her years of interviewing and counselling. That was part of why she trusted her feeling that Phoebe wasn't lying. She'd feel Olga out, and give her impressions to Hayley, who would do the proper police work and interviews if she felt they were necessary.

So much for the bonus Sunday. Julia walked briskly home, phoned the vet for an appointment (politely asking the receptionist for her name, and discovering she was, indeed, Olga), ate an apple and drank a cup of tea, and left the house to walk back to the village. Jake bounded along beside her in ignorant bliss as to the nature of the day's outing.

Julia deliberately arrived ten minutes early so that she and Jake would have to hang about in the reception area. Jake seemed delighted to be there, wagging his tail and doing little jumps of happiness, like he did when Julia prepared his supper. The plan worked perfectly! Olga was at the desk, and there were no other patients and/or owners waiting.

'Well if it isn't Pippa's little fellow,' Olga said, coming round from behind the desk with a dog biscuit in her outstretched hand.

'It is, indeed. Except that he's mine now,' said Julia with a smile. 'It turned out Jake wasn't cut out for a life of service.'

'I heard.' Olga smiled at Jake, who was straining on his lead, wanting to jump at her, his tongue hanging out with pleasure.

'But it's all worked out. We're happy, aren't we, Jakey boy?'

Olga fussed over Jake, rubbing his silky ears, and talking baby talk.

'I know where I've seen you,' Julia said, as if it had just come to her. 'You were at the V.F. Andrews event at the library. We were sitting in the same row. How awful, what happened to that poor man. Such a talent, and I believe he was a lovely chap.'

'So awful,' said Olga, her voice trembling. 'He was. A good man, that is.'

'Oh, I'm sorry. Did you know him?' Julia asked, putting a comforting hand on the woman's shoulder.

Olga nodded, her eyes damp.

'I'm so very sorry for your loss.'

The tears tumbled down. 'I'm sorry. I just haven't been able to talk about it... The loss. It's complicated.'

'Come and sit down,' Julia said, patting the seat next to her. Olga did as she was told, and Jake rested his velvet snout on her knee. 'I have a KitKat here somewhere, the sugar will do you good.' Julia fished the chocolate out of her bag. 'And here's a tissue.'

'I'm sorry,' Olga said again, dabbing at her nose. 'It's just... We were very close. Old school friends, actually. He was my first boyfriend.'

'Ah, a special relationship.'

'It was. I know half of Berrywick is claiming to be his best friend, or saying they're in the book – Mike Garforth is going about saying he's been used in the book and he's going to sue.

But I actually *am* in the book – the main character, the journalist? She's based on me. It's obvious.'

Julia nodded encouragingly. She opened the KitKat and handed Olga a piece. She noticed how Olga didn't even ask if Julia had read the book. She obviously assumed everyone in Berrywick had.

Olga took a nibble of the chocolate, and continued, 'We've kept in touch all these years on and off, and recently we reconnected more... well, more intimately. Me and Vince, we had a real friendship. We emailed each other almost every day and shared our thoughts and feelings. It sounds wrong. And silly. But it was something we both needed in our lives. We had made an arrangement to meet when he was here, to really connect and see if... But now...'

Olga buried her head in her hands.

'How very sad that you didn't get to have that special reconnection.'

Olga looked up at Julia and said, 'I know, I am gutted. I thought there was something very special between us. We were going to see if, you know, when he was here, if we still...'

'If that bond was still there, if it was real.'

'Yes. You understand, you are so easy to talk to.'

Julia felt guilty that she'd used her professional skills to lure the woman into sharing her personal feelings, but it was for a good cause.

'He confided in me. I knew his marriage wasn't good. I would never have allowed myself to have those feelings if I didn't know that he and Sarah were over. And now I hear she's been arrested for his murder. I can't help but think, if only he and I had acted sooner, maybe he wouldn't have died.'

The surgery door opened and the vet appeared. 'Oh there you are, Olga, and Mrs Bird.' He looked a bit taken aback at the little scene – Julia and Jake comforting the sniffing receptionist. 'Is everything okay here?'

'Fine,' said Olga. 'Everything's fine, thank you. Jake is just here for his injections.'

Jake turned to Julia with a look of utter betrayal.

14

Who knew retirement would be so aerobically challenging? Julia set off for home already rather exhausted, having walked into the village, home to fetch Jake, and back to the village for the vet. There was an odd sense of déjà vu, passing the same places for the fourth time today. She passed the library, and then the Buttered Scone, where she considered stopping for a restorative eponymous baked treat, but decided against it. The afternoon was getting on. Better to get home.

The main road was busy with mums fetching kids from school, people popping to the shops for something for supper, a few late-season tourists taking photographs and blocking the pavements. Julia had to keep Jake close at heel on a short leash, to avoid tripping up a day tripper. As they exited the centre, the shops and restaurants gave way to pleasant houses and B&Bs, and the streets became quieter, with a light traffic in afternoon dog walkers and joggers.

Julia could relax a bit, and let her mind wander. It wandered to Olga Gilbert. There was a sharp disconnect between the Olga that Phoebe described – obsessive, deluded, an unhinged stalker – and the woman Julia had just met and spoken to. Which was the real Olga Gilbert? If it was the woman she had just met, then why did Phoebe (or, perhaps more accurately, Vincent) present such a different narrative? If only there was a way to find out what had really happened between Olga and Vince. Was he scared, as Phoebe made out, or had he been planning to meet up with her? The only other person who knew what had passed between Olga and Vince had been stabbed in the library. How could Julia possibly find out the truth?

She'd been so caught up in her thoughts that it came as something of a surprise to find herself once again in front of Sarah's B&B. It was hard to imagine that behind the trimmed hedges, the neat gravel paths and the colourful flower boxes, a bloody knife had been found – likely the knife that had been used to brutally take a man's life.

The door to Sarah and Vincent's cottage was ajar. Had Sarah been released, and was she home? Julia stepped onto the little path to get a closer look. No sign of Sarah. Or anyone. 'Hello?' she called. She took another few steps towards the door. 'Hello, Sarah?' she called again, a little louder.

Julia walked up to the door. It was half open, a bucket wedged between the door and the frame, a mop resting in the murky water. Next to it, another bucket full of bottles and sprays and cloths and brushes. The cleaner must be there. But why no answer? Julia got a strange, unsettled feeling which she tried hard not to put down to the Ghost of Vincent Andrews.

Julia put her head round the door, calling out for a third time, quite loudly this time. There was no one there. The place looked empty. Vincent's jacket still hung over the back of the chair at the little desk. A black laptop bag lay on the seat of the chair, under the desk. As she got closer, she could make out the initials – V.F.A. – embossed discreetly in the corner. The police must not have noticed it.

Olga had talked about emailing Vince every day.

If that was true, then Vincent's laptop would provide answers to some of Julia's questions about Olga, she was sure. If she could just take a quick look at his emails, she would see what he and Olga had written to each other, and know if Olga was a deluded, dangerous stalker and possible murderer, or not.

She told Jake to sit and stay, went inside and grabbed the laptop. She'd take a quick look. She opened the case and pulled the laptop out onto the table. She couldn't believe her luck – or Vincent's trusting nature – when it opened without a password.

At the sound of singing and the crunching of feet on gravel, she slammed the machine shut and shoved it into the bag. The cleaner must be coming. Julia slung the bag over her shoulder and shouted, 'Hello, Sarah, are you here?' very loudly into the empty room. 'Hi, Sarah, it's me...'

'She's not here,' said the voice from the door. 'She's down the police station. But I don't think she'll be allowed any visitors. Not after what *she's* done.'

'Oh, hello,' said Julia, edging out of the door, past the young woman in an apron. 'The door was open. I didn't realise you were here.'

'Just stepped out for a ciggie, no harm done,' the young woman said defensively.

'Of course. And why shouldn't you?'

'Right. And I was only gone a minute.'

'Maybe less... I'd just popped my head in to see if Sarah was here, and there you were. Anyway, thanks for your help.'

They parted on good terms, in full agreement on the central issues – that the cleaner wasn't skiving off, and that Julia wasn't snooping. Julia grabbed Jake's lead – he had been as good as gold, while she had broken about six different laws – and headed down the path into the road, the bag slung over her shoulder as if it were her very own.

Her heart raced and adrenaline pumped through her body. What were you thinking, she asked herself in her dead mother's voice. Breaking and entering. Theft. Theft of *evidence* in a *crime*. A *murder*. Good God. She could be arrested and charged.

Julia felt as if she might be having a panic attack. She wanted to turn around and return the laptop, but how would she explain that? She turned off the road onto the river path and sat on a bench with the bag on her lap, trying to calm her breathing. She watched the water moving slowly past and tried to focus her attention on the ripples. It was working. Her pulse slowed, her breath was deeper and longer. Moira and the clever border collie came running up behind her and overtook at an impressive pace.

A duckish sort of bird floated by on the river, trailed by its teenaged offspring. It was about the only bird whose name she'd managed to remember since she moved to the Cotswolds, and that was only because it was called a wigeon. She thought of it as a water pigeon. It was a ridiculous enough name to stick in her head, unlike the brown warbler or the dunnock or a hundred other instantly forgettable generic names.

Jake had turned his attention to the wigeon too, and was heading for the water.

'No, Jake, come here,' she said, but she could tell from his eager gait that he was going to employ his selective deafness.

'Jake!'

He leapt into the water with a joyful splash and paddled off after the wigeon and its wigeonlings. Or wigoenlets. Or whatever they were called.

Her brief period of calm was over. Her heart rate was back up in cardiac arrest territory.

As a rule, Julia tried not to swear, but this time she found herself muttering a large vocabulary of colourful unacceptable words under her breath.

The only good thing about the situation was that Julia now

knew without doubt that Jake would never catch a duck. Ducks weren't brilliant, but Labradors were less brilliant. They were also less agile than ducks, or even wigeons, in the water, and without the advantage of flight. Jake paddled doggedly after the wigeons, who kept up a steady pace, always maintaining a few feet between the species, but without breaking a sweat. They could paddle to the sea at this rate, and Jake would follow them until he drowned.

Julia ran alongside the river, shouting, 'Get back here, Jake!' in her most authoritative voice.

At one point he turned his head slightly towards her and gave her a sort of sheepish grin, just to acknowledge that he had indeed heard her, but continued his pursuit. She tracked him a few more feet, wheezing and lugging the stupid stolen laptop over her shoulder, until she collided with a man. Her foot caught on a pole or stick and she crashed to the ground in front of him, leaving him staggering for his bearings.

'Are you all right?' the man said, removing a large pair of earphones from his ears. It was the metal-detector guy.

'I'm okay. I think,' she said, getting to her feet and brushing mud from her trousers.

The man reached down and picked up the metal detector from the ground. Then he bent down for the laptop bag and brushed it down too before handing it to her. Jake was still paddling after the wigeons.

'I'm sorry. I wasn't looking. It's my bloody dog...'

The man put his fingers to his lips and gave an ear-splitting whistle and then shouted, 'Come on, boy, come here.'

Jake – whom Julia could actually murder by this point – turned a leisurely half circle and headed towards them.

'Thank you,' she said. 'Are you all right? Sorry to crash into you. I hope your instrument is not damaged.'

'It's quite robust, I should think it's fine. As am I. And yourself?' he asked politely. He had a rather wooden manner, saying all the proper words in the proper order, but without much variation in tone.

'Nothing broken,' she said, as chipper as she could manage. She felt sure there would be some bruising, to add to the fury and embarrassment. She hoped the laptop wasn't damaged. 'I'm Julia Bird.'

'Harry Harbour,' he said, offering his hand. 'Pleased to meet you.'

'We've crossed paths a few times,' she said. 'I'm often out with that hooligan.'

The hooligan had exited the water and was hurtling towards them. He stopped a foot away, braced his four paws firmly on the ground and shook himself, flinging river water in a wide arc, covering them both.

'And this is Jake,' she said, fishing in her pocket and bringing out two clean tissues, both of which she gave to Harry Harbour.

'Thank you. I've heard his name about,' he said with a stiff smile. 'When you shout for him.'

'Well, yes, that happens quite a lot I'm afraid. He does love to chase the birds.'

'But the wigeons were too clever for him, I see.'

'They were indeed. Funny name, clever birds.' She smiled.

'The collective noun for wigeons is elusive, did you know?' he said.

Julia shook her head. What a strange term, an elusive of wigeons. A crash of rhinos, that was a good one. A journey of giraffes. But an elusive of wigeons?

'Yes, quite elusive,' he said. 'Some say a company of wigeons, others a comb or a flight. It has yet to be settled, I believe. Yes, consensus remains elusive on the subject.'

After the day she'd had, Julia felt unable to take this conversation any further. In fact, she had a small but fierce pain developing behind her left eye. 'Well,' she said, with finality, 'Thanks for your help in getting Jake back. Good to meet you properly.'

'You're welcome.'

'We'll be off. I hope you find something good today.'

She walked away and then turned back to Harry, and asked the question that she'd often wondered: 'What is it you're looking for?'

'That's just the thing, you never know what you'll find. Could be a bottle top, could be a missing wedding ring, could be a medieval artefact – that's my area of interest. Worth nothing or worth a fortune. A find could be something that changes your life or your luck. I have a feeling that might happen for me today.'

'Lovely,' she said. 'That's lovely. Good luck.'

15

She would take it back. She wouldn't open the laptop at all, and she would return it in the morning. She wasn't sure quite how she'd manage it, but that was what she would do. She didn't know what had got into her, stealing a laptop. It was entirely out of character, as well as being a crime. This whole matter of Vincent Andrews' death had gotten to her, and she'd lost her way. Well, that was over. She would return the laptop, tell Hayley everything she knew or suspected, and let the professionals handle things.

Julia put the laptop bag by the front door, ready to go in the morning. She felt much calmer having made the decision.

What a long and busy day it had been. She felt quite exhausted. Even Jake, whose energy was boundless, had passed out on the carpet after his supper. She poured herself a small glass of Chardonnay. She felt she'd earned it after all that rushing about. A glass of wine, a couple of her own hens' eggs scrambled in a bit of butter and eaten with sourdough toast, and an early night. A perfect evening lay ahead of her.

And then the phone rang.

'Hi, Sean.'

He didn't even say hello, but got straight to the point. 'I've just heard from the lawyer. The forensics are back. The blood on the knife is Vincent's. The police believe that the knife is likely the murder weapon.'

'Oh, Sean, I am so sorry. What a terrible shock. I know you fully believed in Sarah's innocence. You just can't tell, even when you know someone.'

'What do you mean?' he cut her off. 'She *is* innocent. She didn't kill him.'

'The knife was found in Sarah's bathroom,' she said, as gently as she could.

'There has to be another explanation. That knife could have been planted like she said. Or...'

He seemed unable to conjure up another scenario, and changed tack. 'I had to tell Eleanor of course, once I knew Sarah was going to be kept in custody for longer. She is in a terrible state, crazier than usual. And it seems neither she nor Sarah have money for a lawyer. The money is all in Vince's name and with him, well, dead, they can't access it quickly. She'll have to use whoever legal aid gives her.'

'Oh dear,' said Julia, who privately thought that all women – and men for that matter – should have their own bank account for many reasons, including this type of thing.

Sean was still talking. 'I need to get Sarah released. Julia, what am I going to do?'

'I don't... I don't know. I don't think there's anything you *can* do. The police will do their job, the law will take its course,' Julia said, knowing it wasn't what he wanted to hear. She took a rather larger sip of her wine than she'd intended.

'We need to find the real killer. It's the only thing for it. Sarah still thinks Phoebe did it.'

'I just don't think it was Phoebe, Sean. You were there. You spoke to her. She says she wasn't having an affair with Vincent.

She was sympathetic to Sarah. Everything she said made sense. Do you really think she killed him?'

'No.' He sounded completely deflated.

After a moment's hesitation, Julia said, 'There is someone else if you remember... Someone with a motive. And I spoke to her.'

'Who?'

'I think you'd better come over in the morning and I'll tell you what I know.'

When she woke up the next morning, Julia felt surprisingly refreshed. She'd gone to bed with her head buzzing and had anticipated a night of tossing and turning and fretting and planning. Instead, she'd closed her eyes and slept like the dead. She grimaced at her own turn of phrase.

Glancing at her bedside clock, she saw it was 7.30. Her morning routine in Berrywick was fairly lengthy and Sean was coming at 9.30. She had better get a move on.

With a bowl of kitchen scraps in one hand, her mug of tea in the other, and Jake at her heels, Julia stepped out into the garden. She had on a red woollen jacket and sheepskin-lined wellington boots over her blue and white striped pyjamas. Hardly a stylish get-up, but she considered going about in one's garden in dreadful but practical clothes one of the benefits of living alone. And of being sixty-something. She liked to have her morning tea while she pottered about feeding the chickens and investigating developments in the garden. Touring the estate, she called it.

She didn't know how much longer she would be able to wander the garden comfortably in the morning. There was a definite autumnal chill in the air. She wondered what her first winter in Berrywick would be like. She hoped the wood burner would keep the house toasty, and that the doors and windows would prove well insulated. She might need a hobby, an indoor one. She'd never been much of a one for hobbies. Work had been her passion until it had ended so abruptly, and between her job, Peter, and Jess, her days had been full. What could she do now? Oil painting? Watercolours? Something with wool?

She tossed the peelings into the coop, and the hens fell upon the pile as if they'd been starved since Easter. She loved to watch them – the efficient bustle of their warm brown bodies, their clever beady eyes. Jake loved to watch them too, but likely for different reasons.

Having made a mental note of a few garden tasks that needed doing just as soon as she disentangled herself from the Vincent Andrews situation – imminently, she hoped – Julia went into the house to shower and change and get ready for Sean's arrival. She still had not decided whether to tell him about the laptop. He would be shocked and disapproving. And quite rightly. She had done something terrible and was going to set it straight.

Sean arrived on the dot of 9.30, carrying a paper bag.

'Croissants,' he said, handing them over. 'I'm only on after-noon surgery today, thank goodness. Can you supply the coffee?'

While the kettle boiled, Julia ground the beans and measured out four tablespoons into the French press. She poured in the water, and the smell of coffee filled the kitchen. She took two mugs from the open shelf, and the milk from the fridge.

Sean didn't speak until the coffee was poured, and then he said, 'So tell me, who is this other suspect?'

'Do you know Olga Gilbert?' she asked.

He shook his head.

'I thought you knew everyone in the whole of Berrywick?'

'There are two doctors in the village. If I don't know someone, it means they are either uncommonly healthy, or a patient of Dr Naidoo.'

'Ah. Well, she's an old girlfriend of Vincent's. Possibly a present love interest, too. And maybe – and I'm not at all sure here – maybe someone with a motive.' Julia took a bite of her croissant, making an appreciative noise. It was buttery and flaky and fresh. She chewed and swallowed, and went on to remind Sean what they'd learned about Olga from Phoebe, and her own, quite contradictory, experience with the woman.

'It's too peculiar,' she said. 'It's as if we're talking about two entirely different people. My years of working with people, and troubled people, have taught me to really listen and see people. I know my instincts are good. But I also know that like anyone else, I can be wrong. Very wrong.'

Julia's mind went back to the lowest point of her professional career – she had been horribly wrong, and the consequences had been fatal.

Sean didn't know, of course, of the turn towards the past that Julia's thoughts had taken. He was firmly immersed in her opinion on the present. 'That *is* strange. If she's as obsessed as Phoebe says, her unrequited passion might have turned to rage. She *could* be the killer. We know that she was there on the night.'

He seemed eager to embrace the idea of Olga as Vincent's murderer. Almost hopeful. Anyone who wasn't Sarah would be a good prospect, as far as he was concerned, Julia thought, picking up flakes of pastry from the plate with her fingertip and placing them on her tongue.

'Maybe we can ask around, find someone who knows her. Fish for info,' said Sean, and then, more agitated. 'But it all takes time... Sarah can't stay there another day. I need to do something.'

'There's another way,' Julia said with some reluctance. 'It's... It's not exactly... I wouldn't want...'

'Julia, just tell me.'

'I may be able to get evidence. Written evidence.'

'You can? That's excellent, why didn't you say?'

'It's complicated.'

'Well, it can't be that tricky, I'm sure we can sort it out?'

'I stole Vincent's laptop.'

Sean stared at her in astonishment. 'You have got to be joking.'

'I wish I was,' she said, despair in her voice. 'I don't know what came over me. I was walking past the B&B, the door was open, I saw it and I took it. It was pure impulse. I was going to have a look at Olga's emails to him. But I haven't opened it, I'm going to give it back.'

'Go and get it.'

'Sean, it's not a good idea.'

'But it is! Just think about it. The laptop belongs to Sarah, now that Vincent is dead. We are just going to have a quick look at Olga's emails to Vincent to help prove Sarah's innocence. She would definitely not object.'

Julia was torn. She wanted to solve the Olga mystery. And she wanted to help Sean. But once she opened the laptop and searched Vincent's emails, she was in a different league of culpability.

'I will take full responsibility,' Sean said.

Julia pushed her chair back, got up and walked to the front door. Jake padded after her, half hoping for an outing, and trailed her disappointedly when she came back with the laptop bag over her shoulder, still showing the dusty residue of the fall on the path.

'Here you go,' she said, pulling the machine from its case and putting it on the kitchen table. She kept a hand firmly on it in a protective gesture and said: 'Olga's emails and nothing else.'

Sean nodded.

Julia opened the laptop, hoping that it would work okay after hitting the ground. She found Gmail, put Olga's name into the search bar and a slew of messages filled Vincent's inbox.

'Gosh,' said Sean. 'That's a lot of messages.'

Julia opened the oldest one, from a year ago. It was filled with Olga's reminiscences about their 'special time together when we were young...' and their 'uniquely powerful attraction'.

'Poor thing, she clearly hasn't gotten over her first love. Let's see if there's a reply.'

There were far fewer emails from Vincent than there were from Olga, Julia noted. The response to this one was a polite rebuff.

> *I'm pleased you remember our friendship fondly. It was of course a very long time ago. I hope you have found love, as I have with my wonderful wife Sarah.*

Olga's emails became increasingly passionate and desperate. *We are meant to be together... The feelings are still there... I know you feel it too...* Julia felt sorry for the woman, and ashamed to be reading her humiliation and delusion.

Vincent's emails were becoming increasingly direct and harsh. *Olga, this is inappropriate. I am a happily married man. Please don't contact me again.*

At this point, he stopped answering her altogether. Her emails seemed to peter out for a while, with long gaps between them.

'Look at some of the more recent ones,' said Sean. 'In the weeks prior to the murder.'

There was a renewed spate of emails from Olga in the weeks after the publication of *The Raven's Call*, ratcheting up closer to Vincent's visit. Julia picked one at random.

My dearest. I can't tell you how touched I am to see that you have based your main character on me. My body, my face, which you describe so lovingly. My intellect and sensitivity. It means the world to me that you have immortalised me as Camille Jones.

'I've read that book,' Julia said. 'That character is a feisty young journalist, born to a French mother and English father. She speaks four languages and drives a car in an era when women don't, refuses to settle into marriage and boldly shakes up the man's world of newspapers. Literally the only thing she has in common with Olga is that she's tall.'

She opened a few more – declarations of love, angry letters demanding responses to her own, and a request that they spend the weekend together on his visit to Berrywick on the upcoming book tour. *Leave her behind, let us rekindle the passion of our youth,* Olga had written.

'My God, she's deluded,' Julia said, staring at the screen in disbelief. 'Sean, we need to show this to the police. Olga is quite unhinged and she might be dangerous. I think it's quite possible that she killed Vincent Andrews.'

She closed the last email from Olga. Vincent's inbox filled the screen. All those unread emails that he would never see. The online sales. The bank statements. The holiday specials. The subscriptions to this or that newsletter.

And there amongst them, a familiar name.

Mike Garforth.

And the subject line: *You'll pay for this, you bastard.*

16

If Olga was emotional and unbalanced, Mike Garforth was furious and threatening.

A scan through his emails – far fewer than Olga's, it must be said – indicated that Mike believed Vincent had based Camille's jilted lover, Mick Garland, on him. Mick had Mike's limp, his initials, almost his name.

'You've read the book. Is it true?' Sean asked, leaning back in his chair.

'Well, yes, I suppose so. I didn't know Mike, so I didn't recognise him of course, but now I know who he is, I suspect anyone from Berrywick would have recognised him. The limp is a dead giveaway, and he's got the same colouring – the sandy hair and freckles.'

'I don't quite understand why Mike is so angry, though.'

'Well, the character is drawn as a bit of a comic figure. You know, not that smart, a bit of a loser really, certainly not man enough for the spirited Camille. And he gets tossed aside, eventually. But why would Vincent have used someone everyone would know?'

'Mike dated Sarah years ago,' said Sean slowly. 'Not for long. Sarah broke up with him when she met Vincent, as I recall. She was quite disparaging of him afterwards, although Eleanor stayed quite good friends with him. Typical Eleanor thing to do. Maybe that actually made Sarah a bit more resentful of him. Maybe Vince used that.'

'It's the same story as in the book! Camille left Mick for the smarter, better-looking Felix,' Julia said. 'It seems a bit unkind, doesn't it? Making fun of Mike Garforth.'

'I agree. Vincent had a bit of a mischievous streak though, and I can imagine him planting playful references to people he knew. But I don't think he'd want to hurt someone.'

'Maybe he didn't realise quite how hurtful and upsetting it would be. Or maybe there was some other reason, something we don't know – although Sarah might,' Julia said. 'Anyway, we need to tell Hayley what we've found and we need to talk to Sarah to try and make sense of it all. It's quite a bizarre situation – two different people in Berrywick with a motive for killing Vincent Andrews.'

'Well, it's enough to take the focus off Sarah, and that's my priority – getting her out of jail. The police will work the rest of it out, I'm sure,' Sean said, with a confidence Julia didn't quite feel. 'Forensics, you know. Oh, speaking of forensics, I took a look at the report. There's not much to see. Cause of death was blood loss from a stab wound to the throat. Which any fool could see, of course, you don't have to be a doctor. As far as the blood work goes, there's not much to say – a little bit of alcohol, consistent with having had a glass of wine, but no drugs, prescription or recreational.'

'That doesn't sound very helpful, I must say.'

'You can have a look if you want to. Eleanor gave me a copy. She got one as the only next of kin they could trace,' he said, reaching into his bag.

'Thanks,' she said, taking the folder from him, and putting it down on the table without opening it.

'Let's phone Hayley first and tell her what we know,' said Sean. 'The sooner we do that, the sooner Sarah will be out.'

Anxiety settled on Julia. She didn't relish the thought of admitting to her foolish thievery, but it had to be done.

Sean must have seen something in her face, and correctly guessed at its cause. 'I don't think we need to go into too much detail about how we came upon the laptop. I'll just say that it was there, in the B&B. We saw it and had a look. Which is the truth, or part of it at least.'

She considered his proposal. She wouldn't lie to the police, of course, but she wasn't averse to not being entirely forthcoming if it wouldn't harm the case. 'Okay, thanks. If we can skimp on the details that would be good. Do you want to make the call?'

Sean phoned the police station and asked for DI Gibson, putting the call on speaker so that Julia could hear and speak. He put the phone on the kitchen table between them, resting against a jug of fluffy grasses Julia had collected on one of her walks.

Hayley came onto the line and Sean gave her a rundown of what they'd found on the computer – two separate individuals with grudges, and some explicit or implicit threats to Vincent Andrews.

'I want that laptop,' Hayley said. 'Where did you say you found it? I can't believe my guys missed it.'

'On the seat of the chair pushed under the table by the door,' Julia answered. 'There was a jacket hanging over the chair... It was a little hard to see.'

'Bloody dolts. I'll have them for breakfast.' Hayley spat the words out, and accompanied them with three loud thuds which Julia imagined was her fist hitting the desk.

'What time will Sarah be released, do you think?' said Sean. 'If you like, I'll bring over the laptop when I fetch her.'

'Steady on now, Sean, there's a process that has to be followed. I can't just be springing a suspect on your say-so. I haven't seen the evidence you speak of. And there's the matter of the bloody knife in her bathroom. I'm afraid to say that it has her fingerprints on it. It's a very damning piece of evidence against her.'

Sean looked ready to cry with frustration. He had obviously expected Hayley to release Sarah immediately. Julia laid a hand on his arm and gave him a warm look that she hoped conveyed calm and patience, and the foolishness of shouting at police officers.

He took a beat and said, 'There must be another explanation for the knife. You know as well as I do that she's not the killer. She couldn't stab Vincent, it's unthinkable. Can you not have some compassion for a grieving widow?'

'I do, I do have compassion for her, Dr O'Connor. I don't want to hold her a minute longer than I have to, but the evidence against her is compelling. I'm sorry, but I have to follow the rules and tick all the boxes. This is not a simple matter. First of all, I need to see the emails that you say point to other potential suspects and discuss it with my team. And even then, I will have to get a release signed off before I open the door and usher a suspect out, as I'm sure you can understand.'

'Okay,' Sean said, defeated by the power of police bureaucracy.

'And in the meantime,' Hayley continued in a measured, conciliatory tone, 'it would help me greatly if I could have access to that laptop without jumping through hoops and a whole ream of paperwork to get my hands on it. If what you say is true, it will be good for Sarah's speedy release. If we have another suspect, we might have another explanation for the knife.'

'I'll bring it over after my surgery this afternoon,' said Sean. 'And I've decided to pay for her lawyer myself – so you can expect a call or visit from him very soon. He'll be just as eager as I am to get her out of there.'

17

Julia enjoyed the meditative quality of washing up. The warm water on her hands was soothing, and there was something about the mindless, repetitive task, the dipping and wiping and rinsing and stacking that let her mind wander freely. It wandered to Sean. Their relationship was teetering on a narrow ledge between friendship and something more, something romantic. In the months they had known each other, they had become friends and regular companions, but there had been moments when it had seemed to be leaning quite sharply towards the 'something more'. But they always seemed to pull back onto the ledge just in time.

Julia had avoided thinking about her own reticence, but she mulled over it now. What was it that held her back? She liked Sean and she found him attractive. Hey, he was Sean Connery, 007, what was not to like? No, the problem was with her. She was happy living on her own. She hadn't chosen it; she had expected to be married to Peter until one of them died. It had been a good marriage, admittedly somewhat short on passion as the years had gone by, but they had still been able to have a good conversation, still made each other laugh. When he had fallen in love with their landscape designer, Christopher, she hadn't been able to imagine life on her own. But she'd moved to Berrywick, and found to her astonishment that living alone – well, with Jake and the chickens – suited her.

The washing up done, she rinsed her hands and made at least part of a decision – she would have to have a proper talk to Sean sometime soon. But first, a walk.

It was not until she returned an hour later from walking Jake around the neighbourhood that Julia remembered the forensic report. She picked up the envelope from the kitchen table and opened it, more out of idle curiosity than anything else. Sean had been quite certain there was nothing there that would help their cause.

He was right, as far as she could tell, glancing over the facts and stats and figures and measurements and percentages. To her admittedly amateur eye, there seemed nothing that would shed any light on Vincent's death or his possible killer, but as she read, she was surprised to find it an oddly poignant and intimate document.

The report told the story of a man, from blood type to alcohol level to height. It listed notable physical characteristics – an appendectomy scar, a distinctive birthmark on his thigh, a previously broken ulna in his right forearm, a recent cut on the pad of his right thumb, a fading bruise on his shin.

In a contemplative mood, it struck Julia that these were the little marks unique to every human being, the marks that a lover might know, tracing a finger over the bumps and scars of the beloved and hearing each one's history and provenance. The searing pain of a burst appendix, a fall off a bicycle skidding on a patch of wet leaves, the slip of a knife on a lemon, a bump against a coffee table in the dark.

It was sad, thinking of Vincent alive, flesh and blood, like all of us, and vulnerable to the same illnesses, bumps and bruises. And then killed with a violent stab to the neck.

Julia pulled herself together. There was nothing to be gained by this rather maudlin line of enquiry. She needed to keep her mind on practical matters. She planned to make a big pot of vegetable soup and divide it up for a few meals. There were some bits and pieces in the vegetable drawer that needed using up, and in the garden, she had a few carrots, onions and lots of herbs. It always made her feel pleasantly thrifty and efficient to cook up something wholesome from all the leftovers and her home-grown produce, and have a freezer full of Tupperware, neatly labelled, for future effort-free meals.

She slipped the report back into the envelope and picked up her basket and garden scissors. She took an old straw hat from a peg by the door, plonked it on her head and went out into the garden. Her former colleagues would get a laugh if they could see her now. The old Julia's interest in gardening had gone no further than picking a sprig of mint from the pot by the front door to add to her iced tea. She had been similarly disinterested in cooking – it had been well-known that Peter usually made her lunch, either a tub of wholesome salad, or a nice sustaining sandwich. Julia's passion had been her job as Head of Youth Services, and the prosaic matters of food and such had hardly entered her head.

When the vegetables were brought in, sliced and diced and cooking gently in olive oil, Julia went to put her feet up and read the book that had been languishing untouched. She had expected retirement to have a lot more feet-up-with-book time and a lot less running-around-the Cotswolds-trying-to-solve-murders time, truth be told. Nothing to be done now, though; Sean would deliver the laptop with the evidence to the police, and they would sort things out.

Julia settled down with a contented sigh and opened her book, eager to get back to the story about the romance in

Greece. Who was George, again? Was he the waiter? Or the boyfriend? And there was another one, the airline pilot, what was his name? She flicked back a few pages, but they looked equally mysterious. She recognised bits and pieces, a familiar name here, a phrase there, but she couldn't bring the plot firmly to mind. Was she going senile? God, she hoped not. Maybe retirement and the country life had made her brain rot. She sighed – not in contentment this time, rather in resignation – and started from the beginning.

Not three pages in, Julia remembered the soup.

'Damn,' she said, but only because she had recently resolved not to use stronger language. There was no excuse for it now that she no longer worked as Head of Youth Services, where the temptation to swear had often been beyond resisting, on account of the exposure to the awfulness of humanity.

She leapt to her feet and got there just in time, sploshing water from the kettle into the sizzling pan a nanosecond before the onions turned irredeemably brown.

'Good save,' she told herself.

Her phone was ringing in the sitting room. She walked briskly through and grabbed it, seeing Sean's number. A report from the police station, no doubt. Perhaps he had good news – that Sarah was being released. She hit the green phone symbol and said hello.

'It's gone!' he said. 'Julia, the laptop. It's gone.'

'Gone from where? Tell me exactly what happened,' she said, keeping her voice neutral and without accusation, just as she'd learned in counselling training all those years ago.

'I left it in the car while I went to work. I've just come out of the surgery to take it to the police. I'm here, at my car, and it's not there.'

'You left it in the car?' she asked, before she could stop herself. So much for neutral and without accusation. She may as well have added 'you idiot' to the end of the sentence.

'I know, I know *now*. But I never thought... No one worries about that sort of thing here. It's not London, you know,' he said rather defensively.

'Did they break the window?'

She could hear him moving around the car, opening a door, slamming it. 'No. No sign of a break in. Maybe they jimmied the lock, I think.'

'Damn,' said Julia. She wondered if he had in fact locked the door – it was not something one generally bothered with in Berrywick. She saw no point in asking about that. Instead, she said, 'What did you tell Hayley?'

'That I had the laptop but it had gone missing.'

'And?'

'And she said she'll get one of the office staff to see if they can get a court order to access the emails via the service provider. But that there's – and I quote – "a big difference between an angry email and stabbing someone to death". She also said – and once again I quote – that she's "got a lot on her plate". There was a robbery over in Wakeford this morning apparently; someone lifted a whole lot of expensive orchids from the garden centre. Anyway, at this stage as far as she's concerned, there's plenty of evidence to point to Sarah for the murder, and she reckons she's got her criminal, she's just tying up the case. Of course I told her I didn't believe Sarah would or could do such a thing, but...'

Julia butted in with a thought of her own. 'Who stole the laptop?'

'Well I don't know, of course. And in fact, DI Gibson had the same question. She did say they would investigate, although I don't hold out much hope of a positive outcome. It's not an easy thing to find.'

'Think about it. Who would want Vincent's laptop? Who knew we had it?'

'Good questions, Julia. The first one would be the easiest to answer – someone who might be implicated by something on the computer.'

'Right. That could be Olga or Mike – scared that someone would read the emails and suspect, as we did, that they were involved in the murder. Or it could be someone else entirely, someone else with something to cover up. We didn't search the rest of the emails or the hard drive, so who knows what else was on there.'

'And what about the next question – how would they know we had it? As far as I can see, the only possible answer is that someone saw you leave with it,' said Sean.

'The cleaning lady was there, but she definitely didn't know I'd lifted it. She was too busy making excuses for taking a smoke break, poor thing. And I did a good job of pretending I was just arriving, rather than leaving,' Julia said. She was rather proud of her cleverness in executing this manoeuvre, although ashamed of her thieving behaviour overall, of course.

'I can't imagine how anyone knew it was there, or knew that you took it.'

'Me neither,' said Julia. 'It just doesn't make sense. But someone must've known.'

18

Wilma and Diane looked up eagerly when Julia came into the shop. She got the impression that they had been talking about her, because they stopped abruptly. They covered up their awkwardness with effusive greetings, talking over each other a little too loudly.

'Hello, hello,' brayed Wilma, who was still in her Pilates outfit, with a sort of wrap thing over it. She looked, to be honest, like she was wearing pyjamas and a gown.

'Hi, Julia, how are you?' Diane said, with a concerned frown.

'Hello. Well, thanks. How are you both? How's the shop been?'

'Quite busy actually, for the end of the season,' Wilma said. 'We had to do a bit of a rearrangement of the window display, as you can imagine.'

'We removed the V.F. Andrews books and the welcome sign,' said Diane. 'It seemed in questionable taste to be displaying them when he died so tragically. We wouldn't want poor Sarah to see them when she walked down the road.'

'Although she's in custody, apparently, so that wouldn't

actually be possible, as it turns out,' Wilma jumped in, looking at Julia expectantly.

'Only for questioning, from what I have been told,' Julia said, vaguely. 'Helping with inquiries.'

She was determined not to be drawn into gossip.

'Oh well, that's a relief. I must say, I can't picture Sarah actually killing anyone,' Diane said. She did look genuinely relieved, to be fair. 'I was at school with her. It was a while ago of course, but she was very straightforward, a nice girl, hard-working and bookish, and pretty, of course. Still is. A good-looking woman. The mom's as mad as a bat, of course, but Sarah was solid.'

There was a first round of tea before anyone actually did anything. It was pleasant enough to sit and chat and sip tea.

The tinkling of the bell on the door alerted them to a shopper, the first shopper of the day. It was Harry, the metal-detector guy, looking oddly disarmed without his metal detector.

'Good morning, ladies,' he said, in his oddly formal manner. 'And how is everyone today?'

'Oh very well, thanks, Harry. And yourself?' Diane asked.

'The allergies are playing up a bit, but the pollen count is expected to fall by late afternoon, so I'm hopeful.'

Harry was a very literal fellow, thought Julia.

'Ah well, good luck with that,' Diane said, seemingly unperturbed by his strange manner. 'Felicity well, is she?'

'The academic year started a week ago, so she's been busy. Spent most of the weekend resting up. There is a cold going around. I hope she isn't coming down with that, I can't bear to see her suffer. I thought I would come and do the groceries. And see what you ladies have in stock, while I'm about it.'

'Julia, this is Harry. He's a collector, a buyer and seller of antiques, local artefacts, all sorts of things. One of our best customers, aren't you, Harry?'

'Julia and I have met, in fact. On the river path. And to answer your question, that would depend on your definition. I am a regular customer of this establishment, but I estimate that you might have a few customers who spend more than me.'

'Right,' said Diane who was starting to sound rather tired by this interaction.

'Anything interesting come in?' he asked, perhaps sensing that the conversational part of the morning had come to a close.

'Take a look over in the back corner. A lady came in yesterday with a box or two of this and that. Mrs Hatting, do you know her? She lives over on Kerry Road, but she's moving house. Downsizing. That's the thing these days, isn't it? Especially for the older generation. Anyway, she brought in a couple of boxes and some of it looked quite old. Can't promise, but you might find something that interests you there. We haven't priced everything yet, so best you have a word with Wilma if you find something you fancy.' Diane said this with a bit of an eye-roll, having previously run afoul of Wilma by giving away an unpriced Toby jug.

With Harry occupied, the three women went to work. Wilma, being the manager, allocated the tasks. Wilma herself would be at the tills, assisting customers – the prime job, clearly, in that you got all the chatter and gossip first-hand, and didn't have to delve into the dusty stockroom. Nonetheless, Julia was pleased to be allocated the task of sorting cleaned donated clothing into types and sizes, rather than 'paperwork' and 'filing', which Diane was doing and which sounded horrible.

Diane and Julia went into the back room which doubled as office and storeroom. As expected, sorting the clothing was a job well within Julia's abilities. She found it pleasant enough.

Diane took the opportunity to fill Julia in on the shop's only customer of the morning. 'He's a decent enough chap, Harry Harbour. Funny manner, granted. People say he's one of those geniuses, I saw a doccie about them once, you know the ones who are really, really clever but can't work a can opener. Well, Harry could probably work a can opener, because he likes gadgets and whatnot. But you know what I mean.'

'I do. And there's worse things than a funny manner. "Takes all types, doesn't it?" as my gran used to say.' Julia's gran had indeed said this rather a lot, but Julia suspected she'd intended the remark as a commentary on the diversity of annoyingness amongst humans, rather than an expression of tolerance for their foibles.

Julia hung a pair of trousers, size 12, on the correct rail. Diane moved a sheet of paper from a pile at her left elbow to a tray on her right, and answered, 'That it does. All types. Harry's wife's very clever too. Felicity. She's a history professor. You don't see her about the village much, though. Too busy with her reading and writing.'

Julia made a sort of agreeable noise, having no particular comment to make on a person she'd never met. It struck her that if there was gossip to be had, she would like to hear more about Mike Garforth, rather than Harry and Felicity Harbour.

'So you knew Sarah growing up, did you?' she asked. Julia considered this a fairly subtle play, but she soon discovered that it wasn't necessary to draw Diane out with carefully phrased questions. You simply had to wind her up and give her a gentle push, and she kept on going. While Julia continued the business of allocating clothing to rails, Diane launched right into a series of anecdotes and opinions about Sarah, for the most part warm and positive, but not very illuminating. After a rather lengthy tale about a school hockey team trip to Leeds, Julia realised that she merely needed to nudge her in another direction.

She cut in. 'So were you around when she met Vincent?'

'Oh yes,' said Diane, who had by now completely lost interest in the paperwork. 'That was quite a thing. I had a front row seat for that, quite literally. Shall we have another cup of tea?'

Tea poured, Diane settled into her story. The nudge had worked perfectly. 'Sarah was going out with a local chap at the time. Mike, his name was. Nice chap, but not a keeper, I'd say.'

'Oh really? Why?' This here was what she was looking for, Julia thought, with a prickle of anticipation.

'Nothing wrong with him. He was smart, okay looking, but he didn't have her spark. I'd say he was a safe first boyfriend. You know. The type that the mothers love. Just getting her toe in the water, so to speak.'

'Right, not a bad idea,' Julia said.

'Although I suspect Mike Garforth thought he was going for a big long swim.'

Peculiar metaphor, but Julia got the idea. She nodded encouragingly and reached for her tea, which was cooling on the edge of Diane's desk. She took a sip, as Diane leaned forward and returned to her story.

'We were in our final year, and it was pretty much a given that all those early romances would peter out when people went off to uni, or to a big city. So anyway, this cricket team comes from a few towns over to play a Sunday match. The chaps are a bit older, not school boys. A bunch of us girls go to watch, it being Berrywick, and there being not much to do on a Sunday. Plus, you know, a dozen or so young men to look at. There's this one fellow, such a fine-looking chap he was...'

'Vincent Andrews?'

'Vincent Andrews. Ooh, you should have seen him back in the day. He was something. He had that floppy hair, tall, easy manner. You know the type.' Diane sighed and looked quite misty-eyed at the thought of the hot young Vince. 'He's at the wicket, and he keeps looking over at us, in between balls. He's not concentrating, that's for sure. Gets himself a smack on the head with a ball. Goes down like a stone. Sarah's closest and she runs over to him, to see if he's all right. She's got a cup of water, and she uses her hankie to pat his forehead with the water, and he wakes up and he looks into her face – she was quite the looker, quite besides being a top student, I think I've mentioned – and he blinks and says – wait for it – "Are you an angel?"'

Diane burst into laughter.

'Now there's a pick-up line if ever I've heard one,' Julia said, joining in the laughter.

'My, but that boy was a charmer. The whole thing was like a scene from a movie. Well, that was the end of poor old Mike Garforth and the beginning of Vincent and Sarah.'

'How did poor Mike take it?'

'Not well. And Sarah could be quite mean about him, often joked about him afterwards. He left the village straight after school, went off to uni up north, I think it was. He did well for himself in some business... now what was it? Insurance, I think. Something like that, anyhow. There was an early engagement too, up in London if I remember correctly. It was no one we knew. But apparently it didn't take. He came back to Berrywick eventually and bought a nice big house. He's an upstanding member of the community, all that, but a loner. Never did get married, poor chap. I don't think he ever got over losing Sarah.'

'And her mum? How did Eleanor feel about Vince?'

'Ah, who can ever tell anything that goes on in that woman's head? Such an odd bod, with her strange clothes and crazy ways. But she liked Mike, I remember that. They stayed in touch – you'll sometimes see them having a breakfast at the Buttered Scone.'

The tinkling bell rang at the front door, and a minute after, Wilma came bustling into the back room. 'You've got a visitor,' she said to Julia. There was a tinge of disapproval to her voice, and she looked pointedly at the rails, as if to ascertain whether Julia had been skiving off. 'A girl with blue hair, she asked for you.'

'Oh, that'll be Phoebe. She works for Vincent Andrews'

publisher. I wonder what she wants? I'll go and see. I've finished sorting the clothes here anyway.'

Wilma looked mollified, and went to check on Diane's progress while Julia went out to find Phoebe.

The young woman looked worn down, her usually sleek and shiny hair grubby and unbrushed. She sloped exhaustedly under the weight of a backpack slung over her right shoulder. 'I hope you don't mind me coming here to your work. I wouldn't, except it's important. Urgent. And I didn't know who else to talk to. It couldn't wait. I asked Dr O'Connor, I had his number on my list of locals from Vincent. He said I'd find you here.' She ran her hand through her lank hair and continued, 'Sorry, I'm rambling. I've been awake all night.'

'Here, take a seat,' Julia said, leading her to the sales desk. 'Would you like some tea?'

Phoebe refused tea, but dropped the backpack onto the counter and sank down gratefully into the chair behind the cash register.

Julia cut to the chase: 'What is it? Why are you here?'

Phoebe reached into the backpack and pulled out a thick stack of typed papers, held together with a big black bulldog clip and enclosed in a straining brown envelope. She looked furtively around the shop, like someone in a spy movie. When she didn't see anyone in the front part of the store, she placed the stack of papers on the counter, her right hand resting protectively on it.

Julia could make out the words 'Chapter One'. It appeared to be the first page of a book manuscript, with a lot of notes scribbled in green pen.

'It's the manuscript of Vincent's new book,' Phoebe said. 'The new – the last – V.F. Andrews.' Her voice broke slightly as she said 'the last'.

'Okay,' said Julia, calmly, and waited.

'There's something very strange about it. Something is not right.'

She gave another furtive scan of the shop. 'There are notes on it, unusual notes. And the actual work is... I think it might have something to do with...'

She stopped short when she realised that Harry had appeared behind her, having emerged quietly from the back of the shop, holding an assortment of objects.

Phoebe looked panicked. 'I'll go. I'll speak to you later.' She shoved the manuscript back into the envelope and quickly into the backpack.

Julia felt bad, leaving the girl in such a state, but the shop really was no place for a proper talk.

'Are you still in the B&B in Fairmile Lane? I could come by first thing tomorrow morning, okay?'

'Would you?' Phoebe sounded pathetically grateful. She lowered her voice, even though the shop was almost empty. 'It's important. I need to speak to someone... The notes on the manuscript... I'll talk to you then.'

Phoebe left the shop, glancing furtively around her, as if she expected to be followed out. *What an odd interaction*, thought Julia, her curiosity piqued. She looked forward to seeing Phoebe the next morning, finding out what this was all about.

'I'll take these.' Harry was waiting at the counter. He looked pleased with his haul.

'So you found something, did you?' Wilma said, emerging from the back room.

'Oh, just a few bits and pieces,' Harry said, with a deliberately casual air. 'Nothing special.'

Wilma pulled a very nondescript jug or mug towards her. 'Let's see now, is that delftware, do you think?' She turned it over to view the markings on the back.

'Oh no,' said Harry, 'I am fairly sure it's not an original

piece. And besides, there is a crack, unfortunately. Hairline. Do you see?'

Wilma made a show of peering at the piece, as if searching in vain for the alleged hairline crack. Harry pointed with the tip of a pencil. Wilma frowned and squinted. Julia smiled to herself at the little dance that played out – him trying to get a bargain, her trying to get a good price – no doubt not for the first time between these two.

19

Sean came by the shop just after 3 p.m. He greeted the three women warmly, but only hugged Julia.

'Hope you don't mind that I popped in, I was in the neighbourhood,' he said, addressing her.

'Now that I believe, seeing as everywhere in Berrywick is in the neighbourhood of everywhere else,' Julia said, and they both laughed. 'But it's good to see you.'

Having seen that the visit was in fact a visit to Julia, Wilma and Diane were now blatantly staring at the two of them. Julia realised that their interaction had been quite obviously flirtatious in tone, and her colleagues must be contemplating the idea of her and Sean as a couple, probably for the first time. If there was any doubt, Sean removed it when he said, 'I thought I might walk you home. When do you finish work?'

Diane's eyes, already somewhat poppy, seemed destined to leave their sockets.

'Still busy here till four, I'm afraid,' Julia said, surveying the shop which was, in fact, empty of customers at that very moment.

'Nonsense!' said Wilma, emerging from her paralysed

astonishment. 'Diane and I can handle things for the last hour, you two go along.'

Julia didn't make a show of protesting, she just thanked Wilma, wished them both a good evening, and left with Sean, knowing that they would be the subject of much speculation, starting the minute the doors closed behind them. Oh well, let them talk. At least it would take their minds off gossiping about the murder.

As they walked, Julia filled Sean in on Phoebe's strange visit. 'I can't imagine what was so mysterious. It just looked as if an editor had made notes on the paper.'

'Were they those funny squiggles and arrows and marks, you know, the ones editors use?' he asked.

'No. Actually, from the little I saw, it seemed to be mostly words. So perhaps it was Vincent himself, his notes on the manuscript. Or someone else, commenting. Some writers get their friends to comment on first drafts, I believe? Who knows. Anyway, I'll see Phoebe first thing tomorrow and hear what it is that she's so worried about. How's your day been? Save any lives today?'

'Nothing much to report – just a regular day, all bunions, bruises and backache. Which is good if you're a doctor.'

'Better than births and bronchial pneumonia,' Julia said. She wished she'd been able to think of a third dramatic B on the fly, just to match his three mild conditions. But he chuckled anyway.

They walked on in companionable silence, which Sean broke after a few minutes with a hissed whisper: 'There's Mike!'

As one, they stopped walking, and ducked behind the trunk of a large oak. Julia peered round and followed Sean's gaze. There, sitting on a bench, leaning forward, his elbows on his knees, quietly contemplating the water, was the man Julia had seen leaving Vincent Andrews' event in a huff. A sandy-haired man with a slight limp. The same man who threatened in an email that Vincent would 'pay for this'.

A possible suspect in Vincent's murder.

'What should we do?' Sean whispered.

'We've got to talk to him, of course!'

'Yes, yes of course. What will we say?'

'Just say hello, get onto the subject of Sarah – that's what you two have in common – and we'll wing it from there.'

He raised his eyebrows. 'Wing it from there?'

Julia shrugged, knowing there was no better plan.

'OK,' he said.

'Just play it cool.'

Sean shook his head, took a deep breath, and stepped out from behind the tree. They walked in the direction of the bench and Mike Garforth. As they came up to him, Julia hung back a little, while Sean sauntered up with exaggerated casualness. He stopped suddenly.

'Mike?' Sean said, in an imitation of surprise. 'Well, *fancy* seeing you here.'

He was a shocking, shocking actor. Couldn't lie for toffee! Julia liked that in a man. She only hoped that Mike didn't know him well enough to read the signs. The hyperactive eyebrows, the pronounced articulation of random words, the unnecessarily wide grin.

'Oh hello, Dr O'Connor. How're you?'

'I suppose I'm all right, thanks. Under the circumstances,' said Sean. 'Vincent... And of course poor Sarah... Oh, my manners, this is Julia Bird. She's new to the village.'

Mike gave her a hello, without paying her much attention – just as Julia wished – and replied to Sean. 'Yes, awful about Sarah, I can't believe she's still in custody.' His face was flushed as he spoke about her, the freckles even more pronounced.

Julia moved away towards the river. She felt sure Mike would be more likely to open up if she wasn't around. When she was at a reasonable distance, but within earshot, she stopped and gazed at the water, trying to look like a woman lost in her thoughts, rather than a woman straining to hear every word being said.

'I wish I could help her,' Sean said. His voice sounded true and natural now. 'I know she didn't kill Vincent. I just wish I could find some way to prove her innocence.'

'I know. I've been thinking the same thing. She is such a wonderful woman; of course she didn't kill him. Not that he didn't... Anyway, Vincent Andrews must have had many enemies. Many! He was such an unpleasant man. Nobody liked him.'

Mike Garforth clearly didn't follow the dictum: 'don't speak ill of the dead'.

'Really?' Sean asked. 'How so? I didn't know him well. He didn't come to these parts much. But he always seemed like a nice enough chap.'

'Oh yes, but looks can be deceiving. He was a dishonest man. Devious. And malicious.' Mike's face took on an ugly leer when he said this. 'Eleanor told me – in confidence – that Sarah thought he had had affairs. Disappeared for weekends without a proper explanation, that sort of thing. Eleanor tried to persuade her to leave him, but she wouldn't. It's a sickness, you know. Women who stick with these awful men. And then – then! – I bumped into him last year in Berrywick and he had the gall to ask me not to tell Sarah. Can you believe it?'

Now *this* was interesting information, thought Julia, trying to keep her face impassive, as if she were meditating on the gloriousness of nature – and it was indeed pretty, the leaves on the oaks beginning to turn, their gold reflected and shimmering on the water. But frankly, she was more concerned with the news that Vincent Andrews had been visiting Berrywick secretly. It was Julia's experience that secret trysts never had a healthy explanation.

'Did you agree not to tell?' Sean asked. Sean was nothing if not direct.

'Of course not!' Mike was outraged at the thought. 'I did *not* give him my assurance, what I *did* give him was a piece of my mind!' Mike sounded rather pleased with this neat turn of phrase. 'That's why he put a cruel caricature of me in that turgid book of his. Out of spite.'

'He did that?' said Sean, in what Julia assumed was meant to sound like great surprise. To Julia, it sounded like a child reading lines for a play. But Mike didn't seem to notice.

'You likely wouldn't have recognised me, he was not a fine craftsman of the written word. But it's me.'

'I haven't read the book. But that's most unkind, I agree.'

'I'll tell you what I think, Sean.'

Julia couldn't resist looking round for a peek. She saw Sean lean forward, making encouraging murmuring sounds while Mike continued: 'I think if only people knew the real Vincent Andrews, they'd know he must have put many backs up. Women he'd wronged. Men he'd humiliated. Any number of people might have killed him. You might even say...' There was a pause, and then Mike Garforth said, his voice full of malice. 'You might even say that he had it coming.'

After a bit of mumbling that Julia couldn't hear, Sean called out to her, 'Julia, are you ready? Shall we move on?'

She walked back to join them.

'Good to see you, Mike,' Sean said, shaking the man's hand while patting his shoulder with the other. 'You take care of yourself, and if you think of anything that might help Sarah, do let me know.'

'Will do, Doc. You're a good friend to her and to Eleanor.'

They said their goodbyes and Sean and Julia left him as they'd found him, elbows on knees, gazing at the water.

. . .

Sean and Julia discussed the various scenarios on their way back to her house. At home, Jake welcomed them with the deranged enthusiasm of a dog that had been locked up alone in a cage for a week. He squealed and wriggled and leapt about while Julia let them into the house. She dug for her keys, patting him with her other hand, and said, 'Yes, Jakey, I'm happy to see you too. Hello, my boy. Yes, hello, love. Yes, we're home...'

Julia turned on the lights in the kitchen.

'It is getting dark a little earlier every day,' Julia observed. 'I'd better go and check on the chicks while it is still light. And feed Jakey boy. Do you want some tea?' She had picked up the kettle and was walking to the sink.

'I'll do it,' Sean said, taking it from her. 'You go and deal with the livestock.'

Julia had an efficient evening routine, which she carried out almost unconsciously. She was back in the kitchen in ten minutes. Sean had made a pot of tea and laid everything out nicely on the kitchen table. He was busy at the counter with a breadboard.

'Hope you don't mind, I thought I'd make us each a toasted cheese sandwich. I'm sure you didn't have anything much, being at the shop all day. And all those backaches and bunions kept me working through lunchtime.'

'Of course not!' she said. 'Good idea, make yourself at home. Can I help?'

'No need. But you could pour the tea. It'll be brewed by now.'

Sean was a bit of a stickler in the tea department. None of this 'toss a tea bag in, swirl it around and scoop it in the bin' nonsense for him. His tea was always made in a teapot, and well brewed. 'So the teaspoon will stand up in it,' as he liked to say.

Julia was pouring the steaming black liquid into the cups when she heard the clatter of a knife falling on the counter, and

Sean saying, 'Ow, damn.' She looked up to see him holding his left hand in his right. 'Cut myself. The knife slipped.'

Blood seeped through his clenched fingers. She grabbed a square of kitchen paper towel and handed it to him, saying, 'Come to the bathroom.'

Julia led him by his good hand, giving instructions. 'Now give it a wash. Sit down there on the side of the bath. Keep the pressure on to stop the blood flow,' she said, forgetting for a moment that he was an actual doctor and probably didn't require this piece of advice. 'Hold it tight while I get you a plaster.'

She felt his eyes on her as she reached up to the bathroom cupboard for a box of assorted size sticky plasters. The paper towel was red with blood. She sat down next to him 'Let me see. Does it need a stitch, do you think?'

'I think not, Doctor,' he said with a grin. He opened up the paper gingerly and peered at the wound. 'Just a plaster. It'll be OK.'

Julia chose a large, long plaster. Resting his hand on her knee, she peeled off the backing and placed it carefully on his finger, making sure the soft absorbent square covered the cut. She smoothed the sides down firmly, hoping they would stick well. It was a tender moment, his hand in hers. Her careful attention on this little wound. 'The little battle scars of everyday life,' she said with a smile. And then remembered.

'Sean!'

She dropped his hand and jumped out of her chair.

'The knife!'

He looked confused by this sudden outburst. 'It's in the kitchen...'

'The other knife. Vincent,' she said, so excited that she struggled to formulate the sentence and express it coherently. 'The report showed a cut on his finger. What if that's how his blood got on the knife? What if it wasn't the murder weapon at all? What if he was simply cutting something – a piece of bread, an apple – and he cut his finger, just as you did? He cut his finger and took the knife to the bathroom while he washed the wound.'

His injury forgotten, Sean got to his feet and grabbed her for a hug. 'My God, you're right! You brilliant woman. Vincent dropped the knife to wash his finger, dried it on the hand towel and left them both in the bathroom. They weren't hidden there by Sarah, they were left there by Vincent.'

'Come on,' she said. 'We need to tell DI Gibson!'

20

Hayley looked tired. Tired and grumpy. And not at all pleased to see Julia.

She had agreed rather reluctantly to meet first thing in the morning, and hear Julia out. But she gave the distinct impression of someone with better things to do, submitting reluctantly to this interruption in her busy day.

Now in Hayley's office, Julia felt awkward, even a little nervous. Although she had worked in high-conflict situations, she didn't deal well with personal conflict in her own life. Particularly with someone she genuinely liked. She and Hayley had grown quite friendly after a body had been found under Julia's garden shed, and she'd found herself inadvertently entangled in a murder investigation. They'd co-operated, and even shared a glass of wine and a meal, but now Hayley seemed irritated by her nosing around the Vincent Andrews case.

Julia wondered if she should broach the subject and clear the air, but Hayley pre-empted any conversation she might start. She didn't sit down, or even offer Julia a seat. She simply leaned against her desk and said: 'So, you've involved yourself in another murder investigation, it seems. Poking around the Vincent Andrews case, I hear.'

'It's not like that. I'm not doing any investigating, goodness no. That's not my position. But I did have a thought. Just something that might be useful to you.' Julia spoke carefully, trying not to come over as pushy or critical or a know-it-all. She was merely a concerned citizen who'd come upon a piece of information.

'Okay then, let's hear it.'

Hayley sounded a little warmer, until Julia said, 'It's about the results of the forensic report.'

'How do you know what's in the forensic report?' Hayley asked, sharply. So much for the thawing of relations.

'As you know, Sean is a friend. He has been so worried about Sarah. He gets information, of course, from the family. From Eleanor, Sarah's mother. And he talks about it sometimes. He mentioned the report to me. As a friend.'

'All right, go on.'

'Well, from what Sean said, the report mentioned a cut on Vincent's finger. I wondered if he might have cut himself on the knife you found in the bathroom. Accidentally. That would explain his blood on the knife. And that would mean...'

Hayley cut her off. 'That would mean that Sarah didn't stab him with the knife and hide it in the bathroom.'

'Yes.'

'Okay. I'll look into it. See what forensics thinks of your theory.'

Julia decided to come out with it. 'Look, Hayley, I'm really not trying to interfere. I know it must be irritating to have Sean on your back all the time about Sarah. And to have amateurs coming up with theories about murder investigations. But it's possible that this theory is right.'

Hayley lost some of her bristle. 'Yes, of course. If Sarah isn't the murderer, she must be released from custody.' She offered

Julia a slight smile that held the hint of an apology and said, 'You were right to come to me. I will look into it.'

'Thank you. I wasn't convinced of Sarah's innocence to start with either, to be honest. But the more I look at it, the more I think it's not just Sean being protective. And, Hayley, I'm sure you know that Vincent had troubles and enemies.'

Hayley moved round the desk and sat down on her swivel chair. She gestured to Julia to take the seat opposite her. Between them was a desk with three file trays, each of them stacked to capacity with bulging files, a computer peppered with sticky notes in all the colours of the rainbow, a pile of white slips which appeared to be messages – calls to return, reminders, requests. There wasn't so much as a photograph, a cut-out cartoon or a cute magnet to give the office a personal touch. Even Hayley's mug was a standard-issue white thing with a chip out of it – no doubt one of a dozen identical mugs on similar desks around the office. Hayley was all about work, work, work, Julia thought – and it was piling up and taking its toll.

'What do you know about Vincent's troubles and enemies?' Hayley asked.

'It seems he might have been having affairs. And then there were people who appeared in his books in an unflattering light. There are a lot of people who didn't like Vincent.'

'Well, as my old superintendent said, when I first joined the force, "When it comes to murder, nine times out of ten it's sex or money – if it's not the sex, it's money, and if it's not the money, it's sex."'

There was a tentative knock on Hayley's office door and DC Walter Farmer's face appeared at the little glass window, like a full moon in a Japanese etching.

'Not now,' Hayley said firmly, and turned back to Julia. 'How about we go and get a decent coffee – not the weedy swill that passes for coffee around here?' She gestured to the grey-brown remains in the bottom of her mug with a sour-looking creamy skin forming on the top. It was a distinctly unappealing sight. 'And we can share what we know.'

'Good idea,' said Julia, glad for the thawing of relations between them, and this conciliatory gesture. She reached for her handbag. Hayley stood up.

There was another knock, more insistent this time. The door opened a crack and Farmer's anxious face appeared in the gap between door and frame. 'Sorry, ma'am, but it's urgent. There's something you need to know.'

'What is it?'

'It's about the Vincent Andrews case.' He looked over at Julia, reluctant to speak in front of her, and then back at Hayley.

'Go on,' Hayley said, with an impatient flick of her wrist. 'Just say it.'

'There's been another death, ma'am, a murder, looks like. Over on Fairmile Lane. At the B&B. The cleaning lady called it in just a few minutes ago.'

Fairmile Lane! Julia's blood ran cold. She knew two people who were resident at the B&B in Fairmile Lane. One was safely in police custody; the other was Phoebe Ailes.

'The cleaning lady there found a body this morning, a young woman. A guest, it seems. Not identified, as yet. We're trying to get in touch with the owner of the establishment.'

Julia cut in. 'Phoebe Ailes, Vincent's publicist, was staying there. Next door to Sarah and Vincent. It might be her.'

'Good God,' muttered Hayley under her breath. She closed her eyes for a brief second, more like a long blink. Julia felt the stress and tiredness behind that small movement. Hayley was taking the strain. And another brick had been added to her load.

'Phoebe has blue tips to her hair. Did anyone mention that?'

'Yes. The cleaning lady mentioned that she had blue hair. Ma'am, I said we'd be right over,' DC Farmer said, eager for his boss to get going and take charge.

'Okay. Let's go,' she said. 'Walter, you go with the uniforms. Secure the area. I'll take my car. Julia, you ride with me. You can fill me in on your view of Phoebe Ailes on the way.'

Hayley grabbed a bag and her phone, and pulled a black blazer from the back of her chair in one swift motion. She called after Walter: 'Call forensics to meet you there. I don't need to tell you not to stomp around the crime scene, do I?'

'No, ma'am, Detective Inspector Gibson,' his voice came echoing from down the passage. He'd already set off at something between a walk and a run.

'Come on, let's get over there,' Hayley said a little impatiently to Julia, who was gathering her own bag and jumper somewhat less speedily than the younger woman. Hayley was already heading out with brisk efficiency. Julia had to jog a few paces to catch up with her. She was in her sixties, after all. A good twenty years older than Hayley.

When they reached the car park, Hayley unlocked the car door, swung it open, and got in. She slammed the car door and shoved her seat belt almost forcefully into its holder, until it clicked loudly. Then she turned to Julia – still groping for her seat belt – and said, 'Right, now tell me everything you know about Phoebe Ailes.'

Julia spilled each and every bean she had.

She reminded Hayley about Sarah's jealousy of Phoebe's relationship with her husband, that she viewed her as a potential rival.

She told her about Phoebe's insistence that Sarah loved Vincent and would never hurt him, let alone kill him.

She described Phoebe's sort-of-crush-turned-genuine-friendship with Vincent.

And she relayed Phoebe's insistence that Vincent Andrews was a loyal husband, that there had never been anything physical between the two them.

'You believed her?'

'I did. She's young, and a little star-struck, but I got the impression that she was a genuine friend to Vincent. He even asked her to shield him from an obsessive old girlfriend here in Berrywick.'

Then she reminded Hayley of what Phoebe had said about Olga – at which point Hayley stopped her, phoned the office, and instructed someone on the other end of the phone to run a check on Olga.

'What's her surname?' she asked Julia.

'Gilbert.'

Hayley went back to her call. 'Olga Gilbert. G-I-L-B-E-R-T. Local. Full rundown. And another thing. Can you get the forensic accounting chaps to take a proper good look at Vincent Andrews' finances?'

Driving deftly through the morning traffic, she finished the call and said to Julia, 'If only your boyfriend hadn't lost that blooming laptop.'

'He's not my...'

'This is no time to discuss your love life, Julia.' Which was pretty rich, seeing as Julia hadn't brought it up. Hayley gave her a twitch of a wry smile just to show that she was teasing – mostly – and continued. 'Go on. What else? Everything you know about Phoebe.'

Julia told her about the girl's strange arrival at the charity shop the previous afternoon, carrying a manuscript.

'What was the manuscript?'

'She said it was Vincent's new book. I didn't see any of the text well enough to read it. Only the heading. Chapter One.'

'She came to find you? Specifically you?'

'Yes, she phoned Sean to ask where I was and she came to Second Chances.'

'Why?'

'I suppose she trusted me. After our last conversation. She knew that I believed her about Vince, that I was on her side.

And she didn't know anyone else in Berrywick. Anyone she could talk to.'

They drew up at the B&B, where two police vehicles were already parked. A uniformed policeman was rolling out the crime scene tape. Julia had an unpleasant feeling of déjà vu. Had it only been five days since she'd seen the crime scene team going through the same process at the library?

The car had barely come to a stop when Hayley was out of her seat belt and opening the door. Julia was still extricating herself from the car when the detective said, 'We're going to have to have the rest of this conversation another time. I want to know everything you know about Vincent Andrews' life and the people who were angry with him. But right now, I need to go and look at this Phoebe Ailes situation. Can you make your way home from here?'

'Yes. I'll be home this afternoon if you want to phone to talk. Or you can come over. I can make you the decent coffee you were hankering for.'

'Right,' Hayley said, already walking away, walking towards the room that held the body of Phoebe Ailes.

'Hayley!' Julia called after her. The detective glanced back. 'Don't forget to look for the manuscript. Brown envelope.'

Hayley waved in assent, once more on the move.

Julia felt a sudden and delayed wave of sadness. It hadn't really sunk in until now that that vibrant young woman was dead. Her body lying in the little cottage – God knows what had been done to her. Julia had liked Phoebe. Warmed to her, with her blue hair and her tender feelings about Vincent. It just wasn't right that such a lovely young woman was dead.If Phoebe hadn't been killed, Julia would be talking to her right now, she thought sadly. Phoebe would be describing the mystery of the manuscript, perhaps over tea, in the B&B room in which the young woman now lay dead. Julia would be probing, asking questions, and helping Phoebe think about what she'd found. All the policemen and forensic experts, and DI Hayley Gibson, would be in their respective offices, trying to solve Vincent Andrews' murder, or the Great Orchid Heist, instead of tiptoeing around room in their plastic-covered shoes, trying to work out who on earth killed Phoebe Ailes.

And why?

21

Julia was glad to be home. She was tired, even though it wasn't quite eleven o'clock. She had been up early to get the house and animals in order, and get to Hayley's office. And Phoebe's death had left her feeling bruised and sad. My goodness. That poor girl.

Jake greeted her as if she'd returned from the Great War. He jumped and slobbered and barked and squealed in delight to discover that after four years she'd finally been shipped home and not been bayoneted in the trenches.

'Oh come now, Jake, calm down, love, I've only been gone an hour or two.' She said it with mild exasperation, but in truth it was nice to be missed. Nice to be welcomed home with such love and excitement.

Peter had always been pleased to see her. Even after he'd fallen in love with someone else. And she was pleased to see him, too. Even these days, she smiled when she saw Peter's old Volvo chugging up to the gate, bringing him and Christopher for a visit. Funny, really. Everyone thought she'd hate him after what happened. Her friends had tried to engage in Peterbashing under the guise of sympathy, assuming she'd want that, but she hadn't. She was sad, of course, and surprised, and a little hurt. And it had been a bit of a blow to her self-esteem – was her ageing body really so off-putting that he'd left her for a man? But she knew that was nonsense. She'd come very quickly to the realisation that it wasn't about her. It was about Peter. Peter couldn't help who he was and who he loved. And there was no point in being angry.

And now she had Sean. Whatever that meant.

As if on cue, her phone vibrated in her bag, and she scrabbled around amongst the lipsticks and tissues and pens and keys until she found it, Sean's name glowing promisingly on the little screen.

'Sarah's getting out!' he said, without so much as a hello. His voice was exuberant, almost triumphant. 'She's being released today. Thanks to you. They are busy processing her papers or some such, but I'm going to fetch her from the police station at noon.'

'Oh that's wonderful, Sean! I'm so glad. But really, it wasn't me...'

'It was. Your clever theory about the knife cut on his finger clinched the deal.'

'Sean, is she going back to London, or to the B&B?'

'I suppose she will have to go to the B&B for the night, at least. But I'm sure she will want to get home.'

'She can't go there. Sean, something terrible has happened.'

'Something *else* terrible?'

'Yes, something else. Phoebe has been killed. At the B&B, right next to Sarah and Vincent's place. The police are all over the show. Crime scene tape.'

'Surely not. Another death? Who do the police think might have done it? Was it the same killer?'

She had no answers for his questions. 'Sean, even if they

allow her in, it will be traumatic for her. Take her to her mum's place.'

'I don't know if Sarah will want to stay there. Eleanor lives in a small place full to the brim with her odds and ends and plants and cats and who knows what. I suppose she could come to me. Or I could find her another B&B. I'll see what she prefers.'

'Okay. That's for the best. Let me know how it goes.'

Sean was quiet for a moment and then said, softly, 'But, Julia... Phoebe? I can't believe it. That poor, sweet girl. What happened? It must be connected to Vincent's death, but how?'

'I don't know how she died, but the police are using the word "murder". As for the connection, I haven't had time to think. But I keep going back to the manuscript... She was so concerned.'

He interrupted her. 'Sorry, Julia, I have to take this call. It's Sarah on the other line. I'll phone you a bit later.'

Jake seemed under the impression that after her busy morning out, Julia might like to head straight out for a nice vigorous walk, but she was having none of it. It was an afternoon on the sofa that she was looking for. If she had the energy for it, she'd bake a batch of scones. Her scone baking had come on tremendously. She'd really got the hang of it now – she regularly achieved the exact degree of shiny crisp top and crumbly, buttery inside that defined a good scone, in her opinion. She liked to keep her hand in and bed down the skill by baking regularly. Not excellent for the waistline, but she did give most of the scones away in order to redistribute the calories more evenly amongst the population of Berrywick.

There was to be no scone baking that afternoon, however. Only an hour after she'd made a cup of tea, and a slice of toast and honey, Sean phoned again.

'Just wanted to tell you that I've got Sarah and she's going to stay with me. Thanks for the heads-up on that one. I'm glad we didn't pitch up at the crime scene.' He dropped his voice. 'She's pretty fragile, it would have been traumatic for her.'

'She's been through a lot. It'll be good for her to be settled in at your house for a bit. A nice bath, soft bed.'

'It'll be a bit of a runaround first. Unfortunately, we'll have to go past the shops and buy some things – clothes, and so on. I can't take her to the B&B to fetch hers. I've had to cancel my patients, of course.' The exuberance had gone out of his voice. Now he just sounded flustered and stressed by all the logistics, the poor man.

'Do you want me to go and collect her things from Fairmile Lane?' Julia asked. She could feel her peaceful afternoon slipping through her fingers, but Sean was her friend, so... 'It's close by. I don't mind fetching them. I'll phone Hayley first just to check. If it's all okay with her I'll take the car – it could use an outing – fetch her things, and then I'll drop them at your place.'

'Ah, Julia, I couldn't ask you to do that.'

'You're not asking, I'm offering.'

'Ah, but still...' He hesitated and seemed to change his mind. 'That is very kind of you, thank you. I would appreciate it very much.'

'It's no trouble. I'll be going, then.'

'Thank you, Julia. Really, thank you.' He sounded quite moved by the simple offer.

'Just being a friend.'

Hayley didn't seem particularly interested in Sarah's toothbrush. 'Come and get what you need, just as long as you stay away from the crime scene. Gotta go.'

'Hang on, Hayley,' Julia said quickly, before the detective could ring off.

'Yup.'

'Phoebe. How did she die?'

'Blow to the head. Blunt object. Body gone to the mortuary. Gotta go.'

'And the manuscript?'

The phone went dead before she finished the question. With a bit of luck she'd be able to corner Hayley at the crime scene. Julia felt sure that the manuscript had something to do with Phoebe's death. And if Phoebe's death was linked to the manuscript, then surely Vincent's was, too? And where did that leave her suspicions about Olga and Mike? Would either of them have killed Phoebe? What motive could they possibly have for that? As Julia saw things, Phoebe's death changed everything. It was back to the drawing board in terms of suspects.Jake looked so delighted at the prospect of an outing that she decided to take him. He needed to get used to riding in a car. She wouldn't let him out while she was at the B&B, of course, but she would only be there a few minutes. Then she'd swing by Sean's house to drop off Sarah's things, and take Jake for a good long walk in the woods on the far side of the village, not far from Sean's place.

'I've got a plan,' she told the dog. 'Don't you worry yourself about the details. Get in the car, we'll go and do our good deed, and then it's time for walkies.'

Jake's vocabulary was not extensive, but he did recognise 'walk' and all words derived thereof – walked, walking, and walkies, specifically. He leapt about like a mad dog for a bit and hurled himself delightedly into the car when she opened the door. He sat up straight and proud in the back seat as if he was a prosperous man about town, and Julia was his chauffeur. Julia opened his window so he could enjoy the breeze. As she turned into the main road, he looked out of the window as if he were royalty going out amongst his subjects. They passed Nicky and her boy, Sebastian, who tugged at his mum's hand, pointed and shouted, 'There's the naughty dog! Going for a drive.'

Jake nodded, regally.

'I'll only be a few minutes,' Julia said as she pulled up in Fairmile Lane. 'You just sit here quietly.'

22

Julia opened each of the four windows a couple of inches, to give Jake air (and to avoid coming back to a dog breath sauna), and turned off the car. 'Be a good boy, Jake,' she said, getting out.

A big black BMW almost clipped her open car door as it swung into the parking space ahead of her and screeched to a halt. A tall, distinguished-looking man got out. His thick dark grey hair was meticulously cut and shining, and Julia couldn't help but note how the skin on his face shone too, as if it had been scrubbed down and oiled, like a priceless piece of antique furniture. His suit was beautifully cut to show off his broad shoulders and narrow waist, and underneath it, the top two buttons of his creamy shirt were open to reveal a hint of collar-bone and a thin gold chain with a thin gold ring, perhaps a wedding ring, hanging off it. He would be quite a marvellous sight, were it not for the look of absolute rage on his face.

'Who's in charge here?' he demanded of Julia. Rather rudely, she thought. Jake looked on anxiously through the car window, his brow furrowed over his deep brown eyes.

'That would depend. In charge of what?' she asked pleasantly. Julia knew that pleasantness either disarmed or infuriated angry, bossy men. She suspected that this one would lean towards infuriated.

'The whole mess. The police investigation, for one thing. I need to know what happened to Vincent Andrews and Phoebe Ailes, and I need to know *now*.' He slammed his hand down on the roof of his car as he uttered the last word, causing Jake's face to disappear from the window. Julia reflected that she was right about the man's response, although she took no pleasure in it. The world didn't need more furious men.

'Well, in that case, you would be looking for DI Hayley Gibson,' Julia said calmly, closing her car door and walking towards Sarah's B&B.

'Thank you.' He had the good grace to look mildly ashamed of his behaviour. 'I'm a bit het up, I'm afraid. Vincent was a friend and colleague. And Phoebe a valued employee. So you can imagine...'

Julia stopped. 'You're with the publisher?'

'I *am* the publisher. Vincent's publisher,' he said. He sounded proud, or perhaps prideful. 'I'm just trying to get some answers here.'

Julia felt rather sorry for DI Gibson, who had emerged from Phoebe's B&B, walking towards them, and who would be expected to supply these answers, which she probably didn't have. 'Here comes Hayley now; she will be able to tell you what's going on.' Julia started for Sarah's B&B.

'Julia, have you got a minute?' Hayley called after her, ignoring the man. It was quite a feat, him being so tall and his car so big and shiny. 'I'd like to bounce something off you, if you've got a mo.'

'Sure. I'm here to fetch Sarah's things, like we discussed. She'll be staying at Sean's. But I can talk to you first.'

The tall fellow appeared to be recalibrating his impression of Julia – 'ageing nobody in small ageing car with chocolate Lab', she assumed – now that the head of investigations wanted her input. He blinked and looked from one woman to the other, waiting to be acknowledged. He was not acknowledged.

'Appreciate it. We can talk in the garden, if that's okay. There's a table and chairs round by the plum tree,' Hayley said, still ignoring the big fellow who was right next to them looking on. He was looking at them in confusion, like he couldn't understand why everyone was acting like he was invisible. Julia would be lying to herself if she said she wasn't enjoying it, but she decided to put him out of his discomfort.

'This gentleman is Vincent's publisher, and Phoebe's employer. Mr...?' she looked at him expectantly.

'Frederick Eliot,' he said, offering his hand, and what she assumed was his winning smile, first to Julia and then to Hayley. 'Naturally, I'm most concerned. Devastated, in fact. I've come down from London to see what is being done. I'd be most grateful if you ladies would spare me a minute.'

Julia had come to know Hayley well enough to see that she was calculating whether he was worth her while, or whether she should send Walter or someone else to do the honours. She must have decided that Frederick Eliot would likely have information she could use.

'Come on, then,' she said. She began to move, Frederick starting after her, but Julia stood uncomfortably, not sure whether or not this was an official interview and whether or not she was expected to join them.

'Come on, Julia,' Hayley said.

Julia got Jake out of the car and followed Hayley into Sarah's side of the B&B.

'You're to be a good boy,' she told Jake quietly, in a serious tone. 'This is a police matter. Not a peep out of you.'

Frederick was wondering around, picking things up and

putting them down, much to Hayley's irritation. Hayley gestured for Frederick to sit down. Julia and Hayley followed suit. Jake sat close to Julia's foot, making sure Julia was well positioned between him and Shouty Man.

'Right then,' Hayley said, and then paused momentarily before saying briskly, and rather late in the day, 'I'm sorry for your loss.'

'Thank you,' said Frederick, crossing one long leg over the other and leaning back as if he owned the place. 'It is a shock. A terrible shock. Both personal and professional.'

'I'm sure. How long have you known Vincent Andrews?'

'It must be fifteen years or so. I was a junior publisher when the company published his first book. The publisher looking after him for that first book didn't understand his enormous potential at all. But then I took over from the second book, and I worked with him then and on all the books since, building his brand, promoting his talent. His *prodigious* talent.'

'Would you say he was your top author? In your stable?'

'Well, of course, all of our authors are...'

Hayley gave him a stern look, indicating that this round-the-bush-beating was unnecessary. He looked suitably chastened, and continued, 'Yes, yes he was. He was our biggest seller and top earner. He was the star in the firmament of Prime Publishing. The jewel in the crown, as it were.'

'And Phoebe Ailes?'

'She came to work for me three or four years ago. A valuable employee.'

But not the jewel in the crown, clearly.

Hayley cut to the chase. 'Can you think of any reason someone might want to kill Vincent Andrews?'

Frederick looked surprised to discover that the scene he had imagined – in which he would be the one asking questions and getting answers – had been replaced by one in which he was being questioned and Hayley was getting answers.

'Kill him? Good heavens, no. V.F. Andrews was universally beloved. Why would anyone want to kill him?'

'My question precisely, because clearly someone did,' Hayley said shortly. Short was her go-to attitude right now. This murder investigation was taking its toll on her. 'Did he have any enemies? Professional rivals? Angry girlfriends? Jealous husbands? That sort of thing?'

'Well, I mean, who hasn't...' Frederick stopped short. Was he really going to ask, *Who hasn't got a procession of murderous lovers and rivals?* Julia wondered. Why yes indeed, so it seemed – a flush crept over his buffed golden skin. He rearranged himself awkwardly in his chair and leaned forward. 'Honestly, I don't know about that side of things. As far as I know, he and Sarah were solid, but who knows about anyone's marriage, really?'

'And on the work front? Anything unusual there?'

'Everything is going well. This new book has recently come out, so lots of activity there. Book tours, interviews, press.'

Julia remembered what Phoebe had said when they'd first met after Vincent's death. She hesitated to step into Hayley's interview, but raised a finger and said, politely, 'Might I?' Hayley nodded. Julia asked, 'I heard that you were on the verge of making a deal that would take Vincent to the next level.'

'We were negotiating a Netflix series.' He gave a bitter snort of a laugh and said, 'In our business, everyone's always negotiating a Netflix series. Or says they are. But yes, this one was actually going ahead. It was very good news for Vincent and for the company. We all stood to make some decent cash on that one.'

'Had you noticed anything different about Vincent in recent days or weeks?' Hayley asked.

'Honestly, he seemed a little... on edge.'

'In what way?'

'He kept asking for extensions on the newest book, which

wasn't like him at all. And he wouldn't even send me a few chapters to reassure us. *Quite* unprofessional, and most unlike him.'

'How was your relationship with Vincent?' Hayley asked.

'Our interests were perfectly aligned, Ms Gibson. When Vincent did well, I did well. I can tell you that Vincent's death is a devastating blow for my business. Devastating. So if you think I might have anything to do with this, you can think again.'

'Simply gathering information, sir,' Hayley said. Julia knew well enough to know that these were standard questions.

Hayley switched tack. 'What do you know about Phoebe? Her personal life, interests, so on?'

'She was very focused on work. Loved the work. Devoted to Vincent's career. One of those bookish girls, you know. Read a great deal as a child, studied English Literature. Book publishing was her dream. I don't know much about her personal life. She brought her sister to the Christmas party, I remember that. The others ragged her about it. Not having a date, you know. She was pretty enough, although for my money the blue hair didn't do her any favours. Or the nose stud. Not sure you catch many fish – good fish – with...'

He stopped, presumably arrested by the looks on the women's faces, and mumbled something about, 'Well, each to their own of course. Lovely girl, and clever.'

'Anything between her and Vincent?'

He looked aghast at the very thought. 'Good heavens, no. Vincent wouldn't... Not with Phoebe. Not anyone. Oh no, he and Sarah are – were – devoted. They had the odd row. Let me tell you, Sarah looks like butter wouldn't melt, but she gets her way, that one. Not one to be trifled with. And she watched him like a hawk. She knew there were other women who'd be happy to take him off her hands. But Vincent would never betray her. He couldn't live without her. And as for Phoebe... No, never.'

Julia thought about the manuscript that Phoebe had, the one that had caused her so much concern. She hadn't had a chance to ask Hayley whether it had turned up. She didn't want to pre-empt anything, so she asked a more general question.

'You didn't say – did he hand in the new book?'

Frederick looked defeated. 'I'd given him an extension to the end of next month. I can only presume he was on track, but to be honest, I don't know what shape it's in. Vince always kept his cards very close to his chest. We agreed a time period and a basic plot outline up front, but after that he never discussed the book in detail or showed me anything until he had the whole thing ready for me to read. It was surprising, really, a little at odds with his personality. Vincent liked to chat about things, tell you his every passing thought. But the first thing I would see was the finished manuscript. He always turned in something meticulously written. Every 'i' dotted and 't' crossed. We would bring in an expert fact-checker who specialises in that period, just to be sure that we were right on the historical detail. They were always very complimentary, couldn't believe that a novelist could pull off that level of accuracy and depth. Most of these fiction writers just make things up, but Vincent did the hard slog. It was one of the reasons his books did so well. People loved the detail. The spoons they ate with and arms they fought with. The way this bodice laced – or unlaced, as the case may be. They were quite often unlaced. Oh, Vincent went as this rather charming bumbler, almost lazy, but when he came to his work, he was like a different person.'

Frederick broke off, tapping his fingers anxiously on the edge of the table. The metallic rat-a-tat was starting to get on Julia's nerves, when he stopped and said, 'I'd better get onto that. I might have to get a ghostwriter to finish it. First things first, see what's on his laptop. How soon can I get it? Can you hand it over now, or is there a form or something I need to fill in? I'm staying at the Stag's Head – perhaps you could have it delivered?'

Julia's eyes met Hayley's and they shared a moment of, *Oh God, I guess we'll have to tell him.*

Hayley straightened up and took a breath. 'Well, about that laptop...'

23

'Frederick was apoplectic. Went right back to Big Angry Bloke mode when he discovered the laptop was missing. Poor Jake was trembling in his boots. And when Hayley told him about the physical manuscript, good Lord. It's hardly surprising, I suppose. That book's worth a fortune to him and his company.'

'Oh dear.' Sean looked shamefaced. 'I was such a fool, leaving the laptop in the car.'

Julia felt bad for making so much of it. 'Don't worry. They'll get access to the computer server or the cloud or what have you,' she said with great certainty. Even though she was never quite sure what the cloud actually *was*. Or where it was, for that matter. 'They'll be able to find his emails and the draft of the new book, I'm certain. Hayley said they were busy with it now, so I suppose something will turn up soon. And in any case, the hard copy version should turn up at the B&B, in Phoebe's room. How's Sarah?'

'Relieved to be out, of course, but exhausted. She went straight in for a lie down when we got back. She's been asleep for two hours. She took a pill. What else did Frederick say?'

As if on cue, Sarah came through the door into Sean's sitting room. She had the marks of the sheets on her cheek and the rumpled look of someone who has slept like the dead. She took in the scene – Sean and Julia sitting on the sofa, knees almost touching, deep in conversation.

'Oh, you're here. Sean's friend. June, is it?'

'Julia. Hello. How are you feeling?'

'Like I've lost my husband and been run over by a truck.' Sarah sat down heavily on the sofa opposite theirs and collapsed back into the cushions. There were a lot of cushions. Everywhere. Julia believed that Sean had perhaps found himself in the grasp of an over-enthusiastic decorator when he'd moved into this little cottage after his wife died.

'I'm sorry. How awful for you to be arrested.'

Sarah gave a tired sort of shrug, as if she didn't want to talk about it, and said, 'So what else *did* Frederick say? I presume you are talking about Frederick Eliot, Vincent's publisher?'

'Yes. He came down from London this morning to see if there was anything he could do to help. I happened to be at the B&B fetching your things when he arrived. He was very upset about Vincent, of course. And Phoebe. And asked after you.'

'Well, Vincent was his cash cow, so he must be worried. Vincent kept the lights on in that place, I'll tell you that. Although possibly not for much longer. He was speaking to another publisher about moving when this contract is over. Did Frederick tell you that?'

'I didn't hear anything about that,' Julia said. 'We only met in passing. We hardly spoke.' She felt awkward discussing the conversation she had been party to with Hayley and Frederick. She didn't know quite where she stood. It had, after all, been a police matter. A detective inspector had been interviewing Frederick. She didn't think she was at liberty to repeat it.

'Oh well, that's Frederick for you. He has an eye to the main chance, our Freddie. Not likely to bring *that* up. And it's moot now anyway, isn't it? Now that Vincent is... gone. Frederick will have his last book and the TV show and that will be that. The end of the V.F. Andrews literary legacy.' Sarah teared up as she said it, lifting a cushion onto her lap in a sad little gesture of self-comfort. 'We never had children, Vincent and I. We couldn't. You know that, Sean, of course. V.F. Andrews' work was what he'd leave behind, what *we'd* leave behind. And now it's all over. One more book, and something for the telly.' She drooped even further into the sofa, leaning into the corner for support.

'Oh, Sarah, I'm sorry,' said Julia, getting up from where she was and moving to sit down next to Sarah. 'This has all been terribly hard for you.'

'Nobody understands me,' said Sarah, which was quite a difficult statement to respond to, thought Julia. To say that of course they did felt wrong, but to agree that indeed, nobody understood, felt heartless. Eventually she settled for, 'I'm so sorry, Sarah.'

'Would anyone like tea?' Sean asked, with that strangely masculine way of trying to solve an emotional problem. 'I could put the kettle on.'

'I should be going. I just popped round with your things from the B&B,' Julia said to Sarah. 'They are in the hall, I didn't want to disturb you. I hope I got everything, it was a bit of a rush.'

'That's kind, thank you,' Sarah said, softening. She looked up anxiously at Sean. 'I don't know what to do, really. Do I go back to London? Or stay here and wait and see what happens?'

'Just take your time, you don't need to decide now,' Sean said. 'Your mum's coming over soon, you can have a chat with her. And DI Gibson said she'd give us an update on the investigation as soon as she can.'

'Investigation!' Sarah spat. 'If you can call it that. All that time they wasted on me, they could have been finding Vincent's real killer. Maybe they should look at Frederick. Frederick Eliot, the old smoothie. Not. Hah!'

Sean and Julia looked at each other, silently wondering where this was all going. Julia wondered about the pill Sarah had taken.

'He was always a bit of a snake, and he would have been furious about Vincent leaving Prime Publishing. Could have been him who killed Vincent. I wouldn't be surprised.' She paused, as if thinking, 'Or Phoebe. I would still put my money on Phoebe for it. A woman scorned.'

'Well, she's dead too.'

'But she wasn't dead when she killed him, obviously.'

You couldn't fault Sarah's mad logic.

Sean waded back in with a tentative question, 'Yes, but then, I mean, who killed her?'

Sarah flung her arms about, as if impatient at his silly question. 'Someone else, that's who. God, this world. Killers. Could be anyone.' She gave a huge yawn and said, 'I am *sooo* tired. I think I need to go back to bed.'

Sarah staggered off back to the little spare room, leaving Sean and Julia bewildered. It was more peaceful, though, without her. They exchanged a small smile, an acknowledgement of the passing of the weather.

Julia spoke first, 'What was all that about? Does she really think Frederick or Phoebe killed Vincent?'

'If you ask me, it's the pills talking. They affect people in strange ways. Let her sleep it off and we'll see.'

'Interesting news about Vincent going to the other publisher. It does sound like something that could have a bearing on the case – I wonder if Sarah told the police? I'd better phone and tell Hayley in case.'

'I suppose you'd better.'

24

The missing manuscript was the key to the murders, Julia was sure of it. As she stirred the half teaspoon of sugar into the tea that Flo had brought her, her thoughts went round and round in her head. Had Vincent finished the book? Was the missing manuscript the one that everyone was talking about?

As it turned out, Hayley hadn't heard about the possible change of publisher. 'We got next to nothing out of Sarah. She did put forward Phoebe as the murderer initially, but after the first day, she clammed up completely, refused to talk to us. Just said that we had the wrong person and she was going to sue. I'll look into it. Thanks for letting me know.'

'Of course. Anything that comes up, I'll let you know.' Julia used the opportunity to press for info of her own. 'Oh, Hayley, did you find the manuscript? The one with the notes? In the brown envelope? Only Frederick Eliot was awfully anxious about it, wasn't he.'

'No sign of it. We looked everywhere. In her briefcase, all over. There was no brown envelope and no manuscript.'

'She had it yesterday afternoon when she came to the shop, remember. I was meant to see her this morning to talk about it.

If you want to know what I think, whoever killed Phoebe took that manuscript.'

'Whoa there, Agatha Christie.' There was a smile in Hayley's voice, but also a hint of a warning. Julia was aware that she was overstepping her rather ill-defined role of 'sounding board with good human instincts', dangerously close to 'amateur nosey parker interfering with police business'.

Julia laughed and said, 'You're right, I'm getting carried away. Sorry. But the manuscript... There was something about it that really worried Phoebe. Whatever it was, it could be linked to the murders. The manuscript, Vincent and Phoebe, they fit together somehow.'

'You're right, they do seem to be connected. And I appreciate the input, really I do. It's helpful. I want to solve this murder. I'm sure this poor girl got caught up in this horrible mess by mistake, and next thing, she's dead. Bludgeoned to death.' Hayley went quiet after that.

'Did you find the weapon?'

'There was a big metal doorstop. It's an anvil or something. Like a big old iron? To keep the door open.'

'God, how awful.' Julia felt ill at the thought of the young woman's horrible end.

'Yes. Whoever killed her just swung it at her head. One massive blow. There are traces of hair and blood on it. And some good prints. It all points to an opportunistic, spur-of-the-moment killer.'

'Didn't bring his own weapon, didn't know enough or have enough presence of mind to wipe the doorstop clean,' Julia said. 'Perhaps came to steal the manuscript or to talk to her. Didn't intend to kill her. Something went wrong.'

'Exactly what I thought,' Hayley sounded grudgingly admiring of Julia's quick analysis.

'It all comes back to the manuscript though, doesn't it? Have you been able to access Vincent's backup? Can you see if you can find the document? It must be there.'

'Finally, yes. Got access to the cloud storage. I'll have a word with the data recovery guys about the manuscript.'

There was noise on Hayley's end of the phone call – knocking, an opening door, voices. 'I have to go. It's the computer guys. I'll let you know if there's any news on the manuscript. Later.'

Someone had stolen the laptop. It had been unclear why at the time, but Julia now suspected that whoever stole the laptop had been looking for the manuscript.

Phoebe had been concerned and puzzled by something she'd seen on the physical manuscript.

The day that she approached Julia to talk about the manuscript, was the day that she was killed. And, the day the manuscript went missing.

Phoebe had been killed for the manuscript. But why?

And it really ruled out everyone who had looked like a possible culprit so far. There was no conceivable reason that Olga or Mike would have killed Phoebe. Unless there was something she was missing.

Round and round went the teaspoon. Round and round went her thoughts.

Flo put a plate of French toast with sliced banana in front of her, saying, 'Penny for them.'

Julia laughed. 'Sorry, Flo, you're right, I was lost in my own head. Ooh, this does look good.'

Indeed it did, the French toast all golden and sizzling, topped with rounds of banana. A fat little jug of syrup and a small bowl of whipped cream on the plate next to it.

'Should keep you going for a bit,' Flo said. 'I hear the investigation isn't going so well.'

It had become clear to Julia in the months that she'd lived in Berrywick, that the Buttered Scone was secretly the centre of the entire universe. All people and all information would be drawn into it eventually, as if by some inexplicable gravitational pull. And Flo was the centre of the Buttered Scone.

'These things take time, I suppose,' Julia said. She had learned that the smart money was on *gaining* information from Flo, without being lured into *giving* information to Flo.

'Well, there's some that think it shouldn't be taking as much time as it has. A murder! Two! And after the last lot. Murderers running round Berrywick. And all those orchids still missing, too. What kind of world, I ask you?'

'It's awful, Flo, you're right.'

Julia had come to the Buttered Scone for a pleasant, relaxing breakfast. And she'd so far spent the entire time pondering the murder in the library, and the subsequent murder in the B&B. She looked down at her phone and read the message from Hayley Gibson.

Techies say no sign of the new MS on the cloud. Only the previous books. Still looking but not hopeful. Grrrr.

Grrrr was right. Dead ends in every direction. And not a clue in sight.

Although there *was* a clue. It struck Julia that the absence of the manuscript was a clue in itself. If it wasn't in the cloud with all of Vincent's other books, that meant that:

1. He had put it elsewhere for some reason, or:
2. Someone else had removed it.

If there was one person who was obsessed with the manuscript, that person was Frederick Eliot. And who should appear as she thought that, but the man himself, swaggering past her into the tea room. He didn't see her, head down over her phone at the outside table, and her every instinct was to keep it that way. Julia did not thrill to the idea of talking to the man again. He was arrogant and aggressive, and unnecessarily tall. Also, if Sarah was to be believed, possibly a murderer. Jake – not a fan of Mr Eliot – slunk a little further under the table and rested his brown muzzle on her foot.

While Julia continued to mull all this over, she overheard snippets of his conversation with Flo.

'I would offer a reward, of course.'

Her ears pricked up. Was he offering a reward for information, now? She leaned in closer to the open door, and heard: 'Personal value... Most appreciative...'

She turned to look and glimpsed an exchange of a piece of paper.

Frederick caught sight of her catching sight of him. 'Oh, hello. It's Mrs Dove, isn't it?'

'Julia Bird,' she said, quite proud of how she managed to keep the annoyance out of her voice.

'Quite right,' he said, as if complimenting her on getting her own name correct. He really was the most annoying person. He moved over to her table and sat down. 'I was just saying to Flo here that I've lost a gold ring. It was on a chain around my neck, and the chain must have broken. I've left my number. I'm offering a reward, so if you see anything, be sure to reach out.'

'I'll keep an eye,' she said. 'Speaking of lost things...'

She didn't get to finish her sentence. Frederick Eliot cut her off with, 'Yes, do. And please spread the word.'

'Actually, I've got an idea for you. Something to help you get your ring back.'

'Really? Do tell.'

'There's a chap around the village who has a metal detector. Harry Harbour, his name is. He's always out and about with it. If you think you know roughly where you lost it, he might be willing to take a look.'

'That's a great idea, Julia.' Flo's voice behind her made Julia start. She must have snuck up on her silent plimsolls – Julia suspected that those shoes were the secret of her deep and broad local knowledge.

'Yes, that is a good idea,' Frederick said. 'I believe it dropped off somewhere in the garden of the place I'm staying. Or on the road or pavement outside of the establishment. Do either of you ladies perhaps have this man's telephone number?'

Flo had a good laugh at that. 'No, I don't have his *telephone* number. I don't need to *telephone* him. He's always about the place, wandering around with that metal stick thingy of his, picking up who knows what. Why would a person want to phone him, when he's bound to turn up anyway?'

Frederick looked rather appalled at this – either the lack of telephonic communication in the backward countryside, or the picking up of bits of this and that about the place. He asked, 'Well, do you know where to find him?'

'Harry and Felicity live up on Heath Hill Road. Up the road from you, in fact, Julia. You know where the road splits by the big oak and you can go left to that nice pub, the one with the good Scotch eggs and that sweet little Jack Russell puppy? Well, if you go right there, it's right there.'

'Oh yes, I think I know the house. I walk past it sometimes with Jake. Big sandstone place, with lovely azaleas this time of year.'

'That's the one.'

'You'll take me, then,' Frederick said, pitching the sentence somewhere between a question and an instruction.

Julia considered her response. She was tempted to say no, just out of irritation with the presumptuous man. But on the other hand, if she took him, she could quiz him about the manuscript on the way.

'When I've finished my breakfast,' she said, taking a slow sip of her coffee. 'I'll take you on my way home.'

'Thank you, that's very kind.' It was the first thing he'd said since she'd met him that wasn't annoying. She gave him a small smile and a nod. Maybe he wasn't so bad after all. Doubtless, he was stressed and sad, losing an employee as well as a friend and author. And he was from the city, after all. City ways seemed abrupt and rude in the country. She shouldn't be so quick to judge; she should give him the benefit of the doubt.

'We'll be taking the dog, I suppose? Is it properly trained?' he said, looking down at Jake with a small frown of distaste. 'I can't abide an unruly dog.'

Julia immediately retracted her generous assessment of Frederick Eliot, and took back the benefit of the doubt. Before she could come up with a retort, Flo arrived with Julia's breakfast bill on a saucer.

'Here you go,' she said, handing it to Frederick with a flourish. After a moment's hesitation, he took it and reached into his pocket for his wallet. He put a tenner on the saucer. Flo stood still. He took the saucer back and put a fiver on top of the ten.

Flo looked at Julia with a grin and gave her an exaggerated pantomime wink as if to say, 'That's how we deal with presumptuous fools in our neck of the woods.'

And off she went.

25

It was inevitable that Jake would be on his absolute worst behaviour.

As they left the Buttered Scone, he snatched up the crust of toast Julia had left on her plate, his wide pink tongue scooping it into his open mouth, to be swallowed whole. Julia pretended not to notice, while giving him a sharp pull towards the road. Delighted to be on the move, Jake zigzagged from side to side to take in all the available smells, and on more than one occasion, narrowly avoided tripping up Frederick.

A pheasant, or was it a partridge? – some ground bird, at any rate – dashed out of a hedge in front of them, setting Jake off in a round of frenzied barking and jumping. He pulled the leash from Julia's hands and went after the bird, which had the good sense to dash back into the hedge it had come from. Jake couldn't fit through the hedge, fortunately, but he gave it a good go, hurling himself into the bushes, scattering leaves and sticks, then retreating with a yelp before trying another spot.

The bird would have been long gone, but Jake was not one to give up the chase once he'd started. Julia ran after him, grabbed his lead and continued without a word. Frederick endured the rest of the walk with the long-suffering look of a man undergoing significant discomfort in service of a greater good. His mood was already so bad that Julia thought she might as well just wade in and ask what was on her mind.

'I heard that Vincent Andrews was in negotiation with another publisher. That he was planning to leave Prime Publishing. Leave you. Is that true?'

'Where did you hear that?' he asked angrily.

'Word gets around.'

'Well, it's not true. Vincent would never leave me. I made his career. I took great care of him for well over a decade, and made him a very wealthy man.'

Julia waited.

'If he was talking to other publishers, it was simply for leverage. He was a wily one, was Vincent. You'd be surprised. We were negotiating the next contract, for the next three books and the television rights. He would have been asking around to see what was on offer so he could squeeze me for more. All part of the little dance that is our business.' Frederick gave a fake little laugh, perhaps to show how unimportant it all was.

'That makes sense,' Julia said, mildly. She wasn't sure that Frederick was right, but did not want to antagonise him when she had more questions to ask. 'I'm sure that was what it was.'

They walked on in silence for a minute or two, Jake trotting obediently next to her now, thank goodness.

'Odd about the missing manuscript, isn't it?' she asked in a conversational tone. 'Who would have taken the manuscript for the last ever Vincent Andrews novel?'

'I've been wondering about that myself. Why would someone want it? To stir up trouble, I'd say. But why?'

For once, Frederick Eliot sounded genuine. Not spinning a yarn or trying to get an advantage.

Either he was as stumped as she was – or he was doing a very good job of appearing so.

They took the right at the split of the road by the big oak, as per Flo's instructions, and there was the Harbours' house, right there on the right. They walked up the driveway and knocked on the door, setting off a great deal of yapping of the sort that comes from very small dogs.

Harry Harbour opened the top half of a stable door, leaving the bottom half closed to contain what sounded like an entire pack of yappers.

'Oh, hello,' he said to Julia. And then, kindly, to Jake, 'Hello, good dog.' Which was not something Julia heard every day. She felt warmly towards the strange Harry Harbour.

Harry looked at Frederick without saying a word.

'Frederick Eliot,' Frederick said, offering a hand. Harry blinked and proffered his own, tentatively.

'I hope you don't mind us coming by, Harry,' Julia said. 'Frederick here has lost a gold ring. He's looked and looked. I suggested you might be willing to try and find it with your metal detector.'

'Oh, yes, well, I suppose I could do that,' said Harry. 'I was going to go out for a bit of detecting later anyway.'

'I would offer a reward for a successful outcome,' Frederick said pompously.

Harry looked affronted at that. 'I hardly think so,' he said. 'You'd better come in. You can bring the dog, my lot won't mind.'

He stood back, releasing a tide of small dogs of all breeds and types. White dogs and black ones and dogs with spots. Smooth ones and fluffy ones and wiry ones. Old ones and young ones. Bouncy ones and creaky ones. Julia tried to count them, but couldn't keep track of the seething mass of fur, punctuated with black noses and brown eyes. Eight or nine, she thought. Jake looked utterly terrified, rooted to the spot, leaning against her leg for protection as the little ones sniffed and jumped up on him.

'Rescues, all of them. Good chaps, poor manners,' Harry said. 'Come on in. Come and say hello to my lovely Felicity while I go and put my boots on and get my metal detector.'

He led them into a sitting room. The room was full to bursting with *stuff*. Every wall had been fitted with book shelves and every shelf was packed to capacity. Books on top of books. Books in front of books. Books piled on side tables. Julia even spotted a row of V.F. Andrews books, clearly a full set, which was quite a weird coincidence, given her companion. On the other hand, there were so many books on these shelves, you could probably find just about any reasonably decent author you cared to look for.

There were display cases filled with artefacts – what looked like stones or fossils, the skulls of tiny animals, lumps of metal, pointy rocks that were perhaps ancient tools. One case held a display of knives and daggers. On the wall were bigger items, poles and axes and sticks and hoes, agricultural implements, mysterious things that might have been, well, anything really. Trunks and boxes were pushed into corners, tables cluttered with lamps and globes and books, more books.

'I'm a collector,' Harry said, by way of explanation. 'Historical artefacts.'

It was hard to know who looked more astounded by the surroundings, Frederick or Jake. Frederick seemed literally struck mute and still – an unusual occurrence, thought Julia. Jake immediately lay down, uncharacteristically quiet and still himself.

'And this is Felicity,' Harry said, with pride, gesturing into the gloom.

Julia had not actually seen Felicity at first, so overwhelmed was the slight, grey-haired woman by the hundreds of items with which she shared this space. She seemed supremely unbothered by the clutter, sitting calmly in a red velvet wing-back chair, a big book in her lap.

She dipped her head to look at the visitors over her glasses. 'Hello,' she said. Julia noted her clever, bright eyes. 'Felicity Harbour.'

'Hello, I'm Julia Bird, and this is Frederick.'

'Pleased to meet you,' he said, looking anything but.

'I've just made a tray of tea, Harry. Please bring two more cups for our visitors,' she called after her retreating husband.

'I'm sorry to disturb you,' Frederick said. 'We will be on our way shortly. Harry is kindly going to help me find a missing ring.'

'Well, that's all very Tolkien, isn't it? What fun,' Felicity exclaimed with a laugh. 'Harry will enjoy that. He does like a quest.'

Julia liked the woman immediately, she had a mischievous way about her. Frederick looked as if he couldn't wait to get out of there.

'Yes, the Adventures of Frederick Eliot and the Missing Ring,' Julia said.

'Did you say Eliot?' she asked, peering at him. 'Is your surname Eliot?'

'Yes, but you wouldn't know the family. I'm not from around here. Down from London on business. Unfortunate business.'

'I see,' said Felicity. She seemed a bit taken aback at that. Unlike Julia, she hadn't yet become accustomed to Frederick's rude manner. 'What sort of business would that be?'

'Publishing. I'm V.F. Andrews' publisher. Or, I should say, the publisher of Vincent Andrews' estate.'

'Oh goodness, yes,' Felicity said, looking quite upset. 'I heard about his death. How tragic. Poor family. And what a loss to his readers.'

'His legacy will continue, I'll make sure of that. The V.F. Andrews books will be selling for many years to come. And a television programme is in the works. Oh yes, Vincent might be gone, but there's plenty of life in the property yet.'

There was an awkward silence at this businesslike take on the dreadful situation.

Felicity looked appalled, and then angry. She started to say something, but seemed to think better of it, and instead made a sort of clicking, tutting noise.

Julia really did *not* like Frederick Eliot. There was something off about him. He seemed to lack basic human instincts. But, she reminded herself, that didn't mean he was a killer. Although she had to admit, she'd be quite *pleased* if it turned out to be him, given how objectionable he was. If only there was a way to quietly take his fingerprints and let Hayley check them against the weapon that had killed Phoebe. But you could hardly just demand that an irritating stranger give you a fingerprint sample.

'You're a historian, if I'm not mistaken?' Julia addressed Felicity, changing the subject. 'A professor?'

'Gosh, word does get around, even about a reclusive old lady, recently retired,' Felicity said. In fact, she was about Julia's own age, a young sixty. Now that Julia had become somewhat accustomed to the room, she saw that Felicity had a circle of relative calm around her. At her feet lay a small oriental rug, clean and bright, uncluttered by, well, clutter. At her right elbow was a table and chair, with a lamp, a large A4 book, an even larger dictionary, a little notepad, and a small copper pot filled with pens, as well as the tray of tea. Harry arrived with two teacups, which he put on the tray, and left muttering about something about a jacket.

'I often see Harry on the paths and riverways,' Julia said. 'Him with his metal detector, me with that boundless bundle of energy there.' She gestured to Jake, who was currently far from a boundless bundle of energy. He lay unmoving, while the small dogs had settled down against him or clambered over him, like the Lilliputians over Gulliver.

Felicity poured two cups of tea and added milk without asking. She handed one to Frederick, who took it reluctantly. He really was the most ungracious man. Julia took hers with better grace – a smile and a thank you.

'What period of history are you interested in?' she asked, making conversation.

'Well, I have taught at Gloucester University for thirty-five years, so I have had to cover quite a wide range. Goodness, everything and everyone from Napoleon, to Stalin, to Sankara. And then whatever takes my fancy. I was reading about Britain in the time leading up to the First World War for a while; quite a fascinating period, especially in terms of women. And then more recently I've been thinking and reading about the 1930s and 40s.'

'Fascinating time period, the Second World War,' Julia said. 'That reminds me, someone at my book club was talking about a good new book set in the period. Well reviewed, and she recommended it highly. A novel though, do you read fiction?'

'I do. It's more believable than history, that's for sure. Goodness, some of what happened in real life, you'd just never get away with it in a novel. People wouldn't believe you.'

'What *was* the title, now?' Julia racked her brains. One of the most alarming things about her age was that hard facts like book titles and author names often seemed perched just out of reach. 'It'll come to me in a flash of light this afternoon when I'm feeding the chickens. And with a bit of luck, the author's name, too.'

Frederick sighed deeply, as if the conversation between the two women was the most unbelievably tiresome thing that he had ever had to listen to. Both women ignored him.

'Oh yes, or at three o'clock in the morning. That's when I remember the name of the first Tudor king's advisor, or that of the Berrywick butcher's assistant, whichever one's gone missing that day,' Felicity said, with a warm laugh. 'Well, if the name does come to you, I'd love to know. I'm always on the lookout for good historical novels.'

Felicity reached for the notepad and took a pen from the copper pot. 'I'll give you my number. If you remember the name, please send a message or give me a ring,' she said.

By strange serendipity, at the word 'ring', Harry emerged in boots, a jacket and a hat, his earphones around his neck and the detector in his hand. 'All ready,' he said. 'Time to go.'

Julia and Frederick drained their teacups. Julia stood up, shouldered her handbag, picked up her cup and Frederick's, and took them to the tray. She put hers down, but almost without thinking, she positioned her body between Felicity and the tray, and slipped Frederick's cup into her bag without anyone seeing her. Her heart raced. What had come over her? Suspicion, that's what. Suspicion that Frederick Eliot might have killed Phoebe Ailes, and possibly Vincent Andrews too. Just as Sarah said. Now Hayley wouldn't have to ask him for his fingerprints – Julia had them right there on the cup.

'What are you doing?' Harry asked anxiously, looking at his wife, who was still writing in the notepad.

'I'm giving Julia my phone number,' she said, without lifting her head from what she was writing. She tore out the page and folded the paper in half.

'Don't do that,' he said crossly, reaching for the note.

'Goodness, Harry!' Felicity laughed apologetically, pulling it away from him. 'Don't mind Harry. He's a bit antisocial. Lives in fear of being invited to a dinner party.' She folded the paper again and handed it to Julia. 'Very nice to meet you. Do be in touch.'

26

Having seen more than her fair share of police procedurals, Julia knew to lift the cup carefully out of her bag, using a hankie so as not to smudge the prints. She placed it on a high shelf on the kitchen dresser, feeling simultaneously clever and nervous and guilty and silly. How had it happened that in less than a year in Berrywick, she had become a person who would spontaneously steal-slash-gather crockery-slash-evidence from a professor of History? It was preposterous. And that was without even mentioning the laptop.

She wasn't even sure whether she would give the cup to Hayley. It seemed presumptuous, in addition to being illegal. She still had the option of returning it, somehow, or just throwing it away – which she'd feel bad about, but in a different way. Julia decided that she would put it out of her mind this evening. She would sleep on it, and, in the morning, she would either give it to Hayley or not, as the case may be.

Julia scrambled a couple of her chickens' free-range eggs for supper, and ate them at the kitchen table with a few slices of tomato and a piece of the wholewheat sourdough that she bought from a local baker. It was a good supper, but not quite filling enough. Luckily, she had some home-made butter short-bread, so she had a piece of that in front of the television. An entertaining, if somewhat mindless, reality programme in which a Kenyan tech millionaire determined to put together a team of ice skaters for an Olympic attempt took her mind off things. Julia always enjoyed a story about an underdog claiming an unlikely victory, achieved through dedication, hard work and an opportunity grasped. It affirmed her worldview, at its most optimistic.

She went to bed early and woke early, her mind churning with thoughts about the murders. She lay there and let them float, hoping that they would settle into something useful. A bold insight or flash of brilliance that would lead to a break-through. Instead, she remembered the name of the book they'd been talking about at book club, the one she'd mentioned to Felicity, but had forgotten the name of. *Tell No Lies*, it was called. And the author was Alex Joseph. She only hoped she'd remember it later in the morning.

Her mind went back to the case, and possible motives.

Money.

It was always about money, wasn't it?

The root of all evil, according to the Bible. Or was it Gandhi? Or perhaps Buddha? Michelle Obama? Someone, anyway.

With Sarah now off the suspect list, it was most likely that these two murders were motivated by money. This, she could never understand.

Julia knew that she was in an unusually privileged position. With a decent pension and half the proceeds of the London house, the value of which had grown quite stupendously in the twenty-five years since they'd bought it, she would be able to see out her days in modest comfort in her house in the Cotswolds.

She'd been lucky, of course. Lucky to have a degree and a good job, a husband who earned quite well, lucky to have entered the property market when they did. Lucky, too, never to have had a great desire for more. She liked decent clothes and shoes, and a nice holiday, but she'd never been consumed by a need for the next thing or the better thing. For some people, enough was never enough. It was as if they had an infinite, bottomless hole inside them and they would do anything to try to fill it.

Frederick, for example. Would he kill for money? And how would killing Vincent benefit him?

If Vincent Andrews had been Frederick's 'cash cow', as Sarah had said with bitterness, surely killing him made no financial sense. From what Frederick had said earlier to Felicity, Vincent's legacy would continue to be a profitable enterprise for many years – even in the absence of Vincent himself. Julia knew nothing of publisher's contracts, of course, but it could be that a move to a new publisher would have endangered his revenue stream from all the previous books.

The question was, would Frederick kill Vincent out of greed, with a dash of anger and spite? He might, especially if it meant he could hang on to the rights for all his books and television shows.

Either way, Julia found that her mind was made up about the cup. Dressed and breakfasted, with the washing up done and the surfaces wiped clean, the chickens and Jake fed, Julia set off for the police station, the teacup carefully wrapped in kitchen towel, in a clean plastic bag.

Hayley received the offering without a jot of gratitude. In fact, she seemed aghast. 'You *took* it?' she asked. 'From the Harbours' home?'

'Yes. It was on impulse. I know it was wrong, but my instincts just kicked in. One minute I was putting it on the tray and the next it was in my bag.'

'You do realise that whatever this tells us, it's useless, right? As in, I can't use it. You can't be bringing me bits of stolen evidence, taken without permission, let alone, you know, say, a *warrant*. And you're not even a copper. I have no idea what the legal situation is...' She broke off, and shook her head, exasperated.

'Just hear me out, and we can worry about that later,' Julia said. 'Think about it. Frederick had the rights to the existing books, and would make his money whether or not Vincent was alive. And if no new books were coming his way, there was no downside – financially at least – to killing him. He's a viable suspect. And Sarah seems to think so too.'

Hayley listened to Julia's theory with scepticism. Julia had come to recognise the way the detective cocked her head ever so slightly to the right and raised her left eyebrow just a tad when she was listening to an unlikely tale and wasn't buying it. The bag sat in front of the detective on her desk, a sad little package, like some leftover takeaway.

'He's known the guy for nearly fifteen years, worked closely with him, and he's going to kill him over a contract?' Hayley asked.

Julia found herself selling her theory. 'To hear Frederick tell it, he *made* Vincent Andrews. He was responsible for his career taking off the way it did. His first book was a mediocre performer at best; his second – once Frederick got behind it – was a smash. Think how bitter and angry and hurt he must have been to be thrown under the bus. He was about to negotiate a Netflix series, for heaven's sake. A *huge* deal for him and a big boost to his book sales. And the next thing, Vincent is looking for a new dance partner. Imagine how Frederick felt at that.'

'And Phoebe? Why would Frederick kill Phoebe?' Hayley asked, leaning back in her chair, her arms crossed.

'I don't know,' Julia said, deflated. 'I can't get my head around that. It must have been something to do with the manuscript, perhaps something to do with his new publisher, but I don't know.'

'She was close to Vincent. Maybe she knew something. Something that would have exposed Frederick. Or scuppered his plans,' Hayley said, trying on some thoughts. She ran her fingers through her hair, making it stand up in messy spikes. 'So he killed her to protect his interests.'

The two women sat in silence, both looking at the plastic bag with the carefully wrapped cup inside it.

'Okay, it makes a certain amount of sense. Even if we can't get a fix on the Phoebe connection. Nothing to lose by checking the prints against the doorstop. I'll send it off to forensics. We should get something by tomorrow – I'll let you know.'

'OK, good,' said Julia, gathering her bag and coat without delay. She knew how busy Hayley was, and didn't want to take up any more of her time. 'I'll be on my way.'

Hayley got up with her.

'Julia?' she said, standing at the threshold of her office, her hand on the door frame.

Julia turned to face her.

'Thank you,' she said. 'I mean it.'

27

Julia stifled a surprised smile when she saw Sean. He was all decked out in his gardening gear. A pair of patched khaki trousers which looked as if his father might have worn them before him, and perhaps his father before that. A checked shirt over a long-sleeved vest. Green wellington boots. A wide-brimmed cotton hat.

Somewhat disconcertingly, he had transformed from a handsome Sean Connery lookalike to Old McDonald, who had a farm. E-I-E-I-O. All he needed was a piece of hay between his teeth.

'Gosh, you do look professional. I can see I'm in good hands,' she said, as he enveloped her in a hello hug. It seemed a bit of an odd thing to say, given that she was indeed, in his hands, and arms, so she added an attempt at humour. 'I have full confidence in your ability to help me fulfil my gardening dreams.' That, too, sounded odder than it had in her head, but Sean was kind enough to pretend not to notice.

'Seven years of medical school, that's what you need in a garden helper,' he said. 'I'll endeavour to provide my best flower bed-side manner.'

Why did everything they said to each other sound strange and slightly flirtatious today? Julia distracted them both by taking him to see her purchases.

That morning, she had driven to the local garden centre and purchased a selection of bulbs, a couple of big pots to supplement the few that the previous owners had left, and a few bags of potting soil. Looking at the pile of packets, she wondered if she'd rather overdone it – there were snowdrops, tulips, anemones, daffodils, hyacinths, narcissus and crocuses. She had wondered the same when the young man at the tills had added them up and presented her with a rather eye-watering bill. Who knew that creating the impression of a glorious country meadow which had spontaneously erupted from the earth, would be so expensive? But by then she'd been fully committed, so she'd handed over her credit card.

'What a lovely selection. Your spring garden is going to be dazzling,' Sean said.

'My country garden fantasy ran away with me and I went a bit overboard. I had this vision of masses of colour everywhere, you know, the bounty of spring, and the scent of the hyacinths wafting on the breeze. A couple of striped canvas chairs on the lawn, a jug of lemonade.'

'That sounds perfect. And I think you have just the right number of bulbs for it. Now, what do you want where?' he asked. With occasional consultation to Julia's *English Country Gardening* book, which lay open on the bench nearby, they plotted and planned and then potted and planted. Jake kept them company, and was no trouble once he had been persuaded that this wasn't a fun new version of hide and seek – the roundish things they were putting in the soil had to stay there.

'I was thinking,' Sean said, in a tone that made Julia look up, trowel in hand, from the pot she was filling with bulbs that would produce yellow daffs and deep red tulips. 'It might be time to introduce the dogs to each other.'

Julia couldn't help but laugh. 'Of course. I don't know why we haven't done it before. We should take them on a walk together.' She had met Sean's dog, Leo, a mid-sized brown rescue mutt with the sweetest nature imaginable, and obviously Sean knew Jake. But somehow, Jake hadn't yet met Leo. 'Maybe some of Leo's good manners will rub off on Jake.'

'That's a good start. Once they've met out in the world, when we visit each other, we can bring the dogs.'

'Sure, next weekend?' she asked.

'Yes.' Sean cleared his throat and added, 'And I was thinking that once they get to know each other, perhaps we might take a trip to the seaside. A weekend trip. Together. With the dogs.'

Julia smiled, and managed to maintain an outward air of calm while her heart raced, and a tingle she hadn't felt in a while made its way up her arms and then her neck and cheeks. 'That sounds lovely. I would like that.'

Sean nodded, and then quickly busied himself with opening a new bag of potting soil.

'How's Sarah?' Julia asked, after a brief interval of quiet digging and planting.

'She's doing well, under the circumstances. She's moved in with Eleanor now for a few days, decided that despite the chaos she wanted to be with her mother. Eleanor's been taking good care of her. She'll be going back to London soon, I believe.'

Her pot planted up and ready for watering, Julia stood up and stretched her back. 'One has to get back to real life, I suppose. Face a future without Vincent.'

Julia could hear her phone ringing, but it was nowhere in sight. She scrabbled around, and found it under *English Country Gardening*, just as it stopped ringing.

Hayley Gibson.

She must have news on the fingerprints. Julia felt a thrill of excitement.

'I need to return this call, if you don't mind. And ever since I mentioned that jug of lemonade, I've been dying for some. I'll go in and get it from the fridge.'

'Well that's mighty nice of you, ma'am. I could use a sip after all this labouring in the fields,' Sean said, with an ironic tip of his floppy hat.

'Back in a mo. No slacking when I'm gone,' she said, and went into the house, where she washed her hands and called the detective back, not bothering to check for a message.

Hayley answered without even a greeting: 'We've got a match!' The usually calm and businesslike DI Gibson couldn't keep the excitement out of her voice.

'Between the cup and the doorstop?'

'Yes. There are three sets of prints on the cup, and one little smudge on one.'

'The smudge is probably me, although I was very careful, and the other three would be Frederick, as well as Harry and Felicity I suppose.'

'Well, it's a match. Julia, we've got our man!'

'That's brilliant news. What happens next? You said yourself that the cup was inadmissible. And I'd really rather not be busted for nicking it.'

'We just need to get Frederick's prints, legitimately, so we can close the loop on the evidence. Unfortunately, Frederick Eliot is not on the police fingerprint database. We have millions of prints, but not the entire population. Only people who've had some contact with the police and been printed. Which clearly, Frederick hasn't. So I'm going to have to bring him in.'

'So they take his prints, match them with the doorstop and arrest him for Phoebe's murder,' said Julia. 'But what about Vincent? How are you going to link Frederick to the murder in the library?'

'We know *why* he killed Vincent, and we know that his fingerprints are on the weapon that killed Phoebe. Once he's been charged with Phoebe's murder, and he knows we're onto him for Vincent, Frederick will likely confess, explain the whole thing.' Hayley sounded less sure of this than Julia would have liked. And Frederick Eliot did not strike Julia as the confessing type. More of the deny-and-lawyer-up type. But that was Hayley's problem, not Julia's. Hayley was still sounding pretty gung-ho about her prospects: 'I'm going to try and get hold of him now, get the prints ASAP.'

She pronounced it 'ay-sap', which made Julia feel as if they were in an American crime show, with Hayley as the hard-bitten detective, and Julia herself as the trusty, quiet-but-clever sidekick.

'The lab works on Saturdays. If it all goes according to plan, I might even wrap this up today, take Frederick into custody, and get a full Sunday off for once. And then I will start the week with this case basically in the bag, just a few loose ends to tie up!'

28

Tabitha Too had set herself up in the patch of sun which came in through the front door and landed on the floor tiles in an elegantly slanted rhomboid, just perfect for a cat. Perhaps not perfect for library users, given that its position was such that anyone wishing to enter the library would have to step over the cat. But beauty came at a price, thought Julia as she did just that, stepping carefully over the cat, admiring how her golden stripes glowed tiger-like in the sunlight.

'Hello, pretty girl,' she said, bending down to stroke the cat. Her fur was beautifully silky and warm to the touch. Too opened her eyes a slit and purred – whether at the compliment or because of the stroking, Julia wasn't sure.

'Well thank heavens you're here,' Tabitha the human said, when she caught sight of Julia. She got up from her chair, setting off a light tinkling of bangles and beads, and gave Julia a good hug. 'I have just started on this terrible job, and you've given me an excuse to stop.'

Julia saw boxes and brown paper, and what looked like a typed list. And a dishevelled Tabitha.

'What are you doing?'

'Packing up the display,' she said. 'Historical artefacts from the region. They were on loan for a week or two as part of the V.F. Andrews book event. But I realised we've got a whole lot of activities starting on Monday for Berrywick Book Week – readings, drama, fun stuff for the kids. It's generally chaotic, so I wanted to get all these precious things out of the way before they get knocked over by a bunch of crazed five-year-olds trying to find a guy dressed up like the character from *Where's Wally*.'

'He's the one in the red and white stripy outfit, is that right?'

'Yes. The publisher is sending over a drama student, appropriately attired in red and white stripes, for an event on Tuesday afternoon. I anticipate mayhem.'

Tabitha sounded quite cheerful at the prospect of Wally-induced mayhem. Less so at the packing up, which she was doing on her own time, on a Saturday afternoon, when she might be horizontal on her sofa, reading the detective novels in foreign settings which were her particular favourite.

'I said I'd box the items for collection, but now I can't work out what's what. There's a list, but the labels have got muddled up. This one, for example.' She held up a nondescript hunk of what looked like a blob of metal, or perhaps molten lava, or a very dark rock. 'Would you say this was a handle from an early iron age digging implement, or a stone age axe head?'

'No idea. Sorry,' Julia said, taking the lump and turning it around in her hand, genuinely stumped. 'It could be a fossilised mouse that's been in the library for aeons for all I know.'

'I'll just do what I can and then get Harry to check them when he collects.'

'Harry Harbour? So he lent them to you? That was nice of him. I went to Harry and Felicity's house the other day, and there are thousands of these sorts of things lying around. I shouldn't think he'll miss one if it's lost or missing.'

'You don't know Harry. He's got a photographic memory, or whatever they call it these days. Odd fellow, granted, but he can tell you what day of the week Christmas was on in 1945. And he is meticulous about his collections. What you saw in their house, it looks like chaos, but there's a system of sorts. I guarantee you that if one of these things went missing, he'd know. He's been in to check every now and then. And he'd be very upset. I don't like to upset Harry.'

Speaking of the Harbours, Julia remembered that she hadn't yet sent Felicity the name of the book. She added it to her mental to-do list – she would call as soon as she had finished helping Tabitha. She suggested a solution to Tabitha's problem: 'How about we find the obvious ones first and match them to the list, then worry about what's left?'

'That's a good idea. I did see a few things I recognised – a fork, for instance. And a hair comb. Something that could be an egg cup.'

It was easier with two, and Tabitha lightened up significantly with her friend to help her and keep her company. They went through the items, finding things that looked vaguely familiar, which Tabitha would check against the list.

They chatted, flitting from this subject to that – a worrying medical diagnosis of Tabitha's cousin in Ghana, Julia's gardening efforts that morning, the American elections, a delicious granola Tabitha had tried from the health shop. Julia appreciated the way they could move easily between serious and frivolous topics.

'Here's the fork,' said Julia.

'Right – says here, knife, fork and spoon.'

'Here's the spoon.'

'The knife?'

They surveyed the remaining objects. There was nothing that could reasonably be thought to be a knife.

'Tabitha, it's not here. The knife isn't here,' Julia said. She felt a shiver run from her head to her toes, the kind of ominous prickle that her gran used to describe as someone walking over her grave. 'Did you see it, at all? Do you remember when you last saw it?'

'I don't know. Harry unpacked the exhibit, so it would have been there then, and after that it was all so busy, the event and then the murder...'

They paused, looking at each other, both women coming to the same realisation.

'Tabitha, I think that knife might have been the murder weapon. It might have been taken from the display by whoever killed Vincent Andrews. We need to call Hayley Gibson and tell her what we know.'

Julia fetched her handbag and pulled out her phone to do just that. When she did, she saw a message from Hayley herself, sent ten minutes earlier.

Sorted. Frederick is having his prints taken now. Will keep you posted.

She phoned Hayley, but there was no answer, just endless frustrating ringing. She tried again, thinking Hayley might be there and not taking calls, but that she might note Julia's desperate attempt to speak to her.

'I'm going to go over to the station,' she said to Tabitha. 'Sorry to run out on you, but I need to tell Hayley about the knife. She will be interviewing the suspect today – maybe even right now, that could be why she's not answering. She needs all the information she can get when she does that.'

'That's okay, you go,' said Tabitha. 'I wonder what I should do now?' She surveyed the artefacts and paper and boxes and the glass display case they'd come out of. 'Do you think I should leave them?'

'I think it's for the best. If the killer took the knife, his prints might be on the display case. Although ours too, of course.'

'And the prints of about thirty eager children who've smeared their sticky fingers all over the glass all week.'

'I shouldn't think the police will get much from the glass case, but you'd probably better not touch it any more, just in case.'

Julia exited so quickly that Too looked up in alarm at the clip-clop of her shoes, and moved out of her sunbeam to a spot a safe distance from the door.

Julia turned right, towards the police station.

'Oh hello, Julia,' said Nicky, who was waiting to cross the road with Sebastian. 'How are you today? Been in the library? I was reading this book, you might like it. It's about...'

'Sorry,' Julia said, pushing past them. 'In a hurry.'

Nicky looked alarmed, or perhaps annoyed. Julia hoped that she hadn't just started some inter-generational village feud with the woman – this kind of minor infringement of social norms tended to have more extreme consequences in the village than it would in a town. Julia knew of two families who had ceased to speak a generation ago after a disagreement over the correct pronunciation of the word 'pronunciation'.

But Julia didn't have time for niceties this afternoon. She was on a mission, a time-sensitive mission, that might help Detective Inspector Hayley Gibson solve a double murder.

29

Julia sat on the same row of uncomfortable green chairs she'd sat on before, when waiting for Sean while he visited Sarah in custody. Now she was waiting for Hayley. The young desk sergeant had said, rather unhelpfully, 'DI Gibson is in a meeting. I don't know how long she will be. Probably a while.'

The waiting area of the police station was empty. It was probably a bit early for the Saturday night trickle of drunken tourists, minor bumper bashings, and the like.

Julia had a feeling it might be a long wait. Presumably Hayley was processing Frederick Eliot's arrest. She had no idea what that entailed, but she had spent long enough in bureaucracy and government services to know it wouldn't be a simple matter. She imagined reams of paperwork, and a very unhappy Frederick Eliot.

Julia took out her phone and opened Facebook to pass the time and to give her mind a break from mulling over the murders. She was pleased to see twenty-seven likes for her most recent picture of Jake amongst the rhododendrons, a pink blossom resting fetchingly on his dear little nose. She used to be very sniffy about the number of dogs and cats on her friends' timelines – was there anything more boring? she'd asked Peter in exasperation. But since she had Jake, she had changed her tune.

Scrolling through the news, she got a jolt of surprise. There was Vincent Andrews' face, his floppy fringe and dancing eyes, alive and smiling. It was an obituary, a long one, of the murdered bestselling author V.F. Andrews. There was a brief biography – 'Born Vincent James Andrews, in 1975... read a year of history at University of Gloucester but eventually majored in English... started out in advertising, writing fiction on the side...' – that was something Julia hadn't known – 'greatly beloved... public acclaim for his historical fiction... a number of popular literary awards...'

It was odd reading the last sentence – 'The police investigation into his murder continues' – while sitting in the actual police station where the police investigation was now continuing apace.

A good ten minutes had passed. Julia approached the desk sergeant again. 'If you could get her a message, I'd appreciate it. I have important information regarding a case.'

'Right you are,' said the desk sergeant, and gave her a patronising look as if to say, 'sure you do, dearie.'

'Tell her that Julia Bird is here, and that I have information about the weapon in the Vincent Andrews case,' Julia said, in the voice of the Head of Youth Services – firm and confident and not to be trifled with. 'I will wait.'

It seemed to have the desired effect, because the young woman nodded and went through the door at the back of the room, into the passage with the doors going off in both directions.

Julia took out her phone to check her messages. She wanted to update Sean on the latest news, but it seemed too long and complicated to type with two thumbs. She'd call him later. She noted that their relationship had taken a definite shift, and was now such that she instinctively wanted to tell him what was going on in her life. Especially where the Vincent Andrews case was concerned.

She remembered another thing she'd wanted to do – send Felicity the name of that book. She felt in her bag for the piece of paper with her number on it, and found the hard edge of it, double-folded. She fished out her glasses, opened her phone, and opened the paper. *Felicity Harbour*, it said in a loopy scrawl, with a number underneath, both written in green ink. Julia typed in the number and then the title and author of the book, but she made so many mistakes and deletions and revisions that she took five minutes to finish the message and send it off to Felicity. Honestly, these phones – couldn't live without them, but what a fiddle, she thought to herself, putting the phone back in her bag. She'd saved Felicity's number – another annoying little mission – and was in the process of crumpling up the paper to throw it away when she had a little prickle of instinct that she recognised from her days as a social worker. Something was off. She opened the note again. There was something about it. A flash of recognition, but she couldn't place it.

'Julia. Hi.' Hayley came in at a clip, her face pinched and pale, her arms full of files. 'You have something to tell me? I've got something to tell you, too.'

From the look of her, it wasn't good news.

'Right. I've discovered something significant, I think. Can we speak in your office?' Julia glanced at the desk sergeant who was leaning on the counter, eyes on them, openly eavesdropping. Julia allowed herself a small smirk as she passed on her way to the boss's office.

She sat down opposite Hayley.

'You go first,' Hayley said.

'I think I know what the murder weapon was,' said Julia. 'There's a knife missing from the display of local antiques and artefacts at the library. I believe that was what Frederick used to kill Vincent Andrews.'

She explained what she had discovered that afternoon with Tabitha. Hayley listened attentively and said, 'Julia, that's good information. That knife might well be the murder weapon. But I don't think it was Frederick who wielded it.'

'What? But if he killed Phoebe, surely he killed Vincent too?'

'He didn't kill Phoebe. He came in without protest, and when we explained the situation to him, he was happy to have his prints taken to eliminate him as a suspect. Really, he didn't seem at all worried or resistant. And I soon saw why – his prints don't match.'

'But you said they did! You got a match off the cup.'

'Yes, we got a print off the cup that matched the print off the doorstop. Whoever touched the doorstop definitely touched the cup. But the match wasn't for Frederick Eliot's fingerprint. The prints on the doorstop matched one of the *other* prints on the cup.'

Julia could hardly process this new piece of information.

'But that would mean...' She shook her head in disbelief. It couldn't be true, but it had to be. 'That means Harry or Felicity Harbour killed Phoebe Ailes.'

Hayley raised her hands palms up in a gesture that said either 'you've got it' or 'can you believe it?' or possibly both.

'But why? They don't even know her,' said Julia. 'Do they?'

'I can't see how. How would they know a twenty-eight-year-old publicist from London? Unless there's some bizarre connection, unrelated to Vincent Andrews' death. Like, a family thing...' Hayley looked utterly perplexed. 'Anyhow, I've got DC

Farmer looking into that, and I'm going to bring them both in and get them fingerprinted. And in the meantime, Frederick's release is being processed.'

Julia sat dumbly, trying to do some processing of her own. The Harbours! It didn't make sense. It seemed as though she and Hayley had totally taken the wrong track in their investigations. They'd been wrong about everything. Sarah, the angry, jealous wife. And now Frederick the angry, spurned publisher. Why would a mild-mannered historian or her wonky metal-detecting husband have killed a famous author and his publicist? They had nothing to do with this. There was no connection at all. But there must be...

'All I've got is the fingerprints on that cup. As far as how and why they did it, we're back to square one,' Hayley said, almost as if she'd read Julia's mind.

'What about the techies? Anything useful on the cloud? Emails?' Julia said, grasping at straws.

'Nothing helpful so far. Just an old version of his new book. He must have kept the most recent version on his laptop, but at least it's something.'

'Well that's good, I suppose. Frederick Eliot must be happy.'

'Happy would be an exaggeratedly positive description of his current state of mind. I showed it to him, to make up for the fact that I'd nearly arrested him for no good reason. He was quite relieved to hear it had been found. Although, less so when he saw it.'

Hayley leaned back in her chair and closed her eyes for a minute, then sat up with a sigh and said. 'Better get back to it. Thanks for the info on the knife.'

'Well, I don't even know if it's helpful now.'

'It will be if we find it. Do you know any more about it? What kind of knife was it? Do you know what it looked like? How big? What kind of blade?'

'No idea, just that it was antique. I didn't see it. You'd have to ask...'

Julia stopped in her tracks. How could she not have made the connection?

'What? Who?'

'You'd have to ask Harry Harbour.'

30

The meeting between Julia and Frederick was chilly, to say the least. He had been released from the station just as Julia was leaving the police station. The two of them had found themselves walking across the waiting area and standing together on the doorstep, gazing out at the rain falling on the slick black road. Neither of them had an umbrella, and neither seemed eager to go out into the wet night.

'I'm sorry that you got questioned, Frederick. Pleased it's all been sorted out quickly enough.'

'You'd be surprised how long a day feels when you're in a holding cell, wrongly suspected of the murders of a friend and colleague.'

'I can imagine.'

Frederick ignored her and continued, 'Suspected of murder based on a cup of tea. An innocent cup of tea, and due to the actions of an interfering member of the public.'

'I'm sorry you were questioned, Frederick, I really am. But the cup turned out to be very useful. DI Gibson has some information.'

Julia wasn't sure if she should tell Frederick, but given that the teacup had been used to unjustly accuse him, it seemed only fair. 'It seems that Felicity or Harry must've murdered Phoebe,' she explained, sketching out the process of elimination of the prints.

'How extraordinary,' said Frederick. 'That we took tea with murderers!' He sighed, and said grudgingly, 'Well, I suppose if this all helped find Vincent and Phoebe's killer... Anyway, I'd better be going.'

They looked out into the road where the rain was coming down in that slow but steady manner that looks gentle enough to the uninitiated, but which, as a local like Julia would know, gets inside your collar, and your ears and – given half a chance – soaks you through to your underwear.

'Frederick, will you let me buy you a drink? The Topsy Turnip is one street away. We can sit out of the rain in the pub, and have a pint. Lord knows we could both use one. Not a word about the murder, promise.'

Of course, they spoke about the murder.

After a stilted two-minute discussion about the weather, Frederick said. 'Harry found my ring, you know. About half an hour he was there, waving that wand around like a rather foolish magician. Beeps and pings, you know the sound it makes. And then a longer, louder noise, and he went down on his knees there in the grass and felt around a bit, and there it was. My wedding ring.'

'Well that's good. What did you think of him?'

'A bit of an oddball, but a gentle enough fellow I'd have thought. Hard to imagine him... you know...'

They both pondered the extreme *non*-gentle act that Harry might have committed.

Julia couldn't imagine it. Harry was odd. But he didn't seem odd in a dangerous way. He was one of those awkward, eccentric fellows with strange hobbies and a poor grasp of social conventions and niceties. Julia had seen plenty of clever, strange people who just marched to a different drummer. Or more likely a different bagpiper. Or a different mandolinist.

'Have to say, I agree with you. I would have bet my bottom dollar on Harry Harbour being innocent. What did you talk about, the two of you?' she asked. She had to lean forward to hear him, now that the Saturday party crowd was pulling in in earnest, shouting for friends and bar service, laughing loudly, feeding coins into a jukebox.

'We didn't speak much. You can't really talk once he starts looking; he's got the headphones on, you know. And he's concentrating. But on the way there we spoke about publishing, mostly. He asked about the process, how it works, you know, the writer, the editorial side, the production process. He seemed genuinely interested. He asked a bit about Vincent, too.'

'What did he want to know, exactly?'

'How long I'd known him, how he came up with his ideas. Being interested in history himself, the artefacts and so on, he was interested in the historical side – how he researched the books.'

'What did you say?'

'Not much to tell, really. Vincent studied a bit of history at uni and of course he read a great deal of history in his own time. And more than that, I don't know. As I said, Vincent always handed in a meticulously finished product. He did not show his workings. I told Harry the same, and then he was in the headphones, and that was that.'

'There were three sets of fingerprints on that cup. Yours didn't match. That leaves Harry and Felicity. If it wasn't Harry who murdered Phoebe, it was Felicity. Neither of them seem like likely candidates for murder, on the face of it.'

'I have to say, I agree. I mean, I only saw her for a few minutes, but...'

'And from what I've heard, she hardly leaves the house, just reads and writes,' Julia said. 'He does all the errands.'

'Felicity sits at home for years reading Homer and then out of the blue she gets up and brains some young woman with an anvil? A woman who, as far as we can work out, she doesn't even know? And Harry is similarly unlikely. Murder is hardly the next step from metal detecting.'

'There's got to be some connection between the Harbours and Phoebe. And Phoebe's death must be linked to Vincent's. But how?' Julia tapped her forehead in frustration. She knew that there was a key bit of information missing in this whole affair, something that would explain the relationship between them all. But she just couldn't figure it out.

'You think it over while I get us another pint,' Frederick said, standing up from the table.

She watched Frederick weave his way through the crowd and stand at the bar. The door to the pub opened and a fresh intake of revellers spilled in, bringing a wave of damp cool air with them. They seemed to be a hen party, all of them in clingy dresses in colours and sparkles, and the leader – a skinny blonde – in a sash reading THE MISSUS. The bride-to-be gave Frederick an exaggerated once-over, to which he responded with a deep bow. The young women all shrieked in delight.

Frederick came back with a pint for Julia, and one for himself.

'That was quick,' she said.

'Tall man bar advantage.'

'Thanks. Cheers. And again, sorry about getting you questioned by the police.'

'No hard feelings. Although, I tell you what...' He looked at her over the foam on the top of his glass. 'If you want to make it up to me, you can help me find that manuscript. The one

Phoebe had. The one that went missing. I don't mean to be, um, self-serving, but I really need that manuscript.' His usually arrogant manner had disappeared entirely. 'I don't know what I'm going to do if it doesn't turn up. My career will be over. And as for my finances... the Harbours might as well have smashed that anvil into my head, while they were about it. I'll be as good as dead as a publisher.'

'What about the manuscript they found on the server? Hayley said that you took a look at that.'

'It was useless. Unfinished, of course, but what was there was sloppy, meandering, melodramatic. Amateurish. I mean, I only skimmed it, but from the looks of it there's not much there I could use. I don't know what Vincent did between first draft and final delivery, but if this was the standard, he would have had to have worked some miracles, I tell you.'

He took a deep draw on his pint. 'I need that manuscript that Phoebe Ailes had, the one you saw. Would you say it was complete? How many pages? What size stack?'

He held his thumb and forefinger apart to indicate the possible thickness of the manuscript, making it bigger and smaller, a questioning smile on his face.

Julia thought back to that afternoon in the charity shop, the brown envelope, the manuscript with its heading – 'Chapter One'. She pictured Phoebe's fingers fanning the corners out, the lines of black type, the edits scrawled throughout. And then she saw Phoebe slip it quickly back into the envelope before anyone could see.

Julia slapped her forehead like some kind of cartoon character making a startling realisation. How had this only come to her now? *Harry!* Harry had been *in* the charity shop when Phoebe had brought in the manuscript to show Julia!

'Frederick!'

Her tone made him sit up straight.

'Harry saw the manuscript. That must have been how he knew that Phoebe had it. He surprised us by appearing from the back of the store, where he had been looking at the boxes of odds and ends that had just come in. I'd forgotten he was even there. I'd been in the stockroom until Wilma called me to say someone wanted to see me.'

'Phoebe?'

'Yes.'

'What did she say?'

'She didn't look good. Seemed a bit shaky. Stressed. Said she had to talk to me about something important. That's when she showed me the envelope.'

'Did she say what was in it?'

'The manuscript of Vincent's last book. There was something about it that worried her. Something about the notes. That was what she wanted to talk about.'

'Notes?'

'When Phoebe pulled out the typed pages, I saw there were words scrawled on them, some underlining. Like edits, I suppose.'

'What did they say?'

'I only had a glimpse of them, I couldn't read anything. Then she got spooked. She pushed the pages quickly into the envelope. But Harry was in the shop and he might have seen enough of it to recognize that it was a manuscript. The typed pages, and the writing on it. A big loopy hand.'

'OK, so you think that Harry...'

Julia cut him off, speaking as she rummaged through her bag. 'The edits were in green pen.'

'Yes, well it's more traditionally red, but there aren't any rules.' Frederick seemed amused by his own observation, but Julia wasn't listening. She found the note that Felicity Harbour had given her. She opened it and slapped it down on the bar table, revealing Felicity's name and phone number, scrawled in green pen in loopy handwriting.

'Frederick, I think I know who wrote those notes. I don't know how or why or what they said. But Felicity Harbour wrote them.'

31

Not content with taking over her waking life, the Harbours visited Julia in her dreams on Saturday night. Harry was chasing her along the path by the river, his pack of little rescue dogs running at his heels and yapping. Julia had a heavy bag slung over her shoulder, slowing her down. Felicity walked serenely behind them, seemingly unperturbed by the madness, carrying a ceramic jug, marked with the initials 'V.F.A.' written in green. Dream-Julia somehow knew that whatever she was carrying was fragile and precious, and it made her anxious. In desperation, Julia jumped into the river to escape Harry and the dogs, and was pulled down into the water, the bag slipping from her grasp. Pages of type floated by, and she tried to grasp them, but they kept floating away. She woke up gasping for breath.

She wondered if there was some message in the dream, some clue about exactly what the link was between the Harbours and the manuscript. But she couldn't see anything useful in the swirl of muddled images. She wished her subconscious would be a little more explicit in its revelations. But in the absence of a message from the depth of her brain, she would just have to find out for herself.

. . .

Hayley arrived first.

'I still don't know how you two talked me into this,' she muttered as Julia let her into her cottage. 'It's completely irregular.'

It had certainly taken some persuasion to convince Hayley of their plan, thought Julia, but Frederick had been so desperate to try to get the manuscript that he had begged and begged until Hayley agreed. They'd gone back to Hayley as soon as they'd made the link between the green notes and Felicity Harbour.

'One of them killed Phoebe for that manuscript,' said Julia to Hayley. 'So if we find the manuscript in their possession, then it will be all the proof you need.'

Hayley hadn't been convinced. 'I already have the fingerprints,' she said. 'That's quite enough reason to arrest them.'

'But if you arrest them without first trying to get the manuscript, you might never find it,' countered Julia. 'If we try to wheedle it out of them first, then you've got a cut and dried case.'

Frederick had given a little moan when Julia had mentioned never finding the manuscript.

'DI Gibson,' he said. 'I need that manuscript. And you need an arrest. I've been very nice about the whole wrongful arrest thing, but now I'm begging you to help me. Let Julia and me try to get the manuscript out of the Harbours before you arrest them.'

'You understand that even if you manage to get it, it's evidence,' says Hayley. 'I'd have to keep it.'

'But you'd let me make a copy,' said Frederick, suddenly reverting to the confident man he'd first appeared. 'And even if you didn't, I'd still know that it was safe. We could make plans, keep the public happy.'

Hayley sighed deeply.

'If you don't find the manuscript, the case might get thrown out of court for lack of evidence,' said Julia. She knew that this was a bit of a low blow, every coppers worst fear in a big case like this. Julia had witnessed it a few times in her working life – seen strong police officers cry when someone walked away from a terrible crime just because the chain of evidence had been broken, or some other legal technicality. Hayley wouldn't want Phoebe Ailes' killer to walk free.

'My chaps would search the house and find it,' said Hayley.

'Like they found the laptop in Vince's B&B?'

There was silence as Hayley contemplated the truth of Julia's statement.

'Fine,' she said eventually. 'We'll all go tomorrow morning. You two go in first, and see what you can get. But I'm warning you, any sign of trouble, I'm coming in. Manuscript or not.'

'Deal,' said Julia, with a smile.

'Thank you,' said Frederick, and much to the DI's surprise, he flung his arms around her in a grateful hug.

Which bought them to Julia's house first thing in the morning, with a worried Hayley. Frederick arrived shortly after Hayley, looking quite chipper for a chap about to approach two suspected murderers in their den, so to speak.

'Right then, let's go,' Frederick said, with no time for niceties, jiggling his keys in his hand as he arrived. Jake didn't need to be invited. He was on his feet at the sound of the car keys.

'Not you, Jakey,' Julia said. 'I'll take you out later.'

The dog looked crestfallen and sloped over to the coop to commiserate with the chickens, who never went anywhere either.

'Okay,' said Hayley, taking control of the situation. 'Here's how we play it. You, Julia and Frederick, will walk to the

Harbours. As soon as you are in the house, Julia, you will send me a message. We will follow, and wait outside the house, blocking all possible exits. If I hear anything that sounds like trouble, I'm coming in. After ten minutes, I'm coming in anyway. Do you understand me?' Hayley looked quite fierce as she glanced from Julia to Frederick. They both nodded.

'Okay,' said Hayley. 'Let's tie this up.'

The walk was scenic, and usually Julia was still fresh enough to the country to thrill to the picture-postcard moments – a bird of prey hovering high above an open field, or a newborn lamb suckling from its mum, or hay being piled high on a trailer – but today, she was too preoccupied to appreciate the sights.

Although she wasn't looking forward to the meeting, she felt something like relief when they reached the Harbours' door.

Harry came round the side of the house and saw them there, making Julia realise how sensible Hayley's plan to follow was. 'Oh hello, Frederick and, er...' he said. Julia tried not to be cross. 'Have you lost something else? Do I need my metal detector?'

'I have actually,' said Frederick. 'Nothing metal, though. Something that I hope you or Felicity can help me with. Do you mind if we come in?'

Harry nodded, a little apprehensively, and stood back to let them into the house. He led them into the room they had visited before. Julia quietly reached into her bag for her phone and sent Hayley a quick message that they were in. The room was exactly the same as the last time they'd visited, except that a fire burned in the grate against the autumn chill. Felicity was in the same chair where she'd been the last time they had seen her. A book rested, open, on her knees – the same book or a different one, Julia couldn't be sure. The table to her right held the dictionary, notepads and pens. She looked up as they entered.

'A surprise visit,' she said, sounding neither pleased nor displeased. 'Hello, Julia,' she added, a little more warmly. 'Thank you for the message with the name of the book. It sounds right up my alley.'

'You're very welcome,' said Julia, moving closer. She noted that the writing on Felicity's notepads was green. She felt a little thrill at having already worked out this piece of the puzzle. 'As I predicted, it came to me once I got home.'

'Always does.'

'Frederick has lost something,' said Harry, butting in awkwardly.

'Goodness, well, Frederick, you must be more careful,' Felicity said with a short laugh. 'Maybe Harry will be lucky twice.'

'I do hope so. Or that you might be able to assist,' Frederick said, his voice calm and friendly. 'The thing is, I'm looking for V.F. Andrews' latest manuscript. The last book he wrote before he died. As his publisher, I'm responsible for getting it out into the world – we own it, of course.' He said this last phrase with just a hint of warning in his voice, and then continued in the same warm tone, 'It seems to have gone astray. I've been given to believe that you might be able to help me locate it.'

32

'A manuscript?' Felicity said. 'No, I don't know anything about that. I am familiar with his books, and I heard about his death, of course. A shocking state of affairs. But why on earth would we have the manuscript?'

'Harry?' Frederick said. 'Can *you* tell me about the manuscript?' Julia had to admire Frederick's bravery, and single-minded pursuit of the manuscript.

'Harry's not much one for novels,' Felicity said, before her husband could speak. 'Sorry we couldn't be more helpful. I don't know how you got it into your heads that we would have it.'

She spoke with an air of finality, as if the question had been asked and answered.

Julia spoke. 'Harry, do you remember the manuscript? You saw it that day when you came into Second Chances. The girl with the blue hair had it. Phoebe, her name was.'

'Oh no, I didn't see that,' he said, shaking his head. 'I was looking in the boxes. I found a jug that day, I recall. A nice spec-imen of early English ceramics. I didn't see a manuscript, not at all. Or the girl. I definitely never saw the girl.'

'I think you did. Perhaps I can jog your memory. It was a stack of papers, in a brown envelope. They were typed, with notes written on them.'

Julia turned to Felicity when she added, 'Notes in green pen, like those pens over there.' She gestured to the pot of pens. 'Remember?'

'No, oh, no,' Harry started to speak, a nervous stammer.

Before he found his voice, Felicity stood up and said, 'Thank you for coming by. I'm sorry we couldn't help, but best of luck with finding the manuscript.'

'Do you always write in green?' asked Julia, casually, addressing Felicity. 'Why is that? I always thought red was the colour for edits.'

'I must ask you both to leave,' Felicity said. 'I have work to do.'

'We'll leave when we have the manuscript,' Frederick said. 'I'm not here to make any trouble for either of you. All I want is the book, and I'll be on my way. No questions asked. And this stays between us.'

'Why on earth would we have Vince's manuscript?' said Felicity. Her look of general confusion might have fooled Julia, except for the one giveaway in her sentence.

'Because you just called him Vince,' she said. 'Only his friends call him Vince, I've noticed. Perhaps we should leave this to the police,' Julia said, turning to Frederick. 'I'll ring DI Gibson and she can take it through the official channels.' She felt a bit bad lying to the Harbours like this, knowing Hayley was already party to this plan, and there was no way the Harbours were getting away with the murders. But they needed to get the manuscript to tie-up the case.

'I had hoped we'd be able to sort this out ourselves, but you're right. It's probably for the best,' Frederick said, catching on. To the Harbours, he said, 'We'll be on our way.'

'Wait,' said Harry, by now pale and shaky. 'I did come

across a pile of paper, on my, you know, walks. Perhaps that's your manuscript.'

'What in God's name are you talking about, Harry?' said Felicity, looking at him with confusion. 'You never said anything to me.'

'Well, I don't tell you everything, do I?' said Harry.

'Yes, actually, you do,' said Felicity. 'And you never said a word about a pile of paper. Anyway, you'd...' Felicity stopped suddenly.

'He'd have recognised the writing,' said Julia. 'And he'd have told you.'

Felicity looked panicked, glancing from Julia to Harry.

'If I give you what I found, will you leave us alone?' asked Harry.

'Of course,' said Frederick, before Julia could answer. 'Julia and I will be on our way, not a word to a soul. No questions asked.'

Harry went over to a tall chest of drawers, the surface of which was covered in small figurines of women, dark wood decorated with cowrie shells. He opened the middle drawer, and pulled out a brown envelope, which he handed to Frederick.

'It was me, it's nothing to do with Felicity,' he said. 'I found it, I'm sorry.'

'But why wouldn't you have told Felicity if you'd found it?' Julia asked softly.

'No questions asked, you said.'

'Right you are,' said Frederick, who didn't really seem to care about the bigger picture of whys and wherefores. 'Well, thank you, Harry. Really, thank you. You've been a great help. Really saved the day. Again. I'm most grateful. And all Vincent's readers. Most grateful, too, they'll be. His legacy, saved.'

Along with your bacon, thought Julia. Frederick was so

pleased to have the envelope in his hands that he was gushing, tripping over his words. He seemed to have momentarily forgotten the two murders that had led up to this point and that the police were waiting to arrest the suspected murderers right outside, Julia thought, with some distaste.

'I have a question,' she said. 'The notes, Felicity's notes. What are they?'

Frederick shot her a furious look and clutched the manuscript even tighter. He gestured to the door with a toss of his head. He had what he came for and now he wanted out of there. It was time for the police, his look said.

But a picture was beginning to form in Julia's mind. The threads were coming together.

'You knew Vincent Andrews,' she said, looking at Felicity. 'You called him Vince just now. It was at Gloucester University, wasn't it? I remember you said you'd taught there for thirty-five years. Vincent studied there too, according to his obituary. Did you teach him history? Is that where you met?'

Felicity was uncharacteristically flustered. 'History is a popular course,' she said, not answering the question. 'Lots of people do it.'

'But lots of people don't go on to write historical novels. Historical novels that are renowned for their excellent detail.'

'I don't know what you mean,' said Felicity, somewhat confusingly, as nothing that Julia had said was particularly complex.

'You helped him with the fact-checking, didn't you? Nothing wrong with that,' said Julia. 'If that was what it was.'

'Precisely,' said Felicity, as if that had been her point all along.

'I don't understand why you...'

'I'll take it from here,' came a voice from the doorway. It was DI Gibson, with DC Farmer behind her. 'Good morning, Mr Harbour, Mrs Harbour.'

'Harry Harbour, Felicity Harbour, you need to come with us to the police station.'

'What, why?' asked Felicity, in a very good impression of astonished outrage.

'You are being brought in for questioning with regard to the death of Phoebe Ailes. We have prints from the murder weapon and we need to take both of your fingerprints for comparison. And yours,' she added, nodding her head to Julia. Her prints were on the cup too, of course.

DC Walter Farmer chipped in, saying in his most official tone, the words Julia had heard a hundred times in police procedurals on television: 'You do not have to say anything. But it may harm your defence if you do not mention when questioned something which you later rely on in court. Anything you do say may be given in evidence.'

'It was me!' Harry shouted, loudly enough to startle a cat that was asleep on top of a pile of books on top of a piano.

'Harry!' said Felicity. 'Be quiet.'

'It was me. I did it. I killed Phoebe Ailes and I took the manuscript.'

Felicity started: 'Harry, darling, of course you didn't. Don't say another word. I mean it!'

'And I killed Vincent Andrews too. I confess!' he shouted, holding out his arms, offering his wrists to DC Farmer. 'I killed them. Take me away!'

'Harry! That's not true! Now be quiet!' Felicity stared him down fiercely. He stopped talking, and let his arms drop to his sides.

She turned to the police and said, 'He obviously did nothing of the sort. He doesn't mean it. He just gets anxious and says silly things.'

'Everybody, slow down,' Hayley said firmly. 'Let's all take a deep breath. I want everyone to come with me and DC Farmer down to the station where we will take fingerprints and formal statements.'

Her calm tone brought the stress levels in the room down a notch.

'That includes you, too,' she said to Frederick. 'And I'll take that.' She held out her hand.

'Please, I...' Frederick held the manuscript tight to his chest.

Hayley raised an eyebrow, her hand still outstretched. Frederick looked as if he might argue, or even resist. But he loosened his grip on the manuscript and passed it to her with a forlorn sigh, saying, 'It's very important; his last opus.'

'I know,' she said, reaching for it. 'Pass me the opus.'As the envelope passed from hand to hand, Harry stepped smartly in and grabbed it. In a swift movement he took out the manuscript, tossed the envelope to the floor, and hurled the papers into the roaring fire.

33

The clouds had rolled in and the temperature dropped when Julia and Frederick left the Harbours' house.

Julia had phoned Sean to come and fetch them and take them to the police station as Hayley's car was full, but the atmosphere in his car was chilly. Frederick was seated at the back, his jaw clenched, a vein throbbing furiously at his throat. Julia turned from her position next to Sean, and tried to mend fences with Frederick.

'I do think that...' Julia started, in a conciliatory tone.

'No,' he said, curtly. 'Don't.'

They all drove in silence. Unlike Frederick's, Sean's silence was calm, Julia having quickly filled him in when he had arrived to fetch them. The acrid smell of burnt paper wafted through from the back seat, where the remains of Vincent's final novel lay next to Frederick, damply smoky in a plastic bag. Frederick had thrown himself at the fireplace, hauled the burning papers from the fire and tossed them onto the carpet. There he had stomped on them, while reaching for Felicity's teacup and throwing the remains of her tea onto them to quench the flames. It had been very dramatic and only partially successful in terms of rescuing the manuscript.

Julia watched the brooding landscape through the window, fighting the urge to speak. She could tell that Frederick needed to absorb what had happened – but her mind was churning. Eventually she could stay silent no more, and turned to Sean.

'I'm trying to make sense of things. There's a lot of information missing in Harry's story. Harry says he killed Vincent and Phoebe. But why? Because Felicity fact-checked his work? That hardly makes sense.'

'It does seem extreme,' said Sean, in his thoughtful way. 'It doesn't make sense at all.'

'Felicity must be the connection between the two murders and the manuscript. She's a historian. She knew Vincent from his student days at Gloucester uni. She was fact-checking his draft. But what else is going on? There's something we're not getting.'

Sean took his eyes off the road for a moment and glanced over to her. 'An affair? Felicity and Vincent, back in the day?'

Not impossible. 'Maybe, but why has it come up now? And then, why Phoebe?'

'Jealousy? She thought Vincent was having a thing with Phoebe?'

Julia pondered Sean's idea for a bit. It didn't make sense. Why would Harry then be claiming responsibility for the murders? And what did the manuscript have to do with it all?

'Let's assume for a moment that Harry went to Phoebe to get the manuscript and she was killed in some kind of struggle. Why would he want the manuscript? And then why would he burn it?'

'I've no idea,' said Sean. 'But I've got a sneaking suspicion you're going to work it out.'

Julia tried to work through things in her own head. Starting with the connection between Vincent and Felicity. She was a lecturer, he was a student. He had only done a year of history, if she remembered correctly, and that was a long time ago. And now here Felicity was, fact-checking the drafts of his bestselling novels.

'Frederick?'

A grunt from the morose Mr Eliot, sitting silently at the back of the car.

'Isn't it strange that you didn't know anything about Felicity until now? Never heard her name?'

'Yes, I suppose.'

'I mean, wouldn't the publisher have paid for a fact-checker?'

He stirred somewhat to life. 'Actually yes, that is strange. We actually *do* pay for an expert to look over it. It's damn expensive, but important, you know. Not that Vincent's facts are ever wrong. Far from.'

'So then she wasn't a fact-checker,' said Julia. 'But her hand-writing was all over that manuscript.' Julia turned towards Sean in excitement. 'What if Felicity was a collaborator, even a part-ner? Vincent got the glory, but she did – I don't know – maybe she helped him write. Came up with ideas. Or more. Maybe she even wrote some of it?'

As Sean pulled up outside the police station, Frederick piped up from the back, 'Good God. That would mean that Vincent's whole oeuvre wasn't his. That V.F. Andrews...'

'V.F.!' Julia shouted, smacking the dashboard in front of her. 'F is for Felicity! His middle name is James, did you know? I read it in the obituary. Why would he call himself V.F.? Unless the F is for Felicity!'

'A little nod to Felicity? Her acknowledgement? Just between the two of them,' Sean said, glancing at Julia.

'Yes. If we're right, that means that Harry...'

She was interrupted by a knock at Sean's window. Hayley Gibson's face appeared, Frederick opened the door a crack, and

Hayley stepped back. 'Are you coming?' she asked him. Hayley looked at Julia and said, 'You'd better come, too.'

Julia didn't need to be asked twice. She glanced at Sean, who gave her an understanding nod. 'I'll wait,' he said.

She got out of the car and slammed the door. 'Hayley, a word,' she said, trotting after the younger woman who was already on her way to the entrance, where DC Farmer was leading a handcuffed Felicity and Harry through the door. Frederick brought up the rear, carrying his sad bag of damp, burnt papers.

'Can it wait?' Hayley said, without breaking her stride.

'No, I don't think so. It's something you should know before you talk to the Harbours.'

Her words stopped the detective in her tracks. She turned around. 'What is it?'

Julia explained her theory about Felicity's input into Vincent's novel – that she was more than just a fact-checker, perhaps even a co-writer.

'Interesting,' said Hayley. Julia could almost see her brain whirring. 'Very interesting. It makes a connection, granted. But it doesn't explain why Harry would kill Vincent. Or Phoebe. It's making it much more likely that Felicity is the one whose prints will be a match.'

'His confession doesn't make any sense,' Julia admitted. She still couldn't quite hang it all together. She thought for a moment, and felt something slip into place. 'Well, Phoebe had the manuscript. She'd seen Felicity's notes, and was confused, concerned – she'd brought it to me, she'd likely take it further. Maybe Harry wanted the manuscript back so that no one could make the connection with Felicity. He was protecting Felicity.'

Julia hadn't worked out the full story yet, but this part felt right. Harry adored Felicity and would want to protect her. Even if that meant stealing the manuscript. And possibly, if things got carried away, killing a young woman.

Frederick had caught up now. 'DI Gibson, could you ask Harry about the laptop?' he asked. 'If Harry took the manuscript, he might have taken the laptop too.'

'All in good time,' said Hayley. She seemed a bit brighter now, ready for action. 'Come on. Let's go and see what the prints tell us, shall we?'

DC Farmer was processing the two Harbours at the desk station, with the help of the same desk sergeant Julia had seen previously. The young woman gave Julia a 'you again?' look.

Harry was fidgeting nervously while his prints were being taken. Felicity was waiting her turn.

'The gang's all here, I see,' said Felicity drily, looking at the new arrivals. She seemed remarkably calm for someone who was a suspect in a murder case – the other most likely suspect being her husband.

With Harry printed, the desk sergeant beckoned to Felicity. 'If you could come here, ma'am.'

'You don't need to take her fingerprints,' Harry said. 'I told you, I did it. You'll find my prints match. Just leave my wife out of it.'

'Don't worry, Harry. Let's just get this over with. Obviously, neither of our prints are going to match. We had nothing to do with that poor girl's death, no matter what you claim,' Felicity said. 'Officer, you can take my prints.'

'No!' Harry said, agitated.

He stood up. All the police in the room were on alert. DC Farmer moved towards Harry, who stepped behind his chair. He looked as if he was deciding whether to use it as a weapon, hide under it, or make a run for the door.

Julia could see this going very badly.

'It's okay, Harry,' she said calmly. 'I know you are trying to protect Felicity. It's what you've been doing all along. That's why you took the manuscript from Phoebe, so no one else would see Felicity's green writing and make the connections we did – that she was Vincent's lecturer, and helped him write the books.'

'That's it. That's why. I didn't mean to kill Phoebe. I swear. I only went for the manuscript, but she wouldn't... She didn't...' He looked around wildly, as if hoping for escape or support. 'I'm so sorry. So very sorry. It was a mistake, I never meant to kill that poor girl. But I had to make her stop talking.'

Felicity gave a moan of horror. She had clearly not thought him capable of taking Phoebe's life. Julia could see why. It did seem quite an extreme action for really quite a benign secret.

There was something missing.

Hayley stepped up, 'We'll talk about that some more later, Harry. You'll need to get someone to help you explain it all.'

'A lawyer?' he asked.

'Yes, a lawyer. In the meantime, you'll have to stay here with me.'

'What about Felicity?' He looked worriedly at his wife.

'Felicity will be fine. We'll do the paperwork and release her. We have no reason to hold her.'

'Because she's innocent?' he said. He even smiled as he said it. Julia felt a little sad for him.

'Felicity helped Vincent with the manuscript, it's not illegal,' Julia said. 'She's done nothing wrong. Just helped an old student with his work.'

Harry nodded. 'That's it. She did nothing wrong. She didn't kill anyone.'

'Of course I didn't kill anyone,' Felicity said. Her voice was soft and she suddenly looked frail.

'Exactly,' said Harry. 'You wouldn't. That's what I said. I killed everybody.' Harry nodded, looking unexpectedly pleased for a man who had just confessed to a gruesome murder.

'But *why* did you kill Vincent?' DC Farmer burst out,

breaking his customary silence. 'That's what I don't understand.'

Harry stared at the ceiling for a moment, as if he had hidden the secret of Vincent's murder amongst the dusty corners of the police station.

'I just did. Hated the man,' Harry mumbled eventually. 'He took advantage of Felicity. Took the credit.'

Felicity burst out, 'That's nonsense, Harry. Quite the contrary, he paid the bills. And every time I saw that F in his name – V.F. Andrews – I knew it was me, even if the rest of the world didn't. And you've never hated him. You always said you found him quite amusing.'

Even in all the drama, Julia took a moment to congratulate herself on working the initial out.

'Be quiet,' Harry said to his wife. 'That's enough. I killed him. You don't need to say another thing, darling.'

The whole scene was peculiar, to Julia's mind. Phoebe's murder just about made sense in a warped kind of way, but Vincent?

Felicity said, 'I don't believe you killed him. You wouldn't. And besides, you were with me the whole time on the night he died. We were there together and left together.'

'We weren't together, were we? When we left?' For a moment Harry looked completely confused, and then he seemed to gather himself. 'I mean to say, of *course* we were together. But I went back.'

'No, you didn't. You came home and fell asleep in front of the telly.'

'I didn't, I tell you. I sneaked out. Murderously.'

Hayley interrupted the rather extraordinary marital spat. 'That's enough for today, thank you. I'm going to take Mr Harbour into custody and conduct a formal interview when he has his lawyer present.'

'I'll arrange that immediately,' said Felicity, sounding more decisive. 'This is a ridiculous misunderstanding.'

'Thank you. Mrs Harbour, DC Farmer here will assist with the paperwork in a minute, and then you'll be free to leave. I'll update you as soon as I have more information.'

The police took Harry away through one door. The waiting room seemed unnaturally empty and quiet, with only Julia and Felicity standing there, and Frederick still hunched over his burnt offerings.

'Harry didn't kill Vincent,' Felicity said weakly. 'I just don't know what's come over him. He's not himself at all.'

'But why would he lie about it, Felicity?'

Felicity looked at Julia. 'That's the thing. Harry never lies. You must've noticed, he's a bit... unusual. That's why I love him. And he loves me. He loves me so much, he'd do anything for me. The only time I've ever heard him lie, it's been to protect me. Like when my mother was still alive, and used to phone to nag me and nag me. Ha! Harry used to tell her the wildest stories about why I couldn't come to the phone. It was so unlike him, it made me laugh and laugh.'

'Just now, he didn't seem to think that he had left the book event with you,' said Julia slowly. 'And he seems to have killed Phoebe just to prevent anyone knowing that you helped Vincent with his books. That seems a bit extreme. Unless he was worried that the manuscript pointed at something more.'

'What more could it point to? Although you are right. Why on earth would he kill Phoebe just to hide my identity as Vince's co-writer? Maybe he didn't kill Phoebe either?' Felicity looked so hopeful that Julia hated to burst her bubble.

'No,' she said slowly, putting together her thoughts as she spoke. 'I think he did kill Phoebe. To stop anyone connecting you to Vincent. I think that Harry thinks *you* killed Vincent. He thinks he's taking the rap to protect you.'

Felicity stared at Julia wide-eyed for a moment, her mouth

slightly open as if to object. But nothing came out. It made a strange sort of sense.

'But why would he think that?' said Felicity.

'Because it makes sense, in a way,' said Julia, watching Felicity carefully as she spoke. 'Vincent had taken all the glory for the writing, giving you a bit of money and an initial. You might be bitter? Was he going to share this latest TV deal with you, I wonder? I must say, Felicity, I can see a lot of reasons that Harry might think you murdered Vince.'

'That's... that's ridiculous,' said Felicity, her face flushed. With guilt or with anger, Julia wasn't sure. 'I'm phoning my lawyer right now.'

While Felicity went into the passage to make a phone call, Frederick looked up from where he sat. He'd been rifling through the unburnt scraps of manuscript, reading a bit here and a bit there, deaf to the drama around him. For Frederick, the manuscript was everything. In a sombre tone, he said to Julia, 'This manuscript is terrible. Hardly better than that early version the coppers found on the cloud.'

'How very strange. Even for a first draft?'

'I don't think he wrote this at all. It's not his style. It's not *bad* Vincent. It's someone else. Someone else wrote this book. I'd stake my life on it.'

Possibly not the best choice of words, thought Julia, given that two people had already died.

'What about Felicity? It must have been her,' said Julia. 'She said she was helping. But maybe she was doing more. Could Vincent have had some kind of writer's block? Got her to write more? And it went horribly wrong and she killed him?'

Felicity, having finished her call, walked back into the room.

'Did you write this?' Frederick asked, waving the pages. He was not one to mince his words, even speaking to a possible murderer. As he wafted the papers, they gave off a bitter smell and a light sprinkling of ash.

'I most certainly did not,' said Felicity, looking down at the messy pile with the contempt it deserved. 'I helped him define the historical period, and I wrote in the historical elements. When he was finished, I checked the final manuscript and added in more historical details – and Vincent was such a good writer that it was easy to do. Usually. But this one... God, I even said to Harry that I was worried. The money we get from helping Vince makes a huge difference, so if he'd lost his touch it would be terrible.'

'You didn't write it?'

'Believe me, Mr Eliot, if I had written such appalling prose, you wouldn't have to murder me. I would gladly stab *myself*. Heavens.' She gave a dramatic shudder. Julia felt quite warmly towards her for the whole performance.

34

'Good Lord,' Tabitha said. 'Felicity's quite something, isn't she?'

'Oh yes, she certainly is.'

'I would gladly stab *myself*.' Tabitha chuckled heartily, setting her bangles jiggling and jangling. 'She really said that?'

'Yes. Those very words.'

'I wish I could come up with clever things like that on the spur of the moment. I'm always struck dumb. But not Felicity. I *do* like her. It would be a pity if it turned out she stabbed Vincent.'

'There's certainly a lot of evidence pointing at her,' said Julia. 'But there's something that doesn't add up about it. For a start, with Vincent dead the Harbours take quite a financial loss. Felicity didn't have a formal arrangement so she would not get any royalties going forward.'

'Well if it wasn't her, who did it?'

'A most excellent question,' Julia said. She stroked Too rhythmically, the motion of her hand following the cat's even breath. It relaxed them both.

'Did you notice the Harbours leave the event that night, Tabitha?'

Tabitha frowned. 'I'd noticed that they were there. They don't often get involved in village events, especially not Felicity. I think most of her friends are at the university. I remember thinking that perhaps they saw it as some sort of date night. An event that met both their interests. I'm almost sure that they left together – I think I would have noticed if they hadn't. It would have been awfully odd.'

'And if they left together, it's hard to think how Felicity would have had the opportunity to murder Vincent.'

They both thought about this for a moment.

Tabitha tried another tack. 'So who do you think wrote the appalling prose?'

'Honestly, I don't know. I'm hoping that Felicity will find Vincent's laptop. I'm ninety-nine per cent sure Harry took it. I had a brainwave in the middle of the night. I remembered that I met Harry on the path when I walked home with the laptop. I ran into him, literally. I dropped it when I fell and he picked it up. Vincent's initials were on the laptop case. He must have seen them.'

'Why did you have Vincent's laptop?' Tabitha asked. A reasonable question indeed.

Julia blushed. 'I took it. It was an impulse thing.'

'Julia Bird, well I never!'

'I know, it's terrible. I don't know what came over me. But if I'm right, the laptop is at the Harbours' house somewhere. Harry hid the manuscript there; I think it's quite likely he hid the computer too. I've asked Felicity to look today.'

'And if she finds it?'

'If she finds it, we can look at the names on the document. The author, who originated the document, and who else contributed what.'

'You can do that?'

'Yes.'

'Gosh, you're clever.'

'Not really, it's a feature of the word processing programme. It's built in.'

'Well I never,' Tabitha said. She looked amazed and impressed at this miraculous feat of modern science. She was more of a pages-between-covers sort of person.

The two women sat in companionable silence in the comfy reading section of the library. The area – which hosted their book club, and after-school hangouts, and, quite recently and unexpectedly, V.F. Andrews' murder – was quiet that Monday morning.

'No sign of the knife?' asked Tabitha.

'None.'

'If only we had one of those security camera things. We could see who was standing by the display, and who left when, that sort of thing.'

'That would be handy indeed. The first thing I'd like to know is exactly when Vincent disappeared. Where he went, and who with. Let's go through it again. Start from scratch. Tell me what you remember from the end of the evening.'

'He was signing books. Phoebe was doing the payments, and he was signing.'

'Right. That I remember.'

'I was clearing up. Think I'd just put the dirties away in the kitchen. In and out, I was. And at some point, I came out and he was gone.'

'Who was still there?'

'Hardly anyone. Eleanor and Sarah. Phoebe. Maybe one or two last stragglers.'

'Did you ask where he was?'

'I did. I asked Eleanor and she said he'd gone home.'

'But Sarah and Eleanor were still there?'

'Yes.'

'That's a bit odd, isn't it?'

'Now you mention it. I thought he might have a headache. Or a tummy ache.'

'I'll go and ask her,' Julia said.

'Ask who?'

'Eleanor. It's not making sense. Sarah said she left with Eleanor, but didn't know where Vince was. But Eleanor told you he'd gone home. Maybe we've missed something.'

'I'm sure the police will have asked.'

'They probably did, but I'm starting from scratch, remember?'

'Honestly, Julia Bird. When you get your teeth into something...'

Eleanor seemed pleased to see a visitor.

'No bother at all!' she said, when Julia apologised for the intrusion. Julia had come up with a story about canvassing for Friends of the Library. She even had forms, legitimate ones, which Tabitha had given her. She was rather pleased with her cunning ruse.

Eleanor ushered her into a stiflingly warm room, filled with cushions and plants and brightly coloured pictures. The whole windowsill was full of orchids of all types in pots. A large reproduction of some Gauguin painting of island maidens hung across the fireplace, which wasn't lit, but filled with more plants: a miniature forest of ferns and white anthuriums. The trailing plants Julia's mum had called 'hen and chickens' sat on the mantelpiece amongst a collection of semi-precious stones. The little striped 'chickens' hung down on their pale runners. A small heater blasted forth, and the air felt humid, as if recreating the atmospheric feel of Gauguin's beloved Tahiti.

'What a lovely room. So unusual. It doesn't even feel like the Cotswolds. It's as if we're on a tropical island.'

'Exactly! That's what I wanted. I've lived abroad, you know.

The tropical climes. Once you've seen a bit of the world, experienced different things, it opens your eyes, doesn't it?'

'That's certainly true,' said Julia, and it was, even though the Cotswolds was her rather less exotic life-change. Eleanor showed Julia to a green velvet chair matted with cat hair. Just looking at it gave Julia the prickles. Instead, she took an upright wooden chair in front of a desk, on which was a most unusual black-spotted orchid in a white pot. 'My back,' she said, by way of explanation.

'Oh, don't I know that one,' said Eleanor, rubbing her own back. 'Sciatica. If it wasn't for the Pilates, I don't know how I'd walk.'

Eleanor was, in fact, a very trim and upright woman. Good looking, and with a youthful manner, younger than her years. Julia wondered if she should take up Pilates herself.

'You're my cousin Sean's friend, if I'm not mistaken?'

'Yes, I am. I'm seeing him later, in fact. We have a walk planned.'

'Do send him my best. He's my favourite cousin. He's been such a help and support after the awful thing with Vincent.'

'I think we met at the library that night,' said Julia. 'I'm sorry for your loss, Eleanor.'

'Thank you. It's been terrible. Just terrible. My poor Sarah is just devastated. You were the one who found him, weren't you? You and the librarian lady, Tabitha.'

'Yes. I went to help her clear up the next morning, and we found him.'

'Must have been awful. And I don't understand it. That he was killed there, in the library. He'd already left, I thought.'

'Yes, it's very strange that he wasn't seen.'

'There were only one or two people there.'

'Do you remember who?'

'There was the librarian and the PR girl, the one with the

blue hair who was killed. Perhaps a couple of stragglers from the audience, but I couldn't say who. And me and Sarah.'

'What time was it that he left?'

'It must have been about nine. Well, I didn't see him leave, exactly. Not myself, personally. Sarah told me he'd gone home, not feeling well.'

Before Julia could ask the next obvious question, Sarah spoke from the doorway.

'Oh hello, it's Julia, isn't it?' She looked paler and thinner than when Julia had last seen her. The poor woman seemed to be held up by the door frame.

'Yes, hello, Sarah. I just popped in on library business. I'm helping with the fundraising...'

Julia realised as she said it that the library fundraising cover story might not have been her finest, given the family's recent experience of the library. She was pleased to have her phone ring and disrupt the awkward moment.

'I'm sorry,' she said, fumbling for it in her bag. 'I forgot to turn it off.'

She pulled it out and saw Felicity's name. 'Do you mind if I take this?'

'Go ahead,' said Eleanor, although she did look rather disapproving.

Julia stood up and moved slightly away, to lessen the rudeness of taking the call.

'Hi, Felicity.'

Felicity didn't even say hello. 'I found it!'

'The laptop?' Julia said. 'Oh good. And the document?'

'I think so, yes.'

'Right, well if you go into the Word document and click on "file". You'll see the author, and then collaborators... No, not open the file. Click on it... No, not the icon... Not to worry, if you can't work it out I'll come over and show you. Later, but I need to go home first. Jake's been alone. OK, I have to go.'

She ended the call and apologised to Eleanor and Sarah. 'I'm sorry. Well, I should be getting along. Thank you for letting me take up so much of your time, Eleanor. I'll leave the forms with you, have a look in your own time.'

And she made her way through the damp orchid forest of Polynesia, to the front door, and out into the blessed cool air of the Cotswolds in autumn.

35

'Come on then. You're going to make a new friend,' Julia told Jake, while she gathered up her coat and car keys, and took his leash from the hook by the kitchen door. 'Best behaviour, please.' Remembering their fateful visit to the dam some months back, she muttered, 'And if we could make it round the dam without finding a body, I'd appreciate that.'

Jake never required a second invitation for an outing. He was waiting next to the car by the time Julia had closed the front door. When she opened the car door, he jumped into the back seat and assumed his usual position, sitting upright behind the passenger seat and gazing thoughtfully out of the window. Julia took up her own position as his driver, glancing into the rear-view mirror occasionally to smile at her funny dog enjoying the view. Her heart felt full with love for the good boy. Goodness, she had turned into a soppy dog person.

Sean must have drawn up to the little parking area just seconds before her. He was opening the hatchback boot to let Leo out. The slim brown cross-breed jumped lightly onto the grass and immediately started sniffing for clues as to previous visitors. Julia pulled up next to them, waving through the window.

'Hey there,' she said brightly, as she got out. 'Great timing.'

She opened the car door and Jake leapt out like a bullet from a gun, dashing to the nearest tree for a wee, then hurling himself at Leo, who took it all in good humour, gambolling elegantly with the galumphing chocolate lout. Julia and Sean set off down the path towards the dam, the dogs off lead.

Julia told Sean about her day and her discoveries, and her visit to his cousin's house.

'You didn't tell me it was so exotic,' she said.

'You didn't tell me you were going to visit my cousin under false pretences,' he said with a smile.

'Well, not exactly. I *was* dropping off the forms. And I just nosed around a bit at the same time. I was trying to find out more about the time around Vincent's death.'

'Did you learn much?'

'Not really. According to Eleanor, Sarah told her he'd gone home ill. But remember that Sarah said she didn't know where he was when she was questioned. So, what I'm wondering is, did he actually leave the premises and go home, or not?'

And if he had left, why had Sarah stayed, she wondered? Was Sarah punishing him, letting him go off alone, sick? And why had Sarah lied about it when she first spoke to the police? She'd definitely implied that she left first and that Vincent just never came home. A fight, she had said. Nothing about feeling sick. 'I don't think he was ill. I think there was something else going on,' she said to Sean. 'Think back to when Sarah first talked about that night. That he never came home and she thought he'd stayed out after their spat at the signing.'

Sean nodded. 'So he didn't go home sick at all. Maybe Sarah told Eleanor that because she didn't want to admit he'd gone off in a huff.'

'That makes sense. Mothers can be funny.'

Their conversation was interrupted by the ringing of Julia's phone. She looked at the screen: Felicity Harbour.

'Do you mind if I take this?' Julia asked, showing Sean who was calling. 'She might have found something on the laptop.'

'Of course, go ahead,' Sean said. He turned away politely, and picked up a stick, which he threw for the dogs. The dogs chased after it, as if they had been friends forever. Not a care in the world, Julia thought. How nice to be a dog. She answered the phone.

'I've figured it out,' Felicity said, without so much as a hello. 'Gosh, I do feel clever. I did what you said, but I had to go into edit mode for the names. Worked that out and the funny thing is...'

'What?' said Julia, impatiently. 'Who?'

'Well, it's interesting. Vincent *and* Sarah worked on the document. At the beginning, it's mostly Sarah for about three chapters. And then suddenly Vince takes over, and there's nothing from Sarah. It's so odd. At first I thought maybe he'd used her laptop, but you can see which bits she wrote and the styles are *quite* different.' Felicity paused for a brief – a very brief – breath before going on. 'It's funny he would ask her for help when he never wanted her to know that *I* gave him help. He said she'd hate to know how I helped him with the history bits. Said we could never tell her, that he needed her to believe that he did it all himself. And then here it looks like she helped him, too. The really odd part is that what she wrote is good, and what he wrote is complete drivel. But anyway, if she was helping him, I guess he must've told her about me.'

Julia realised she was never going to get a word in edgeways. But that was not the only thing she'd realised.

If Sarah had written the first part of the book, it changed everything. How would Sarah feel if she had realised that Vince had asked another woman for help before he asked her? And if that was the case, how would she feel about that woman? And what if Vincent had told her about that woman? And why had Sarah stopped writing? Especially if her part was actually better.

And then Julia remembered where she had been standing when she'd taken Felicity's last call. And who had been listening, as Julia had happily given directions as to how to find the authors of a document.

She covered the mouthpiece and said to Sean. 'I think you need to phone Hayley. Now.'

He stopped his stick throwing, startled. He reached for his phone. The dogs looked on expectantly, jumping in advance of the throw that never came.

Felicity was in full flow, 'I just don't understand why Vincent's part was so awful – he's usually such a good writer. I wonder if Sarah knows how long I've helped him? What a fool she must feel if she does.'

Sean waved his phone in front of her face, mouthing, 'Hayley.'

Julia finally managed to speak. 'Hold on, Felicity. Don't hang up.'

She took the phone from Sean.

'Hayley, where are you? You need to send someone to the Harbours' house now. Felicity is in danger.'

Hayley said. 'What's going on, Julia?'

'Please, Hayley, I'll tell you now – but send someone first.'

A phone in each hand, she quickly went back to her first call.

'Felicity? Are you there?'

'Yes, but there's someone at the door. I'll just go and see who it is.'

'Don't open the door!'

'Don't be silly, it's not locked.'

'Felicity, listen to me. Felicity?'

'Oh hello, Sarah,' Julia heard, over the yapping of the Harbours' pack of dogs

Julia went back to Sean's phone and said, 'Hayley? Are you on your way?'

'Yes, but we're in the next village. Driving as fast as I can. I phoned it in, so the uniforms will meet me there. What's going on?'

'I think Sarah's the killer. She's there now, at Felicity's house.'

'On my way,' said Hayley, and killed the call.

In her other ear was Felicity, her voice mild and friendly. 'I didn't hear the bell. I see you let yourself in. What a nice surprise, Sarah. Shall we have tea?'

And then the phone went dead.

36

'What on earth is going on?' Sean said. 'What do you mean about Sarah? She's not a killer.'

'Call the dogs,' Julia instructed, already jogging towards the car. 'We need to go to Felicity's house right now. Sarah is dangerous. I think we've had it all wrong, and Sarah *did* kill Vincent Andrews after all. And I hope I'm mistaken, but I think she's going to kill Felicity Harbour too.'

Sean and Julia went together in his car, with him driving and Julia filling him in on the details on the way. The two dogs sat alert in the back, curious about the strange turn their walk had taken. Sean was, understandably, absolutely floored at the suggestion that Sarah might be a murderer.

'How well do you know Sarah?' Julia asked. 'Is there any history of... anything?'

'Quite well.' He paused. 'I was close to Eleanor growing up, although we grew apart as we got older. She's a bit unusual, you might've noticed. But still, I've seen Sarah at family events since she was a child. She was a good student, clever and competitive. Top marks in her year in the whole county. She got a special scholarship or something to university, as I recall. She read

English at Cambridge. She didn't finish, though. Everyone was very surprised, and Eleanor was furious, and bitterly disappointed. But Sarah left to marry Vincent, and then she worked in, what was it? Public relations, I do believe.'

'Any mental health problems? Discipline issues?'

'I don't think so, but honestly, I can't remember too much detail. It was so long ago. I haven't seen much of her since she moved away.'

Four minutes later, they were at the Harbours'.

Four minutes. More than enough time to kill someone and be gone.

Or, perhaps, just enough time for a village lady to boil the kettle and make a pot of tea and lay out a plate of biscuits. To pour a cup for her visitor and herself, and to settle into a chat about village matters.

Julia hoped with all her heart that they would find Sarah and Felicity engaged in the latter activity. But she feared the worst.

They pulled up out of sight of the house, in the shade of a big oak. Sean opened the windows halfway to give the dogs air, and turned off the car.

'Be a good boy, Jake,' Julia said in a low voice, patting him through the window. 'You stay here with Leo and be nice and quiet.'

'Let's walk quietly round the side of the house, see if we can peek in,' she whispered to Sean.

'This is ridiculous,' he said, although clearly he didn't think it so ridiculous that he didn't whisper too. 'Sarah isn't dangerous.'

'Nothing would make me happier than for you to be right,' she said. 'Now come on.'

The Harbours' garden was – as one might expect – not a

manicured affair. As they crept down the side of the house, they had to step carefully past overgrown rhododendron bushes and watch their step on rough paths with weeds growing happily undisturbed between the stones. Julia caught her foot on a half-concealed rockery and might have come a cropper had Sean not caught her arm and steadied her.

When she got to the corner, Julia peered round it to the front of the house. She felt a bit silly, like some sort of cartoon spy, but she wanted to get the lay of the land before revealing their presence.

She heard Felicity's voice faintly through the open windows.

'But you must have realised before, even if he never told you? All those weekends when the two of us met up in some far-flung place. What did you *think* was going on?'

'I never knew. All this time, I thought I was the one. The only one.'

Julia couldn't believe what she was hearing. It wasn't what she had expected at all. Vincent Andrews and Felicity Harbour? It was unimaginable. Had the affair started when he was her student, she wondered? She looked behind her and saw Sean's face, as shocked as own.

'What did you think he was doing, all those years? When he disappeared for days?' Felicity asked, incredulous.

'I thought he was seeing another woman. Or women. For, you know... For sex, not *history*.'

Sarah said this with distaste, as if an extramarital romp would have been preferable.

'Good heavens, no.' Julia could hear the appalled shudder in Felicity's voice. She edged closer, confused as to what she was hearing. Had there been an affair or not?

'This is a worse betrayal,' said Sarah, angrily. 'He strung me along all these years, making out we were a team, we were in this together. It was a partnership – he came up with the historical background and themes, and all the detail of the period. I came up with the storylines, I structured the books, wrote his first drafts. By the end I was doing everything except the detailed historical side of things.'

Julia nodded to herself. That made sense. It was Sarah who was the good writer, and Vincent who had made a mess of the latest draft. Not the other way around.

'But I did the historical side,' said Felicity, speaking slowly, as if realising the implications for herself. 'And because of that, my husband is now a murderer. He killed Phoebe, you know, because he thought I killed Vince. He thought that seeing as Phoebe had realised I wrote part of the novels, she would think I had killed Vince. And the poor stupid man thought I had indeed killed him. But why would I have done that? Vince's books put the cream on our scones.'

There was a moment of silence. 'Only they weren't Vincent's books at all, were they? I'd always thought that he could at least write a good story.'

'He couldn't.' There was no trace of bereaved wife in Sarah's tone. Just anger.

'I must say, I can hardly... I'm shocked. All these years, you wrote the books,' Felicity said, in wonder. 'So what did Vincent actually *do?*'

'Nothing. Well, that's not completely true. He looked pretty and spoke well, which went over with the book club set. And he charmed the publishers and cashed the cheques. But as far as the books were concerned, he went over my drafts, typed comments on what to change. But now I think about it, the comments were yours – and you know, he changed a thing here or there – the shirt was red, not blue. The hero brought gardenias, not roses. They ate veal, not lamb.' She said this dismissively, bitterly. 'Of course, after that he thought he'd practically written the whole thing. Which is what led to the latest fiasco of a manuscript: he thought he could do it all himself.'

There was a moment of quiet, eventually broken by a sob, and Sarah's voice: 'Our life together was a sham, a lie... I thought I was married to this brilliant history buff, that I was helping him make his knowledge and insight more accessible to the world through his novels. And then I saw the actual hand-written notes – not the comments that he usually wrote on the Word document. And I realised it wasn't him at all. But I didn't know who it was.'

'It must have been terribly disappointing for you,' said Felicity, in a soothing tone over the sound of clinking and gurgling – the sound of more tea being poured. 'I honestly have to say that you did a marvellous job. You have real talent.'

'I do, don't I?' said Sarah. 'I'm Vincent F. Andrews, but no one knows it.'

She gave a harsh laugh, entirely without humour.

'I was going to be a writer, you know. I was the reader. I was the one who was good at English. But I got pregnant in my second year at uni and we decided I would drop out. I lost the baby and nearly died in the process. But I never went back to uni.'

'I'm so sorry, Sarah,' Felicity said. 'That is truly tragic.'

Sarah started to weep, softly. 'I couldn't have another baby. Vincent wanted to adopt, but I didn't. I started writing, histor-ical fiction. I threw myself into the novel. Vincent showed an interest, helped on the history side. Or I thought he did – all along it was you.'

'Yes, he came to me for help and advice, and I gave it to him.'

'He took the book to a publisher. I was so damaged, I wanted nothing to do with it. I was just writing for my sanity, to take my mind off things. I didn't care about publishing. They loved the book. They signed him. He said it was to protect me, in my fragile state.'

'While he took the credit. It's appalling, Sarah.'

'I know. But we were doing so well. The book sold, and I wrote another and another. I had fun – like the character I based on Mike. How that made me giggle! And we were partners, you know. He always said. Partners in everything. But now I find that we weren't.'

'What happened with the newest book, though?'

'He'd been negotiating the Netflix deal, and I told him I wanted my name in the credits. Such a small thing, but then he got ugly. Said he could write the book that I had started without me. He never really understood what I did, what went into it. So I said he should go ahead, I was done. Obviously, his book was rubbish. I think after he saw your notes, Felicity, he realised that.'

'I am a bit blunt sometimes,' said Felicity. 'I was surprised at how bad the draft was. Usually I focus on the historical accuracy, but this time the plot was all over the place, and the writing! Well, now I know why.'

'On the way down here he asked me to write a new draft, using what he had done. He said something about how he'd mail me his version. But then I saw the manuscript lying next to his computer with your green notes all over it, I couldn't believe it. I realised someone else had been helping him. He admitted he'd had help all along.'

'Yes, right from the first book. He brought me his draft.'

'My draft.'

'Yes, yours.'

'That night at the library, I was still reeling from what I'd learnt. And there he was, saying all those nice things about me to try to butter me up so that I'd do what he wanted. But it was like I could see him clearly for the first time. And I hated him.'

There was a moment's silence as Felicity presumably took in what Sarah had just said. Outside the window, Julia had the same realisation – that Sarah had killed Vincent.

'He took terrible advantage of you. But you are a writer,

Sarah. A fine writer. I'm sure you will have a fine solo writing career,' Felicity said, trying to placate her. 'It's not too late, you know. You're a young woman. You have your life ahead of you. A great future.'

Julia noticed that Felicity's voice had changed. She sounded nervous.

'Do I, though?' Sarah asked. 'Do I have a great future? Well, that depends.'

Julia took a chance and leaned forward for a better view. She saw Sarah's back, her arms hanging down, a short knife in her right hand. Felicity saw it too, and then she saw Julia. Had Sarah taken the knife with her? Then she can only have meant it for one thing. Julia's eyes met Felicity's for a second, then Felicity went back to Sarah. 'Now, Sarah, of course you do. As long as you don't do anything rash, this can all be explained. Let's talk this through.'

Julia stepped away from the window. She motioned to Sean to move ahead of her, back the way they'd come. 'We need to get in there,' she whispered. 'The front door...'

As she did so, she heard Sarah's voice. 'I'm sorry, Felicity, you're the only one who knows I killed him. You have to die.'

This time, they didn't make much effort to creep silently. Speed was of the essence. And besides, Sarah was too deep in her own pain and anger to notice them.

Sean rounded the corner and headed for the front door, with Julia hot on his heels. The sound of Sean's heavy breathing and the crackle of breaking branches under their feet was joined by Jake's barking, and what she assumed to be Leo's. She glanced up without slowing, and saw the dogs' excited faces at the car window. There was a chase, and they wanted in on it.

Sean stopped on the doorstep, looking to her for guidance. Julia didn't hesitate. She took hold of the big doorknob, wrenched the door open and went in. She reached the doorway to the room just in time to see Sarah, knife in hand, make a lunge for Felicity. With surprising agility, the older woman aimed a kick from her seat in the wingback chair. It was enough to deflect the hand with the knife and send Sarah crashing against a display cabinet filled with clay pots and vases. The glass front shattered and the pottery fell and broke. The noise was shocking, but Sarah was right back at Felicity in an instant.

Julia flung herself into the room, shouting, 'Stop, Sarah! That's enough.'

She grabbed Sarah's arm, trying to make her drop the knife, but Sarah held on tight. The left side of Sarah's chest was wet with blood – she must have fallen onto the blade. Nonetheless, she twisted herself out of Julia's grasp, the knife still in her hand. As she did so, the knife nicked Julia's arm. Julia cried out in surprise and pain – the small cut stung sharply.

Jake came running, making a worried, high-pitched bark Julia had never heard from him before. He must have squeezed himself through the car window. Sensing the violence and tension, he did the only thing he knew how – made a lot of commotion. He ran between Julia and Sarah, jumping and barking.

The noise was deafening, and enough to stop Sarah in her tracks. Julia took advantage of the moment and grabbed at her again. This time, Sarah dropped the knife. It clattered to the floor. Sarah wasn't giving up. She dropped to her knees to pick it up, but Felicity kicked it out of the way. The knife skittered across the wooden floor to the door, where DI Hayley Gibson was just in time to stop it with her foot.

Sean held Sarah from behind, his arms tightly over hers, saying kindly, 'Come now, love, it's over.'

37

The dogs were fast asleep on the carpet in front of the log fire – the first of the season, and the first Julia had made since she'd bought the house. They lay curled, Leo's back to Jake's tummy, Leo's tan nose resting on the Lab's chocolate brown front leg. The glowing coals at the centre of the fire were mesmerising, and Julia felt her own eyelids growing heavy, even though it was not yet 7 p.m. She straightened up in her seat on the sofa, hoping that would wake her up a bit.

Sean, who was similarly slumped in the opposite corner, did likewise. 'Shall I check on the soup?' he asked.

'Yes, thank you.' Julia liked that he'd thought to stir it, and that he felt at home enough in her house to do so. 'I'll come and set the table. Tabitha will be here any minute.'

In the kitchen, a pot of beef and barley soup was warming on the stove, and a loaf of bread was in the oven – both pulled from the freezer for a quick, impromptu supper.

There was a freshly home-baked apple pie on the counter. Sean had helped with the slicing of the apples – Julia's arm was still a bit sore from the nick from Sarah's knife. Only when she put the pie in the oven did Julia remember that she'd planned to make an apple pie for a Sunday lunch at Eleanor's, to welcome Sarah and Vincent, and introduce Julia to Sean's family. Now, Sarah was awaiting trial, and Vincent was dead. Julia had met them all, but not under the cheerful circumstances she'd anticipated. And there had been no pie.

There was a knock on the kitchen door. They smiled at the timing, and Julia said, 'There Tabitha is. I'll get it.'

DI Hayley Gibson was on the doorstep.

'I left the station and was passing,' she said, a little awkwardly. 'I thought we might speak.'

'Come in,' Julia said, stepping back to let her into the kitchen.

Hayley looked past her at Sean, standing at the stove, stirring the soup. 'Oh, I'm sorry, I didn't know you had company,' she said stiffly. 'I can go, we can talk in the morning.'

'That's okay, stay,' Julia said. 'I'd like to hear what's been going on.'

'Soup's ready, I've turned it off,' said Sean, tapping the spoon sharply on the side of the pot. He put the lid on and turned to face Hayley. 'Hello, DI Gibson. Don't mind me, come in. I'd like to hear, too.'

There was a bottle of wine and three glasses, set out for supper, along with a jug of Julia's lemonade. 'Long day for you,' Julia said. 'Sit down.'

She gestured to Hayley to help herself, and she reached for the lemonade. The detective looked tired, and her work clothes – the black trousers paired with a green shirt today – looked rumpled. The three of them sat down at the kitchen table.

'The family's been in touch with the lawyer, I take it?' Hayley asked Sean.

'Yes. I know that Sarah confessed to killing her husband. Stabbed him with the knife she took from the display cabinet.'

'Forensics have confirmed that the knife she used to threaten Felicity was also the murder weapon. It looks like a pretty open and shut case. The only thing that might have a bearing is her, um, mental state.'

'Good Lord,' said Sean, shaking his head. 'I've known her since she was born. I can't believe I didn't see how fragile she was, how damaged. And how dangerous.'

'I'm sorry, Sean,' Julia said, putting her hand on his arm. 'She lost so much – her degree, the baby, and her recognition as a writer. Then to discover he wasn't even writing his side of the books, that there was another woman involved, it was worse than an affair. She was so hurt and angry, she did a terrible, terrible thing.' 'Did Sarah say what happened that night at the library?' Sean asked the detective. 'When Vincent died?'

'She arrived at the library to see Phoebe hovering around Vincent, anticipating his needs, clearly doting on him. She got the idea that they were having an affair – on top of the recent revelation that another woman was helping him write, she cracked. She said that it was too much betrayal,' said Hayley.

She took a sip of her lemonade and continued, 'After the signing, when things were quieting down, and you were clearing up, she confronted him about Phoebe. He didn't want a public scene, so he led her away, between the shelves. The fight turned to the new book, and Sarah said she wasn't going to help him. He said fine, she wasn't irreplaceable. He'd find somebody else. Writers were ten a penny. Phoebe could probably do it.'

'That would have pushed her over the edge, I suppose,' said Sean. 'She wasn't thinking like a sane person anymore.'

'Indeed. Sarah was devastated and furious. She grabbed the knife from the display case nearby. She stabbed him.'

'Thank goodness you worked it out and got to Felicity's in time,' said Sean. 'Or there might have been three deaths. Sarah was...'

They were interrupted by a knock. Julia got up and opened the door to Tabitha, who was accompanied by a chill breeze that promised winter. She bustled in, her tiny frame encased in a soft flowing brown coat, and a scarf in a paisley pattern of red and orange. She looked like autumn. Sean got up and fetched a fourth wine glass from the dresser, and then opened the bottle, pouring them each a little glass.

'I've been at Felicity Harbour's place,' Tabitha said, taking her place at the table. 'I phoned to let her know a book she wanted had come in. She didn't want to come into the village. Obvious reasons. By which I mean gossip,' she said sternly. Tabitha did not approve of gossip. 'I said I'd drop it off for her, which I did. And collected her overdues. Poor Harry used to do all that. I don't know what she'll do without him.'

'It's very sad about Harry,' said Sean. 'I've known him forever and he seemed the most harmless man you can imagine. I still can't quite believe he killed that young woman. And so violently.'

'No question there,' said Hayley. 'DNA, prints, confession – the whole trifecta.' There was a hint of satisfaction in her voice.

'You'd be surprised what the most gentle people will do to protect the ones they love, Sean. Harry thought he was protecting Felicity,' Julia said.

'Really? Protecting her from what?' asked Tabitha.

'Harry thought that Felicity killed Vincent. There had been some tension, some spats between them, apparently,' said Julia.

'That's right, Julia,' Hayley said, and continued the story. 'We found some of the emails. Vincent had complained that he was giving her too much of the pie. He wanted to reduce her fee. Seeing as he was the big name author, you know.'

'Even though Sarah and Felicity wrote the books,' Sean said in disgust. 'From what Julia tells me, he was not much more than the face of the operation.'

'Well, Felicity was having none of it. And there would've been no contract between them, of course. Their arrangement was hush-hush. Harry knew all this, so when Vincent turned up dead, he thought Felicity had done it. He thought the business relationship had fallen apart irreparably, and Felicity had killed him out of anger.'

'That's why he wanted the manuscript back from Phoebe,' said Julia. 'Because the handwriting on it would link Felicity to the murder. When he overheard Phoebe talking to you in the shop, he thought she had made a link to someone else being involved with the books, and perhaps the murder... Anyhow, that's why he stole the laptop, too. So he could get rid of the evidence there.'

'He explained how he did that, by the way, Julia,' Hayley said. 'You were right, he saw the laptop bag with Vincent's initials when he bumped into you. He followed you, and then saw Sean with the laptop. He couldn't believe his luck when Sean left it in the unlocked car.'

Sean blushed and cleared his throat in an embarrassed sort of way, and took a sip of his wine.

'Harry went into the library at some point and saw the knife was missing. He thought Felicity had killed Vincent with it, and tossed it on the path on the way home,' said Julia. 'That was why he was so busy with his metal detector.'

'I'm sure that's so,' said Sean. 'We kept on bumping into him on the same path, didn't we?'

He got up and checked the status of the bread, tapping it to see that it was hot and crisp. He turned off the oven and turned on the burner under the soup. Julia caught his eye and gave him a smile of appreciation, before continuing. 'Harry tried to protect his wife by stealing the incriminating evidence. But once the police collared him on Phoebe's murder, he found what he thought was a sure-fire way to keep her out of jail – he confessed to a murder he didn't commit, the murder of Vincent Andrews.'

'He thought seeing as he was sure he was going to jail for

life anyway, he'd protect his wife and go down for that murder as well,' Hayley said.

'Will he go to jail for life?' asked Tabitha. You could see she felt torn between a fondness that the whole village felt for Harry and the knowledge of the horrific crime he had committed.

'That will be for the court to decide,' said Hayley.

'Supper's ready,' Sean said, from the cooker. 'Shall we eat?'

'Perfect, thanks, Sean,' Julia said, clearing a space in the middle of the table, where two mats had been put down to receive the hot, heavy pot. She fetched bowls and plates and handed them round. The smell of the fresh bread made her mouth water, and the soup looked rich and good. 'Help yourselves. I'll go and toss a few more logs on the fire; we can have our pie there, where it's nice and warm,' she said, walking through to the sitting room. The dogs woke up – whether to the smell of soup, or to her footsteps, she wasn't sure. They wagged their tails sleepily, making a pleasant *thump thump* sound on the carpet.

'What lovely chaps, you are,' she said, stepping past them to reach into the big basket of logs. 'Let me stoke it up for your majesties, shall I?'

She took a big log and tossed it onto the burning coals, then followed it with another.

'More logs for the dogs, how's that?'

'As good as bogs for frogs,' came Sean's voice, startling her and making her blush.

'I know, talking to the hounds...'

'And making jokes for them, that's the best part,' he said affectionately.

She threw on a third log and straightened up, standing in front of him. He put his hands on her shoulders and bent to kiss her. This time, there was no confusion. This was no peck, no friendly touching of lips. It was a proper kiss, soft and hard and just wonderful.

They drew apart and smiled into each other's eyes.

'I think we can say the dogs are properly introduced,' Julia said, playfully. 'You can book that weekend away.'

He gave her the Sean Connery grin that made her heart flutter like a Bond girl's eyelashes. He kissed her again, quick but firm, and said, 'Consider it done.'

Hand in hand, they returned to the kitchen, where their friends were serving themselves soup and chatting about matters other than murders.

'Hayley!' said Julia. 'I've got a little present for you.'

'What?' the detective asked, her spoon poised in front of her mouth.

'I think I've solved a crime.'

'Well, it was a group effort, I'd like to think.'

'Not *that* one,' she said with a smile. 'Another crime. Would you like to know who has a veritable *forest* of brand new orchids?'

'I would indeed.'

'I'll tell you after the apple pie.'

A LETTER FROM KATIE GAYLE

Dear reader,

Katie Gayle is, in fact, two of us – Kate and Gail – and we want to say a massive thank you for choosing to read *Murder in the Library*. If you enjoyed the book, and want to keep up to date with all Katie Gayle's latest releases, just sign up at the following link. Your email address will never be shared and you can unsubscribe at any time.

www.bookouture.com/katie-gayle

We have loved exploring more of Berrywick with Julia and Jake. We hope that you have too. If you haven't read about Julia's first few weeks in Berrywick, then please grab a copy of *An English Garden Murder*.

We look so forward to introducing you to more of the colourful characters of Berrywick, and finding out what happens between Julia and Sean... and Jake, of course! You can follow us on Twitter for regular updates and pictures of the real-life Jake!

We hope you enjoyed reading about Julia's second adventure, and if you did we would be very grateful if you could write a review and post it on Amazon and Goodreads, so that other people can discover Julia too.

You might also enjoy our Epiphany Bloom series – the first three books are available for download now.

You can find us in a few places and we'd love to hear from you –

Katie Gayle is on Twitter as @KatieGayleBooks and on Facebook as Katie Gayle Writer. You can also follow Kate at @katesidley and Gail at @gailschimmel.

Thanks,

Katie Gayle

facebook.com/KatieGayleWriter

twitter.com/KatieGayleBooks

Made in the USA
Monee, IL
06 September 2022

13314438R00146